HEAT, DUST
&
ROCKET
LAUNCHERS

HEAT, DUST
&
ROCKET
LAUNCHERS

By

I.R.TYLER

QCBC

Copyright © 2015-I.R.Tyler, ianrtyler.com, Hope without Borders, COCET, GOPOL, CB Network, GOPOL 360 child alert system, Tom Ross and all COCET characters. Published by QCBC, Tasmania. Paperback edition 1, Vol 3, of the 'Hope without Borders' trilogy.

ISBN 978-0-6453869-0-5

A catalogue record for previous books in this series, Hope Arises, and COCET are available at the National and the Alexander Turnbull Libraries of New Zealand. Heat Dust and Rocket Launchers is deposited at the National Library of Australia.

DEDICATION

This book is dedicated to Jane, from Spreyton, Tasmania, who together with thousands of other Tasmanians have been subject to child sex abuse, and still seek justice. In Jane's case, Project Prevail, her final attempt to secure redress clearly displays that law enforcement from any state or federal agency must never accept the word of a child sex abuser when seeking to use them as an informant, and never, ever ever, contemplate using a violent paedophile as a registered informant.

If they do, they cannot be surprised, if years later, they find out that the deal they made was like a German 16th century 'Faustian Pact,' a deal with the devil at the crossroads at midnight, where the commodity exchanged wasn't just a lighter sentence, but also included the lives and souls of Australian victims who desperately needed their voices to be heard.

ACKNOWLEDGEMENTS

Heat Dust and Rocket Launchers was written during the lockdown period in the Australian state of Tasmania following the breakout at the Northwest Hospital, in Burnie. The period was difficult for everyone including the following editors who I wish to thank: Tim Ford, Mary Loweth — for their unending support and advice through some of the most difficult times in their lives.

Victim Advice

If you are a victim of child sex abuse, or an adult that was subject to sex abuse as a child, and need assistance; you should go to the Police, your Doctor, the Samaritans or other similar victim advocacy group. Their details can be found on the internet or in the telephone directory.

If you are a hidden victim, such as the mother, father, brother, sister, husband, wife or partner of an offender, and want to understand more about what happened to you, then the helpline through www.ianrtyler.com is available to you for free wherever you are in the world. This helpline is also available free to victims who are considering reporting a crime, but wish to know more about the process before they do.

Advice for Child Sex Offenders

If you are a child sex offender, internet viewer, maker or supplier of child sex abuse images, or someone who sexually assaults a child of any age and you read this book, stop what you are doing, your actions are criminal. If you become distressed through guilt or fear, seek assistance or hand yourself into the nearest law enforcement station together with your hardware.

If you are living with the disorder, are managing it and have not offended, then your thoughts alone do not make you a criminal. But it does make you much more liable to offend. Help is available to you from confidential helplines that are designed to keep you from acting on those urges such as, Circles of Support.

CHAPTER ONE

At COCET's headquarters in Aylesbury, it had been a painful week. Debrief after debrief, meeting after meeting; the content distilled, stripped back, analysed, then summed up in a single report. The aim, in corporate language, was 'future learning', 'better practices' and 'working smarter'.

Looked and sounded non-threatening, and on most occasions it would be, but on others it could be used against you. The bottom line was: they had been outmanoeuvred. Close, yet tactically miles off. And, because of it, they had missed the chance to arrest Michael, who was now in the wind. If they were to gain the backing for what they wanted to do next, it was critical the report was pitched just right.

Tom looked across the table at Acting Detective Sergeant, Jane King.

"Well, if you were Maggie, would you accept this?"

Jane lifted her head up slightly, flicked her eyes up at Tom, before returning to the report: her expression not giving anything away. He could see she was nearing the bottom of the last page.

"Yes, I would," replied Jane, now head up, facing Tom.

"If you were John Troy, would you?" Jane shot back, with a smirk on her face.

Tom had to think about that for a few seconds. Maggie would make a decision on a single read. John Troy was far more political. His decision-making would factor in the 'what ifs', and how they might change his future golf handicap.

"My guess is . . . he will steer away from it."

"The Chief knows his risk-averse style," Jane replied, in a manner that was more of a statement of the obvious.

Something that Tom didn't disagree with.

"Anything missing?"

"Nope."

"Still happy with the intel?"

"Yep."

"Deena, all lined up?"

"Yep."

Tom shrugged his shoulders and hit the Send button on the email he had waiting.

"I'm going to get a presentation ready," Jane declared, now at the doorway, disappearing out of sight.

"OK, I'm getting a brew. Do you want one?" Tom replied, raising his voice.

"Sure," Jane shouted back.

For a very long time Tom had realised that 'no' was the default word most used within British policing. It was simply the easiest option. It required less thinking, less work, and, when challenged, required the least amount of justification. It was also, almost always, the cheapest option. Most cops, when they began their careers, would be full of motivation and belief, but after a while they would fall victim to second-guessing a course of events in an investigation, and just not take any action in the first place. This attitude wasn't confined to new cops. It would happen all over again as officers were successful in promotion. It was the same 'no', just a different operational environment in which to say it. After dropping off Jane's tea, Tom sat down to wait and began to ponder if he was stretching the policing envelope too far. What would he do if 'no' was the answer? At this precise time, he didn't have a plan B.

Superintendent Maggie Burrows moved her chair to one side, pulled the speakerphone closer to her and read the conclusions once more before calling Detective Chief Inspector, Tom Ross.

"Hi Tom. Well, the plan looks better on paper than I thought it would . . ."

"Do you feel the same way about it?" Tom hurriedly interjected, suddenly realising he had been too quick off the mark.

"I think more so."

"In what way?"

"Hmm ... you can't say 'no' to this and then expect to be taken seriously on a global level. The Chief put the GOPOL group together for just this sort of case. He made himself its first CEO. This is where he gets vindication for what he stuck his neck out for," Maggie replied, staring at her speaker and then looking up to the ceiling in her office and wondering, if she were in the Chief's shoes, what she really would do.

"The operational risks: thoughts?"

"The plan to negate them is good," Maggie replied, letting out a sigh which Tom could hear.

"This will stand or fall on legality, Tom."

"I know, but the Canadian Ambassador will be doing something with or without us."

"Is she lined up?"

"Yes."

"Prepped?"

"I don't know what you mean Boss."

"I will take that as a 'yes' then. OK, I will support this and send it on. Both you and ADS King to be available at short notice."

"Yes, Ma'am."

Maggie's stare remained fixed on the speakerphone well after the line went dead. She was about to support an operational plan that was, at its very best, only semi-legal. Worst case scenario, she was breaking the law of another country and putting the lives of her own staff in great danger. She had her own mentors that she trusted, some senior to her that she could go to for advice on this, but she knew that they would all give her the same answer: 'No.'

She had a few years left to do, had long given up hope of further promotion, didn't give a monkey's what JT thought, and would never forgive herself if she did nothing. She had said 'no' more times than she cared to think of and would live with the consequence of saying 'no' for the rest of her life, just as much as saying 'yes' if it all went wrong.

Maggie intertwined her fingers and flexed her hands outwards before beginning her written support. She was confident that, together with Tom, they could neutralise the risks, rescue children from abuse and break up a paedophile network that may or may not contain their missing suspect Michael. Also known to COCET as LB.

The following afternoon in Kidlington, Maggie Burrows, Tom and Jane arrived at Police Headquarters and made their way to the Chief's office.

"The A Team! I've been expecting you. How are we all?" Margaret Thrinton said, with a beaming smile and the genuine warmth of a caring mother tending for her children.

Tom went to speak, but abruptly stopped, realising that Margaret, who was the consummate professional, was looking at Maggie, rather than him.

"I'm fine. Can't speak for the others," Maggie replied, in an upbeat tone, before making her way to the new coffee machine, which made better coffee than she could buy at Caffè Nero and was free.

"I want to take the opportunity to thank you both for the work you do," Margaret said quietly, with a look of admiration on her face, before picking her tone up again.

"Jane, is the Canadian Ambassador lined up, and has she got my personal number?"

"Yes."

"Well, you'd better ring her. The Chief is running 20 minutes late, and I warn you, he is not in a happy mood today."

Jane moved off to the seating area and texted Deena Potts, the Canadian Ambassador to Cambodia, who was currently in Toronto.

Tom, who had followed Maggie to the new coffee machine, relayed the information that the Chief was in a bad mood.

"Fricking marvellous. I wonder if I can get two coffees down me in the time we have."

As Tom was making his mind up whether to have tea or hot chocolate, he glanced over to Jane who smiled at him and mouthed, 'Flat White'.

With all three seated and sipping, Jane got a text back from Deena Potts confirming the delayed start time.

A few minutes later, and without warning, the Chief's door opened abruptly, and he stormed out of his office, making his way past the coffee machine and into the kitchenette, which was on one side of the corridor. Tom looked over to where Margaret was seated. She had a pair of headphones on and was busy typing. She stopped briefly, intuitively knowing that she might be needed, just as the Chief shouted, "Margaret! Where're the bloody chocolate Hobnobs?"

Tom, had he known, would have shouted back where they were. But Margaret, who was immaculately attired in a dress with no hint of a crease in it – although she had been seated most of the day – walked slowly and elegantly into the kitchenette.

There was a short pause before the Chief reappeared, armed with an unopened packet of biscuits, walked briskly past the three of them without any acknowledgement and back into his office closing the door firmly behind him.

Margaret made her way back to her desk and smiled at Maggie, who was sat at rigid attention with a surprised and concerned look on her face.

"No need for the A team to be worried. A couple of those and all will be well again!"

About 20 minutes later, and without any appearance of being warned, Margaret got up and approached Maggie.

"The Chief is ready for you now."

As they entered his office, Tom could see that the Chief was sat at the table to the left of his desk, along with Detective Chief Superintendent John Troy and another man he did not know.

"Come in, take a seat. You all know John. This is Toby Spencer-Drummond: he's a government lawyer."

As Toby stood, Tom could see that he was wearing a three-piece, pinstriped suit that looked like it had come straight out of Savile Row.

Maggie shook his hand and introduced herself, leaving the way for Tom and Jane to follow suit.

"Sorry for keeping you waiting Maggie, but we have probably saved everyone some time. JT?"

"Jane, you won't be required to present the operational plan. Maggie, we've read the report; the operational side of it, if authorised, will be for you to manage, and you will be responsible for it."

'This is looking good,' Tom thought.

"The issue is one of legality," JT continued, "that's why Toby is here. Can we speak with Ambassador Deena Potts now, please?"

Jane, who had her phone ready, texted Deena and within moments the speakerphone console in the middle of the table rang.

"Hi, you're speaking to Chief Constable James Galloway of Thames Valley Police."

"Hi James, it's Deena Potts, pleased to meet you."

"Pleased to meet you too," he said, before introducing everyone in the room.

"Deena, I'll say upfront, I want to make this happen. I created Global Online Police for exactly this sort of case. I also authorised the inception of the Combined Online Child Exploitation Taskforce, COCET, within my own force. They are the UK's representative for GOPOL. I have a great deal personally invested in this, so, what I authorise at my end needs to conform with the law."

"Sure, I fully understand," Deena replied confidently, a soft Canadian accent starting to become apparent.

"So, I am going to hand you over to Toby: he has a few questions."

"Ambassador, is your Minister for Foreign Affairs aware of what you are proposing?"

"Yes."

"So, there is a written record of it and its authorisation?"

"It has been recorded within activity updates by my office to the Minister. There isn't a need for authorisation, as all my actions are covered by my appointment from the Prime Minister."

"OK, but, if things got a bit sticky, there would be communication from the Minister's office to you surrounding it. There would be here, certainly where anything occurred that might lead to a diplomatic incident."

Maggie had no idea what Tom had said to Deena, when he had briefed her, but was hoping Deena knew enough to see off Toby's concerns.

Tom was thinking, 'Ahead and waiting, Toby.'

Jane was thinking, 'Eat him up, Deena.'

"I can't speak for how you run your Diplomatic Service, Toby. But I can, and do, speak for Canada's. What I and my staff do when in country is down to me. That authority was bestowed on me by the PM. If and when things get 'sticky', as you put it, I sense it long before it happens and update my briefings to the Minister to ensure no blindsiding."

"So, what you are saying then, is that the Minster knows, and there is no need for your proposals to be questioned?"

"No. I'm not saying that. I'm saying that I tell the Minister what I am doing and, depending on the nature of what I am doing, that will determine the level of briefing he gets. That's not questioned. That's how I operate and have been doing so for the past eleven years, and I enjoy the complete support of both the PM and the Minister."

Tom had been watching Toby's body language. If he had felt the diplomatic slap down, he wasn't showing it.

"Your intelligence indicates that children have been going missing in Phnom Penh, and this started shortly after the suspect known to COCET as Michael or LB, escaped arrest in Bangkok?"

"Yes."

"And COCET has intelligence that indicates that this suspect might be Canadian: is that right?"

"Yes."

"And you have a source that says that a Caucasian male is behind the children going missing?"

"Yes."

"And both you and COCET feel there is merit in thinking that this unidentified male in Phnom Penh, could be the suspect COCET wants to locate?"

"Yes."

"I understand your reticence to approach the local police with your intelligence, but why not use your own law enforcement such as the Royal Canadian Mounted Police? Why is it you want to use COCET staff?"

This time, Tom thought that the Ambassador didn't reply quite as quickly.

"I think what you are really asking, Toby," she replied slowly, "is, if it all goes wrong, why can't it just be Canada's fault? Why drag the good name of the British Diplomatic Service into it? Spoken like a true diplomat!"

"That's not what I am saying," Toby interrupted.

"Oh yes, it is. And I am not used to being asked a question and then being interrupted. So, kindly let me finish. Yes, if GOPOL, of which COCET is part of, isn't allowed to work on this, then I will request RCMP assistance. It makes sense that GOPOL supports this operation: there is a strong possibility that their wanted person is behind the children going missing, and GOPOL has been set up to achieve exactly what we are proposing here. It's an obvious solution. Don't you agree?"

"Whether I agree or not has no bearing on this. The law, however, does, and I have to make it clear that UK law enforcement cannot be undertaking law enforcement activity in another country without the host country authorising it."

Toby ended his statement with a sense of finality, which the Chief picked up on.

"We aren't here to discuss operational tactics, Ambassador. We were seeking to fully understand your position, and you have made that quite clear. Thank you very much for your time. You can expect a decision on this very soon."

With the call complete, the Chief turned to Maggie. "I need to speak with JT and Toby. Can you wait outside for a moment?"

"Well, Toby?" the Chief said, once the door was shut.

"As long as the operational plan keeps UK Police out of law enforcement activity inside the Kingdom of Cambodia, then you are fine. My personal thoughts are though, you will be very lucky to achieve that. If it all goes wrong, we should be able to manage it on a diplomatic level, but GOPOL's reputation, and you, its inaugural CEO, will be tarnished badly before it's even got off the ground."

"You can't seriously be thinking of trusting Ross on this, can you?" JT said, as soon as Toby had left.

The Chief stared at JT, but didn't reply.

"It hasn't even been a year since Fiona was murdered. You give him an inch, and he'll take a mile . . ."

"That's a bit unfair, and you know it!" the Chief snapped back.

"Sir, he's been proactive all his career; he's been an undercover officer and a detective nearly all his service; he's a shit magnet, he can't help it! Doesn't matter what restrictions you place on him, he will find a way around them if it means getting the result."

By the time JT had finished, the Chief had moved back to his desk and was seated facing him.

"That's exactly what I am counting on, JT. Bring Maggie in please."

JT paused, not really believing what he was hearing, his incredulous expression causing the Chief to smile.

"Maggie. It's only fair you should know that JT strongly disagrees with what I am about to say. And, if this all goes pear-shaped, he will not only tell me that he told me so, but he will hold you personally accountable, and that will be career ending for you. Do you understand?"

"Yes, I do."

"I'm not sure you do; I really need to emphasise that this could have huge personal impact."

"I understood that before I signed off on this. This is my choice, and I fully accept the consequences if it all goes wrong."

The Chief looked at JT, staring impassively at him for a moment.

"You need some of her concrete pills, JT!"

"Authorised," said the Chief, who was now looking at Maggie, with JT still shaking his head in disbelief.

By the time Tom and Jane got back to COCET's offices, the rest of the staff had left work for the day. Maggie had told them to get an early finish, but neither of them was in the mood to go home.

"You want me to text Deena the result?"

"Yes, and set up a conference call for tomorrow afternoon."

"Any decision from Maggie about who is going to Cambodia?"

"Not yet. She will be here at eight tomorrow. Says she'll make the decision then."

"How soon will it begin?"

"No time to waste—as soon as. You got an operational name yet?"

"Yes, 'Veritas'."

"How you fixed at home? You alright to get away?"

"Mum and Dad can help out, but it would be better that I run this end. We are well advanced on the intelligence case for operations Blackwood and Laverton. I would expect the UCs to be deployed within the next ten days."

"What about their instructions?" Tom asked.

"You would have to do it before you leave or via Skype if you are away. What did Maggie say?"

"Not a great deal. She was a bit sombre to be honest. Said JT was clearly against it, but that the Chief had overruled him."

"Nothing more?"

"Nothing," replied Tom.

"I'm off then. See you tomorrow."

Before going home, Tom checked and read a few emails that had come in during the time he had been away—mostly new policy updates relating to Thames Valley Police. None of them had any impact on him at the moment, but, with what he was about to embark on, he might need to know them. He knew only too well how things could change overnight, with a sudden punishment move. After all, that was exactly what had got him into the position he was in now, one where he was about to commence a covert operation with an ambassador from Canada. He had an ominous feeling that things might turn full circle.

The following morning Jane was in Tom's office when Maggie arrived.

"Jane, can I have a few minutes with Tom please?"

"Sure," replied Jane, not showing any concern for the request. Back at her desk though, she stared at the closed door and wondered why she had been asked to leave. Her gut instinct told her it was a danger sign, and that she needed to be on her guard.

"Tom, let's be clear here, if this all goes wrong, there can be no misunderstanding or claims of communication breakdown. Do you understand?"

"Yes," Tom replied, thinking her tone was quite harsh.

"I was called into an early meeting with JT before coming here. He thinks you can't be controlled, are a liability, and has put that in writing."

"I think highly of him as well," Tom replied, with a noticeable hint of sarcasm.

"He has put me on notice that if you mess up, go outside the confines of the operational brief, we are both finished. He has made it quite clear that he intends to ensure that, policy-wise, he is totally covered to come out of it smelling of roses, whilst you and I are on the dung heap!"

Tom didn't have a huge beef with JT. He was the DCS. Part of his job description was to instil the fear of God into the detectives below him. They weren't buddies, didn't play golf together and, as a result, Tom never mixed in the same circles. On this case though, he was clearly drawing red lines and was prepared to act on it.

"The last thing I want is for you to get hurt in all of this," Tom began, before being interrupted by Maggie.

"This is my decision, Tom. They won't be able to sack me. But they will you. You must understand, unless you stay as an observer on this deployment, JT will use it as a means to sack you."

Tom, in all his career, had never been faced with the sack. The reality was, it was far more difficult to achieve than threaten, and, even at JT's rank, he couldn't secure it alone unless he was given the green light from above. Then there was the Police Federation. Tom was a paid-up member, and they would provide considerable support to him if things got tough, whether he was in the right or the wrong. The threat though, caught him off guard. He felt disturbed, and it took a few moments to lay those feelings bare. The Chief had authorised the job. From a Constabulary point of view, he could not go any higher, had never been known to harbour any desire for the top job at the Met, or Inspector of Constabularies. Which pretty much left him retiring on a bad note. That didn't equate to sacking him just to get even.

JT, had he any desire for further advancement, would have had to undertake further training at Bramshill College in the preceding years, which he had not done, and so had reached his own personal pinnacle. The desire to personally be responsible for the sacking of an officer must be coming from somewhere much deeper. Tom was missing a piece of the puzzle and needed more information.

"I know JT's on the square, and he hasn't got a completely clean sheet from Operation Hope as far as I'm concerned, but why is he after me? Why the threats?"

"Goodness knows, Tom. But you really need to be careful. He is lining you up, whilst at the same time he's planning his own escape route."

Tom believed Maggie. If she didn't have a clue, then that was the truth.

"There can only be two reasons, Maggie. It is either: he's been promised a job, and a senior one that needs him to have a clean sheet, or his Masonic mates mean to do me some harm."

Maggie had long known that Tom was critical of Police officers being members of the Masonic Lodge. She knew many that were still members, even though they had been told it was incompatible with policing, and JT was one of those. She had also known for many years of the rumour of a cabal within the Force, one which looked to achieve further advancement of its members. It had come into the tip line numerous times when she worked on Professional Standards. They had never identified the group, but had concluded it was more likely than not that it existed, and, therefore, it remained an open investigation. It certainly wasn't something she could tell him about.

"I share your concerns about Masonic influence, Tom. Let's face it, it's misogynistic and has no place within the police. However, I can't see one or some of them wanting you sacked just because of the past."

"Maybe you're right. But JT has made this personal. He isn't stupid, sacking isn't in his gift. He can try, he might get me demotion, but he can't guarantee the outcome on something he has been party to, the Chief has authorised, and where we are working with, and for, another country."

"Your best bet is to ensure that you stick to the rules of engagement; if you stray, you don't stray far, and don't get caught. And, it might be a good idea to speak to someone from the Federation before you go—someone that you can trust. If you don't know anybody, then I can recommend someone."

"Send me their name," Tom replied, in a tone that enquired if they were finished.

With Jane back, Maggie began.

"Jane, where are you with Operations Blackwood and Laverton?"

"We'll be ready to submit surveillance authorities early next week."

"In that case, I want you to remain here, take charge of COCET whilst Tom is away and provide support for Operation Veritas."

"Yes, Ma'am."

"You must be available to join Tom should there be a need, so be prepared. Passport, inoculations, whatever Tom gets before he goes, you get as well."

"Yes, Ma'am. Who will cover for me if I leave?"

"I will."

"Yes, Ma'am."

"Tom. The away team will be you and Sarah Dorsey."

"I was planning to take an Intel Officer," Tom said quickly, interrupting Maggie.

"I know, but I've decided otherwise. If you come under the spotlight of local authorities, the fewer the better. It fits your cover story: Sarah can deliver a communications presentation, and the Chief wants her there for later maximisation of the GOPOL brand."

"Does she know?"

"Yes, she has the authority from her home force, and the NCS is happy for her to go."

Tom thought about arguing for the Intel Officer but agreed three was too big, whilst at the same time wondering if all those clearances had been obtained overnight. His gut started to tell him that there were other forces at work in the background.

"You and Sarah will deliver the training to the NGOs that Deena has lined up. The training has to look and feel slick, with Canadian branding. As you know, the Ambassador has arranged for a joint capacity-building initiative with another Commonwealth country to be circulated within her Cambodian network as your reason for being there— it's your cover story. Questions so far?"

"None," Tom answered.

"I have changed your operational parameters slightly. To bolster the cover story, you only get the day you arrive to acclimatise, so you'd better let Deena know so she can make the necessary changes at that end. It's being proposed that you deliver three training sessions, roughly one day apart. That might change when you get there. It should give you about three spare days at the end. If you don't need them, then go and do some sightseeing or shopping, otherwise the operational plan and the options are all the same, apart from exit staging. Don't return straight home. You should return via Bangkok, as that is the most likely location you will need to go to, being as that was the last location we have for Michael."

"OK, does that mean we now need to include the Thai overseas liaison officer?"

"Not at the moment. All other operational activity stays the same, and, just to re-emphasise for Jane, you are not to go outside the operational brief. This is just a look, locate, observe and report back to the Ambassador. Understood?"

"Yes, Ma'am."

Tom nodded, "When do we leave?"

"As soon as all three of you have inoculation clearance from Occupational Health, and you Tom, have had a first aid refresher."

CHAPTER TWO

The Thai Airways plane began its descent into Phnom Penh, Cambodia. Tom and Sarah quickly stowed away their belongings and fastened their seat belts, ready to land. Looking out of the window the foreign, sun-baked countryside came into view, and Tom began to feel cut off from home, separated from the security of the wider Police family— naked, as if some power had been stripped from him.

He had a plan; it was simple and straightforward. Stick to the plan and it would be fine, he told himself, with Maggie's warning of not straying from the path following hard on the heels of his own thoughts. His contemplation was suddenly interrupted by the hard landing, followed by the loud noise of the plane's engines being placed into reverse thrust to help it lose speed.

As he entered the airbridge leading from the plane to Immigration control, the Far East tropical heat began to penetrate his senses. A heat that he knew, had lived in as a child, experienced on holiday, but, as a predominantly Northern Hemisphere human, he was part of a group less able to acclimatise to the heat quickly; exacerbated by clothing that was too light for the country he had just left, but, now, seemingly too heavy for the country he had just arrived in. Sarah moved alongside him, her skin taking on a glisten as her body began adjusting to the extreme temperature.

"God, that's lovely."

"Nice to be warm?"

"Sure is."

Not having time to apply for visas meant they had to go through the landing procedure to obtain them. Passports, photos, application form and US dollars. The whole procedure very manpower intensive, with not a woman in sight. One person to take the documents, another to check them. The documents then handed to a third person who reviewed them again, before splitting them up, handing some over to other staff, who viewed them again, before passing them to yet another who had more braid on his shoulder than the rest. That person rubber stamping the passport, before handing it back. A human chain of immigration staff.

With their passports back and the requisite visa attached, they were asked to produce them again by more staff, only metres away and in full sight of the issuing officer, just to ensure that the work really had been done – and that they weren't just imagining it – before being allowed through to the carousel area.

"You been to any Communist country before?"

"No, you?"

"Nope, feeling like we're in one now though!"

Sarah laughed at Tom's comment, just as she saw her luggage come into view. Not seeing his, he went in search of a trolley and returned just in time to see it snaking its way around. Two large suitcases on board, they made their way out to the Arrivals area, which was miniature by Heathrow standards but just as packed.

The heat hit Tom with ferocious force, followed by the cacophony of foreign voices from taxi drivers offering their services, many with handheld placards written in English. The air hung heavy and wet, even though it was a bright sunny day, making it difficult to breathe. As he scanned the now screaming throng of potential taxi drivers, he eventually spotted the sign he was looking for at the very back, held high by just a pair of arms, the person out of sight below the pleading mass in front.

"The shuttle is right at the back."

Moving slowly through the waiting crowd, they made their way to the back, out of the shade and into the full sun. The rays hit his head, making his skin feel like it was becoming immediately sunburnt. The bright light seemed to reflect off everything, even the black asphalt which, within a short distance, threw up a convection of air temperature, making a road mirage appear. Without sunglasses, his eyes automatically squinted to minimise the intake of sunlight as they fought to adjust to the sudden change.

He could see the sign holder was a small female who, unaware of their presence, was still looking down at the ground with her hands held high, her face covered from the sun by a white cloth hat.

"Your arms must be aching?" Tom said, by way of an announcement, with no idea if she could understand English.

As the woman spun around, they could see a badge with the name Chenda, and the Canadian Maple leaf emblem.

"Hi, you Mr Ross and Miss Dorsey?" Chenda said, in almost perfect English.

"Yes, we are," Sarah replied, whilst positioning herself so as to avoid the glare, quietly wishing that she hadn't packed her sunglasses in her suitcase.

"Lovely to meet you both. If you follow me, there is some shade where you can wait whilst I get the car," Chenda said, whilst offering her hand in a Western style handshake to both Tom and Sarah, dipping her head slightly as she did so.

Chenda was difficult to age, Tom thought. She was small to him but not when compared with the other Cambodians around her. Dressed in a combination of black and white and yet without a hint of perspiration on her skin, she had an infectious smile.

They followed Chenda. Just the act of pushing the trolley a short distance caused sweat to break out on his neck and run down his back. He felt extremely unprepared and uncomfortable.

Chenda led them to a waiting area next to the pick-up and drop-off lane.

"Just leave the trolley here when I return," she said, before walking towards the car park opposite.

Sarah smartly shot into the small area of shade that the roof canopy currently provided due to the position of the sun.

"Her English is flawless!"

"And no local accent," Tom replied, joining her.

Minutes later Chenda arrived driving a white Toyota Land Cruiser.

Loading the suitcases only took seconds, but it was enough time to generate more sweat, which he only recognised once inside the cool of the air-conditioned car.

Chenda quickly negotiated her way through the airport barrier-controlled exit and onto the highway, before dialling a number on the phone in the vehicle. It rang three times before it was answered, and the voice of Deena Potts came on the line.

"Hi both. Good journey?"

"Yes, it was very good."

Sarah wasn't sure in which direction she should be speaking. Chenda picked up on it, even though her eyes flicked between the road ahead, both sides of the vehicle and behind her as she wove her way around the traffic in her lane. It was a sight. Lorries, cars and small motorcycles carrying what looked like three generations of one family, perched in front of and behind the driver, perfectly in balance; others with bamboo cages containing live ducks overhanging the slim motorcycle, the width of a car: all moving in and out and alongside each other. It looked like chaos to him.

Chenda pointed her finger at the centre of the dashboard, and Sarah spotted the small microphone.

"Sorry I couldn't be there to meet you, but I had some unexpected meetings that I had to attend."

"That's OK, Deena, we weren't expecting you."

"I had planned we would meet tonight at the Embassy, but that's changed. Chenda has organised a private conference room at the Sunflower, where you are staying. I suggest we meet at five."

Sarah looked back at Tom, for confirmation.

"That'll be great."

"Good. In the meantime, get checked in and get some rest. Chenda, once you have dropped them off, can you meet our police source, normal place, he has some urgent information for us."

"Sure, Deena."

"See you all at five then."

With the call finished, Sarah couldn't take her eyes off the road, her feet making imaginary braking motions, as if she was driving and taking emergency action to avoid a collision. "How long will it take to get to the Sunflower Hotel?

Chenda spotted Sarah's feet movements. "Don't worry, Sarah," Chenda said, whilst letting out a whoop of laughter, "all this is normal. This is Cambodian driving. Everything in Phnom Penh takes 15 minutes, so we will be there in 15 minutes, for sure."

Sarah wondered if she was flushing after being caught out, and involuntarily looked around at Tom, sitting in the back. He grinned back at her and got a poked-out tongue gesture in return.

"Everybody that comes from Canada or the UK cannot believe the driving here, but do not worry, I am an expert and you will be safe. Take in all the sights . . . check out this billboard!" Chenda said, pointing to her right.

As they passed, they could see it read, 'Abuse a child in this country, go to jail in yours.'

Tom was wondering, 'If you are here, did you read this?'

Sarah was thinking, 'That's a very good communication strategy.'

For the rest of the journey they were silent, not because they didn't have anything to say, but because of what they could see and hear. It was so different from what they normally witnessed that it kept them captivated.

Tom was trying to draw from his memories as a child living in Singapore. He could remember some streets and stores, looking exactly like the ones he could see now. Yes, it was cool in the car and hot and humid outside, but the two things that really struck him were the brown dust and the lack of fear in the faces of the road users. The road was dulled from the constant rays of the sun, then stained a light brown from the soil where the highway met the side of the road; with no walkway, it was able to creep onto the road. The asphalt was in pretty good condition, and the road, although two way, was wide enough that a lorry could be overtaken on both sides simultaneously by motorcyclists. Most of them had more than two passengers, some of them children and babies – with no safety clothing or helmets – wearing no more than flip-flops, trousers and a T-shirt. They were all smiling and happy as they rode along, not showing any concern for the dangers that existed should an accident occur. There was every shape and size of vehicle on the road, all travelling at different speeds, some limited by their state of repair, as evidenced by the black exhaust smoke that belched out as they tried to keep up with others.

It looked so chaotic to Tom, and yet at the same time it was a perfect masterpiece. They all braked and accelerated, as if dancing to a rhythm they all knew. Chenda knew it, and so it held him in a trance as he watched the dance progress from a slow waltz to upbeat, and then back again, swaying seamlessly in and out of danger.

He felt something at that moment, something that he couldn't identify, something ethereal. Was it the souls of the many murdered Cambodians he had been reading about, or was it just the memories of the abused children that were always there with him? Whatever it was, the dancers never once touched each other, all the way to the hotel, in exactly 15 minutes.

Tom had agreed to meet Sarah downstairs at 4.50pm. It was now 11am, and he had a scheduled 1pm Skype call with Maggie. He set his alarm and laid down to see if sleep would come. It did, but at 12.50pm.

"You look like shit, Tom," Maggie said, smiling.

"Just dropped off. The picture at your end must be good then!"

"I won't keep you, just need a short update."

"Here, safe and sound. Spoken with Deena, meeting her here, not at the Embassy. Meeting is at five. That's all there is."

"OK. Email me once you've had the meeting, so we can Skype again."

He laid down again, and this time quickly dropped into a fitful sleep.

Later, he was awoken by the alarm. For a few seconds he didn't know where he was. Even though the air-con was on and the room cold, he found himself damp from sweat, feeling hungry and a bit mentally uneasy. Sitting on the edge of the bed, he attempted to analyse why he was feeling the way he was. With nothing other than where he was to pin it on, he got up and had a long shower.

With fresh clothes, feeling clean, dry, and armed with a counsel book, Tom stepped out of the room and made his way downstairs. It was one flight and he used the lift, but by the time he got to the meeting point he was already hot and wondering where the next air-conditioned room was. With no sign of Sarah, he sat down to wait and watched staff and tourists enter and leave the lobby area. Out beyond the entrance he could see a busy road that ran alongside the Mekong River, which the hotel overlooked. The sun had disappeared, replaced by clouds that looked heavy with rain. His clothes were already limp, an indication of the moisture level in the air.

"You get any sleep?" enquired Sarah, arriving from behind Tom, wearing a beach dress, swimsuit, and carrying a beach bag.

"I did. You?"

"A bit, then I woke up and couldn't get back, so I came down to use the pool. Got a bit more there."

Tom, who was already feeling a little bit out of his comfort zone, struggled to adjust to the new environment, with Sarah sitting close to him clothed in a figure-hugging, one-piece swimsuit and a mostly transparent beach dress. He could see that her bag contained her notebook and guessed she wasn't intending on changing for the meeting.

"Are you hungry?" Sarah asked, whilst quickly running a hairbrush through her hair, then tying it back with a scrunchie.

"Hank Marvin starving!"

"Me too. How about we order something to tide us over as soon as Deena arrives, and we know how long this is going to take?"

"Sure, I'll go and get a menu from reception."

"No need, I've got one in my bag," Sarah said, turning towards Tom with a big self-satisfied grin, having finished her hair.

Tom found himself staring, whilst catching a slight hint of perfume or suntan lotion.

"See, I'm not just all Comms, I can do logistics too."

Tom was about to take up the offer of banter when he spotted Chenda, who, arriving outside the open lobby, stopped and quickly got out to open the rear offside door of the Land Cruiser they had been in earlier. This time, there were small flags attached to the front of the vehicle. The hotel staff, whose job it was to receive guests as they arrived, seemed to act more urgently at the sight of this driver and its occupant. All three had spoken over Skype, so each knew what the other looked like, and Deena walked confidently, with an air of authority, towards them.

"Tom, Sarah, lovely to meet you in person," Deena said, with a beaming smile and genuine warmth, shaking Sarah's hand first, and then Tom's, meeting their eyes as she did so.

"I see you have found the pool already Sarah. Good girl. Start as you mean to go on!"

"The heat is so lovely, Deena, I just couldn't resist it, and I was struggling to get some sleep."

"Yes, the dreaded jet lag," Deena began, stopping as Chenda arrived. "Can you find the room and check how long we have it for?"

"Yes, sure."

"It takes me a full three days before I am back into it. I'm guessing you will be getting hungry about now?"

"I am, I mean, we both are!" Sarah said, hardly containing her surprise at Deena's perception.

"We need to sort that then, but first it might be good to see what comes with the room."

"We have it for the evening," Chenda announced, arriving back, whilst pointing towards two large doors behind them.

"Let's get inside so we can talk. I have a lot to tell you."

The conference room, which thankfully was air conditioned, contained a large oval table with plenty of seating and two easel stands with fresh flip charts and pens. At one end there was a long counter with serving plates of fresh fruit, pastries, water, tea and coffee.

"I suggest you eat tonight at the Foreign Correspondents' Club. It is known as the FCC and is just down the road. Chenda can drop you off, then pick you up again when you're finished. That will be about 7.30, so will this tide you over?"

Sarah looked at what was on offer, before turning to Tom and then Deena. "The way I'm feeling right now, that looks like starters and pudding to me!"

"In that case, Chenda, can you get a menu?"

"No need, I have one," exclaimed Sarah, producing a menu with a flourish from her beach bag, offering it straight to Tom. "I'm having the club sandwich: it comes with fries."

Tom, having already checked the snacks menu in his room, didn't need to look.

"Same for me. I'll go and order."

On his return he found all three, eating fresh pineapple and watermelon.

Deena began.

"In the short time I have been away, two more children have gone missing, one local, and one foreign—a dual national, who went missing from the Riverside area whilst in company with his mother, who is from Belgium, and his father, who is French."

"What have the police done?" Tom said interrupting, with a sense of urgency in his tone.

"We don't have a direct police contact; we work through informants who work for the police. Sounds strange I know, but this way we can guarantee a level of truth, because with the police you never get it.

"In relation to the local child, nothing. In relation to the foreign child, very limited. They went to the scene the next day, made a fuss in the area, stopping cars and people, then left. Official line is they have no leads but are working hard to establish them. Our information is that they will poster the foreign child at the borders, but that could take days, if not weeks, as they need authorisation for the money to be spent. The French Ambassador has made numerous attempts to motivate them into more action. He has offered to pay for the advertising. They will take it, and it will get done, but it will be way down the line."

"How long have these two been missing?"

"It's been two days, Tom. They were both reported as missing on the same day, and two hours apart—roughly the same area as well."

"Has this been centralised with a squad heading it up?"

"Doesn't work like that here. The police say that children go missing all the time, some turn up weeks later, some turn up in Western charity houses having been rescued off the streets, the NGO's thinking they have been abandoned and are starving. Some of them have been."

Sarah shook her head in disbelief. "Two days is a long time. They could be anywhere by now."

Tom ate some pineapple; the unbelievable taste being negated by the information he was hearing.

"Is there anybody in the police that we could engage with?"

"No. There is an Immigration Police officer who is new to us. Well connected on the Cambodian scene, influential family, extremely wealthy, educated in America, fluent English, has all the right connections and is probably destined for one of the top jobs. At some point we will need to reach out to him, but not yet."

"Immigration: this isn't his area though, is it?"

"Again, doesn't work like that. He will be able to do whatever he wants. He will be our best bet."

"How do we get to the point when we can safely ask for his help, without giving the game away?"

"Well, I have a plan," replied Deena, getting up and walking over to the counter to get a bottle of water and a glass.

"First up though, intelligence update from our Phnom Penh informant is that a Caucasian male is believed to be behind the two latest missing children."

"How can the police not link this all up?" Sarah said, in an incredulous tone.

"I am trying to manipulate that, but not getting anywhere yet. I have a list of all the known NGOs and other charities that are operating in Phnom Penh. Chenda, do you want to update us on that?"

"Yes, absolutely, for sure. I have a small army of spies," Chenda said, with a proud smile. "They were tasked to visit all the houses run by foreign charities or private NGOs to see if any of the children that had gone missing had turned up there. And they haven't."

Tom could see where the investigative thought process was heading and agreed with it.

"My thoughts, Tom, were to feed that back to the informant, who in turn could bring it to the attention of his manager, in the hope that it might instil some urgency. As of yet, nothing."

"I like your thinking."

"Through Chenda's spy network we have spent money to track back and find out where the Caucasian male description started. They all fizzle out either on the street or the Russian market from someone they don't know and have no way of contacting."

"I have since put a process in place," Chenda said, with an earnest expression and matching tone, "so, if they are in that position again, they will get details and we will know straight away."

"What is the Russian market?" Tom enquired.

"It is a large market where everything in the world is either sold or made—frequented by the locals and tourists. If you go there, take Chenda with you. And remember, anything with a Western name on it will be fake!"

Sarah looked at Tom with a wry smile.

"Sounds like one to miss."

"Not at all, Sarah, you must visit it. It is an experience. I look forward to taking you."

"On the way to the FCC Chenda can show you the locations where the children were last seen but, in short, that is all I have at this end and you can take it from me that the police don't even have that."

"We're only here for a short time; we really need one of those spies of yours to come up with something in the next few days if we are going to investigate this and identify him," Tom said, knowing he was stating the obvious.

"Luckily for us we have a second informant, one from Battambang, which is a city about 4 to 5 hours drive away from here."

Tom sat up alert, with a look of surprise.

"Go on!"

"Well, he won't say much over the phone, we have to go and see him. He wants payment, which I can authorise in exchange for the information."

"Has he given anything that suggests he is worth the money?"

"Yes. He says he knows who is behind the children going missing, why, and a possible location for them!"

Tom looked at Sarah incredulously, eyes widening, before looking back to Deena.

"When can we see him?"

"I suggest we leave straight after the first training session tomorrow. We will need to overnight there, and then travel back the next day. Your second training engagement isn't until the following day, so we will have plenty of time for a debrief."

Tom was thinking that in the UK they would just go that night and couldn't see why this should be any different.

"Can we go now?"

"No. I am well known for cultivating informant opportunities. This may well be just another person trying to make a fast dollar – I get plenty of it – and to be honest this has all the hallmarks of one of those cases. He was evasive, and when pushed just gave me a location and time, and that is tomorrow, late evening, in Battambang."

Tom felt a chill go through him, with goosebumps appearing on his arms. He knew it wasn't the air conditioning.

"Do you have a gut instinct?"

"Yes. My inner woman tells me it could be good!"

Sarah smiled and laughed. She was beginning to take to Deena.

"This is what I have planned for tomorrow. Chenda can pick you up from here at 8am and take you to the Intercontinental. That should give you plenty of time to get set up and to be finished around 11.30. Chenda and I will collect you at 12 noon, and we leave straight from there for Battambang. We'll have lunch on board and there are places we can stop."

"Do we need to vacate our rooms for the night?"

"No, keep them just in case this all falls down in the meantime. You will need to bring an overnight bag though. We will check in once we get to Battambang, have something to eat, and then go to meet the informant. Next day we travel back. Questions?"

Tom had plenty, but felt it wasn't the right time for a long list of 'what ifs'.

"Nope, sounds good."

"Sarah?"

"Nothing from me."

"In that case, I will leave you to your food. Enjoy your visit to the FCC, it's a 'must do' when in Phnom Penh."

"I will meet you in reception at 7.25?"

"Yes, see you then, Chenda," replied Sarah, just as the waiter arrived with two club sandwiches.

It was dark, hot and humid when Chenda arrived to collect them, and the Embassy vehicle was a cool refuge that they climbed into eagerly. Chenda quickly negotiated the vehicle back out onto the highway, turning right and accelerating to avoid getting caught up in oncoming traffic, in what looked like an illegal manoeuvre.

"Alright then. On the right here coming up shortly is the area where the European boy was last seen by his mother."

Chenda pulled over to the right side of the road, straight across the path of oncoming vehicles, which had to take avoiding action to prevent a collision. Yet it was all done smoothly, as if they were taking part in some sort of rehearsed manoeuvre—one where everybody was expecting it to happen, and they all knew their role in it. Tom, who was in the front seat on this occasion, fell into the same subconscious trap as Sarah, realising after the event that his feet were reaching for the imaginary clutch and brake below him.

Chenda, who was looking away from Tom whilst parking at the same time, still spotted it and let out a long laugh.

"Don't worry, Tom. I am an expert driver. I have been on an Embassy driving course in Toronto. They said I was the best driver they had ever seen from Cambodia."

Chenda looked at Tom through the darkness of the car, and he thought he could just see a slight wink, but he wasn't sure.

"We all drive like this. They expect it. It's not a problem."

Sarah had just cottoned on.

"Wasn't just me then!"

Tom turned and thought about poking his tongue out.

"Captured."

Sarah laughed, "Happens to us all, eh?"

"No need for you to get out. If you look right, there on the grass on the other side of those small trees is where he was last seen."

Sarah could see that there was a wide strip of grass that ran alongside the road and was bounded on the far side by a stone wall which looked to be over waist height: probably too high for a small child to clamber over.

"What's on the other side of that wall, Chenda?"

"That is the mouth of the Tonle Sap River; it is where it meets the Mekong. If a small child went into the Mekong there, he or she will never be seen again," Chenda replied, correctly reading Sarah's line of questioning.

The area was deserted and dark. Not the sort of place you would want to be walking alone at night, Sarah thought.

"What's it like here during the day?"

"Much busier, plenty of people around. Especially just by the trees, because of the shade they provide. Locals go there to eat their lunch."

Tom disappeared into his own thoughts, wondering how the abduction went down, if that's what really happened. How many were there? Where would the getaway vehicle have been parked? It was broad daylight, and busy. How come nobody stopped it? There must have been some witnesses, even if they didn't recognise what was going on as illegal. The fear and confusion that the child must have felt. How are the parents feeling right now? He felt a wave of anger rising in him, one that he knew well. He grabbed hold of it, placing it in his memory bank for later use.

Chenda double-parked outside the FCC and handed Tom an Embassy phone.

"The code is your room number. I'm under Chenda. Call me five minutes before you are ready to leave."

The FCC was an old building, dedicated to an era long since passed. It oozed of the French colonial era; shabby looking with its washed-out yellow paint; peeling in places with signs of crumbling on the elaborate stone facades. The adjacent buildings were of the same design, a home above a shop, with the immediate area a hum of street activity, congested with shoppers, tuk-tuks and rickshaws. Tom felt he was following in the footsteps of foreign correspondents who would meet to drink and swap stories from a war that had occurred in his lifetime. The stairway up to the first floor was adorned with old pictures from the country's turbulent history, taking you on a journey back in time before you got to the top. The bar, centrally located, gave way to a seating area that provided a view over the street scene below and opposite to the river, blacked out by the night.

The warm wind blew in through open and what formerly would have been, wooden-shuttered archways, adding its own ambience to the busy Asian scene below. Sarah took a long drink of her cocktail, waiting for the alcohol to take effect. With the assistance of the jet lag, heat, and location, it didn't take long.

"I can't imagine what must have gone through that kid's mind. Do you think he's still alive?"

Tom had already drunk most of his bottle of Tiger beer, was wondering why it tasted better than others he had drunk at home and beginning to feel guilty for its enjoyment.

"I hope he is, but if we can't find him soon, the longer this goes on, the slimmer his chances are."

"I'm going to have nightmares about this!"

Tom thought about that statement. Whether it was the location, the heat, the beer, or the crimes, he didn't know, but he was on the brink of confiding a deep secret; one that he had only confessed to Fiona after being caught out.

"Goes with the territory," Tom said, in a matter of fact manner.

Sarah was watching Tom as he spoke, and his comment wasn't lost on her. She was weighing up what to say next, when her mind was taken off the subject by her tummy yelling, 'feed me!'.

Chenda was outside and waiting in the five minutes she said it would take her, and they were back at the Sunflower and in their rooms within minutes. After a quick Skype call to Maggie, updating her of the new intelligence and the proposed plan, Tom, feeling tired, got into bed and closed his eyes. But after 20 minutes of trying, he realised sleep was not going to come any time soon and thought a nightcap might help. Getting dressed again, he went to the bar and ordered a double whisky over ice, then meandered out into the warm night, only to find Sarah there already.

"In all the gin joints in all the towns!"

Sarah, startled from her thoughts, jumped in her seat.

"Great minds, eh?"

They both sat silently, sipping their drinks, looking out into the darkness to where the mighty Mekong River was. The warm, moist, tropical air flowing over them, helping the location and alcohol find their targets.

After a while Tom became aware that Sarah was looking at him. He met her stare and could see she had a troubled look on her face, as if she was making an internal decision on whether to say something, or not.

Sarah held eye contact briefly, before looking away again into the darkness, where she knew the Mekong was flowing.

"What you said earlier," Sarah began, then paused, unsure if she should continue.

"I said quite a lot earlier: what bit are you referring to?"

This time Tom looked away, thinking it might be easier for Sarah to speak if she wasn't being stared at.

"The bit about going with the territory. Before we left, I was briefed on you by both JT, and Dr Clayworth... I know."

CHAPTER THREE

Police academies of the modern era teach their recruits that mere suspicion, of itself, is not enough to act upon. Some of those students later become detectives, a few then spend a large part of their investigative lives analysing those suspicions from an early stage, using the results to further an investigation: their experience having taught them that if it looks dodgy, feels dodgy and smells dodgy, it is more likely than not to be dodgy.

For Tom, the knowledge that JT had spoken to Sarah about his personal history was chewing away at him. It was causing his finely-tuned sixth sense to work overtime; then send messages to his brain. It had bothered him through the night, at breakfast, and during the training presentation, to such an extent that he had found it hard to remain focussed during and afterwards in question time. If his mind wasn't on JT, then it had been on what awaited them that night; he felt exhausted.

For some reason, his thoughts kept winding their way back to Maggie, and what she had said about JT before they left. The main comment that bothered him was that she thought he was being lined up for the sack. He hadn't contacted the Union Rep, whose details Maggie had given him before they left either, which was now weighing on his mind. Something was not adding up, but he couldn't carry on thinking as he was; he had to put it in a box, otherwise it would consume him. He decided to draw a line under it for now, by making a promise to himself that he would lay another marker down with Stuart Simmons, in Professional Standards. That way, he at least had a lifeline should it all go wrong.

"We'll be arriving at Battambang in 15 minutes," Chenda announced proudly from the front of the people carrier they were in.

The vehicle had been specially adapted, with a higher horsepower engine, stronger suspension, tinted windows to the point of blackout, bulletproof glass and extra reinforcement below where Deena Potts was currently sitting; to mitigate attacks involving improvised explosive devices.

Tom was sitting in the centre row, having swapped with Sarah at the midway point. It provided him with unrestricted views and the added advantage of being able to speak to Deena. The journey had been, and was still, an eye-opener. The roads, mostly asphalted, were in a very bad state of repair and had clearly been in that condition for a long time. Some holes were so big that traffic slowed to a crawl to manoeuvre around them, with Chenda driving on the wrong side of the road against oncoming traffic, as if it were natural to do so.

Once outside Phnom Penh, the buildings of its colonial past quickly gave way to dry paddy fields and flat unused agricultural land that looked baked hard by the heat. The land was bordered on one side by the road heading north, palm trees and jungle on the other. It looked impoverished. The small wooden shacks dotted around, propped up on stilts, housed many generations of one family, who smiled and waved happily as the car sped past. It made him feel both privileged and guilty at the same time.

Battambang, the capital city of Cambodia's north-west, now 15 minutes away, was not yet apparent, the countryside showing no signs that it was close to a major trading centre until it abruptly gave way to a mixture of wooden, single-storey shacks and French colonial stone buildings, some with three floors. The foreign influence was so strong, especially in the well-preserved ones, that you could have been mistaken for thinking you were in France for a split second. The roads became busier, wider, traffic slowing to a crawl as vehicles were signalled into line by two traffic police officers ahead.

"We'll get stopped here," Deena announced. "What do you think it's for, Chenda?"

"It will be car tax for sure."

Sarah, who was in the front seat, turned to Tom and gave him an upward lift of her eyebrows and a small smile, which told him she was interested to know what it was like being stopped by police in Cambodia.

Chenda opened the window and immediately began conversing in Khmer, as first one, then both officers came to her window. After a short exchange, Tom watched one officer go to the front of the vehicle and check the licence plate, then return to say something in Khmer to his colleague, who then began speaking quicker, with more authority, whilst pointing his finger at the Toyota. Chenda responded with a volley of sentences, at least matching the officer's urgency and upping the authority in her tone, indicating at one point to the rear of the vehicle in the direction of Deena, which took the officer by surprise. He peered into the car, looking backwards as he did so. The other officer, Tom noticed, stayed silent and was looking at Sarah, transfixed. The first officer withdrew his head and smartly took one step back as Chenda began again—her tone unmistakeable. She was on the offensive. It ended with an emphatic 'umph' as she closed the electric window, lifted her head slightly, faced forward, paused and then slowly drove off, before picking up speed.

"What was all that about?" enquired Deena.

"The blacked out windows again. He wanted to impound the car and kick us out on the street. I told him he was stupid, he and his family wouldn't be eating rice tonight or for the next month, if he insisted on kicking the Canadian Ambassador out onto the street."

Chenda let out a small giggle, dropped her voice as Deena explained to Tom the rules relating to blacked out car windows in Cambodia.

"I think his sidekick had the hots for you. He was cute, not my sort, but quite cute, nonetheless. You have a boyfriend or husband, Sarah?"

Sarah, who was already smiling from Chenda's exchange with the police, let out a laugh.

"Neither."

"Really? I find that hard to believe. All that blonde straight hair! For sure, that is what the sidekick was staring at. Khmer men love blonde hair."

"Don't embarrass Sarah, Chenda," Deena shouted, from the rear of the car.

"Perfectly good question, Deena. But yeah, sure, no problems. No more questions about boyfriends or husbands," replied Chenda, looking up into the rear-view mirror at Deena.

She waited until Deena looked away, before looking back at Sarah, with a smile and a wink; at the same time negotiating traffic from all sides.

Having checked in at their hotel, Tom opened his bag, removed some clothing for that night and then took his wash kit to the bathroom—stopping in front of the mirror. He had to get some sleep before they went out tonight, and that wouldn't come until he got hold of Stuart Simmons.

He went in search of the number, sitting on the edge of the bed as the call connected. After two rings he quickly disconnected, suddenly pondering if what he was about to do was right or not. Deciding to trust his gut, he rang again.

"Stuart Simmons, Professional Standards, how can I help you?"

"Stuart. It's Tom Ross, how are you?"

"I'm fine, thanks. How are you? Where are you? This is an awful line!"

"Yes, it is. I'm in Cambodia, working. I guess how I'm doing, is why I'm ringing you. I need to lay down another marker, same as I did with you on Operation Hope."

Stuart, who was sat at his desk, leaned forward, and silently pressed a record button on a device attached to the phone he was using—one that Jerry Stone from IT had given him just two days earlier.

"You do seem to attract trouble, Tom. What is it this time?" Stuart said, with a just enough of a jovial tone to disguise the seriousness of the situation.

"I'm here tracking down an outstanding offender from a previous operation. It has personal authorisation from the Chief, as head of GOPOL. I'm working in partnership with the Canadian Ambassador to Cambodia, with Maggie heading it up at that end.

"Before I left, I found out that JT was against this deployment, me in particular, and told Maggie he will ensure I'm sacked if I go outside the boundaries of the operation whilst here. Cambodia is a far cry from British policing; I have every intention of sticking to the script, but the threat from JT is stopping me from focussing on what I need to do.

"I want it recorded with the PSU, you in particular, that I have every intention of doing what is legally and morally right whilst here, but the threat of the sack hanging over me is total bullshit and just brings back all the issues and concerns I had with Operation Hope."

"Come on, Tom, you know as well as I do, JT will sometimes flex his authority, and he doesn't care who comes off the worse for it. I am sure it's just sabre-rattling."

"Well, I hope you're correct. But I want it known that I feel that something isn't right. I can't put my finger on it, but my gut tells me it isn't just sabre-rattling. He has an agenda, and I'm written all over it!"

"Look, Tom," Stuart replied slowly, in a caring tone, "we've been here before. This time you're operating away from home, in a totally different environment. It's bound to make you feel on edge. You have a clean bill of health. If you say something isn't right, then, from experience, that's good enough for me. Consider it logged."

"I don't want an intelligence sheet submitted on my gut instinct!" Tom quickly replied.

"I know, it stays with me. If you need to chat something through, or need a steer, just ring me. We go back, just remember that."

With the task complete, relieved, Tom got into bed and quickly fell asleep. Back in England, Stuart Simmons switched off the recording device, picked up his phone and rang Maggie Burrows.

"I just took a call from Tom Ross."

"Recorded?"

"Yes."

"What did he want?"

"Touch of the jitters I'd say. Hardly surprising. Wanted to lay down a marker surrounding JT."

"What exactly?"

"What we anticipated: just his survival instinct. Nothing more. I've opened the door so he can call me again if he needs to."

"Good. The game's afoot."

Maggie Burrows got up, went to her office safe and spun the dial the required number of times before entering the combination. She retrieved a mobile phone, switched it on, then rang one of only two numbers contained in its directory.

"Yes?"

"Margaret, it's Maggie. Tom just rang Stuart, as anticipated. Survival instincts, laying down a marker—that's all. You should get the recording soon. Can you let the Chief know?"

"Yes, of course."

Tom woke to the sound of his alarm. Pulling back the sheets, he sat on the edge of the bed, searching his feelings, mood, instinct and their combined effects. Making the call was the right one. He felt better, relieved and hungry. Getting quickly dressed, he was down in reception with a minute to spare, but still later than the others who were there ahead of him and who must have been waiting a while.

"What time do you call this? I thought a good Marine was always ten minutes early?" Sarah exclaimed, with a cheeky grin on her face, whilst looking at her watch.

"I'm Hank as well!" she added.

Tom was about to claim he was, in fact, not late, but looking at Deena and Chenda, who were both wearing self-satisfied looks, he became acutely aware he was manifestly outnumbered, so decided against it.

"Point taken. I'll be earlier next time! Let's eat!"

They went to a restaurant known to Deena, one that served Cambodian and Western food. Deena, Tom and Sarah all ate the same Lok Lak Cambodian dish, whilst Chenda went for Australian steak and chips. The meal also provided Deena with the opportunity to get a feel for

Tom and Sarah. She had noticed that Tom, who had been distant on the journey to Battambang, was not showing any signs of that now, whilst Sarah was the normal, confident, self-assured, communications professional that she had thought she was from first speaking to her weeks before. They were a strange combination of skill sets for this type of deployment, and it interested her.

She had requested the Canadian Embassy in London to supply her with an intelligence package on COCET, GOPOL and Tom. They had more on them than she had expected; the file was an eye-opening read. The work that COCET had started had been both explosive and tragic. The intel was mostly open source material, with a small amount of unevaluated intelligence from a single source. The real surprise though, was that the intelligence officer thought it prudent to make a search with the Canadian Security Intelligence Service. The search report came back negative, but nothing to see here, does not mean there isn't anything there. It just means you haven't got high enough security clearance, or someone doesn't want you to know. There was no need to make a search with the Security Service on this level of request, unless you thought something would be found. She had probably seen other intelligence in the course of her work, then, when the negative search came back, had left the search on file as a flag for her. It was a subtle way of telling a reader that there might be other things going on in the background, and, if there were, other things, it was her view that neither Tom nor Sarah had any knowledge of it either.

Back at the hotel, they went straight to Deena's room, where Chenda rang the informant, as requested, at exactly 10.30pm. They heard the call answered immediately. Chenda had a short conversation in Khmer, before placing the phone to her chest.

"I need pen and paper."

Deena quickly grabbed some hotel stationery and a pencil from the desk in her room. Chenda sat down and continued the call in Khmer, whilst writing down instructions in English on the paper she had been given. As the call ended, she stood up.

"OK, we have to drive along Street 616. I know it, it's on the east side of the River. We have to find Street 601, drive down from the junction two kilometres, then pull over and wait. I don't know this Street 601, but I have a map in the car. We will find it."

"How long will it take to get there?" asked Deena.

"If we find Street 601 on the first attempt, then 15 minutes!"

Although in Cambodia's third largest city, they were driving on roads with no street lighting, reflective lines, or road studs. Outside it was pitch black, with just the lights of the vehicle they were travelling in as a means to see. The lights of the car were powerful, especially when on full beam, but the darkness was so black that they quickly failed to penetrate the night. The only traffic on the road was the occasional small motorcycle with two to five people on board; otherwise, the streets were practically deserted, as if there were a curfew in place.

"This is eerie," Tom announced to nobody in particular.

"What does that mean?" Chenda asked, eagerly.

"Strange, sort of scary. It's very dark compared to the roads we are used to travelling on. The bike riders—they seem to come out of the darkness without warning."

"Tom, don't worry one bit. This is normal driving for me. I am an expert. You cannot see these riders, but they can see us, so, take it from me, they want to live. They will not be crashing into us for sure."

Tom was impressed that Chenda was so full of confidence, but it wasn't enough to convince him otherwise of the danger. After about ten minutes, Chenda started to slow down to look for a junction on her right. Out of the darkness, a street appeared, causing her to stop in the middle of the road and get out a small tourist map.

"Ok, Deena, I think this is it. We should try it, and, if he doesn't turn up, we should then come back and go further. But I am sure my superior map reading skills mean that this will be the right one!"

"I bow to your superior knowledge and skill on the matter, Chenda," replied Deena, in a jovial tone.

Chenda turned into the junction and set the odometer. After a short distance the vehicle slowed and came to a halt on the nearside.

Whether it was the vehicle's extra cladding or its security features, Tom didn't know, but he could hardly make out the noise of the engine running or the air con, which was keeping the inside temperature cool in comparison to the outside night: that was a humid 23°c.

He had been on many, if not hundreds, of night observations but nothing quite like this. He was a British cop, effectively on covert operations, in the middle of rural Cambodia. The street was deserted, with the only thing he and the team able to see being the poorly maintained road ahead, some immediate land to either side of it, lit up by a halo of conical light created by the headlights, which Chenda quickly extinguished. It was nothing if not surreal.

Chenda maintained watch in her offside mirror. After a couple of minutes, she spotted a single light in the distance.

"We have a rider coming."

Tom couldn't see the light from his mirror, but Deena was able to see through the rear window.

"It's slowing," she stated.

Tom turned around and looked in the direction of Deena. He could hear the motorbike engine as it pulled up behind them, the light penetrating the darkness of their vehicle and causing him to look away to save his night vision. The engine and headlight were quickly switched off, allowing the night to envelop them again. The rider approached Chenda's door, stopping just short so Tom couldn't see. There was a short conversation in Khmer, followed by the rider opening the central sliding door, stepping in and sitting down in a rear seat next to Deena. Sarah, who was sitting in the central row, switched on a roof light so everybody could see as Tom and Chenda climbed through to join them.

The rider was in his early forties, Tom thought. He was slim, with smart close-cropped hair, dressed in jeans, a short-sleeved shirt and was wearing a pair of stout-looking, highly polished black shoes.

Chenda immediately began in Khmer.

"No need to speak Khmer. I speak good English!" the rider announced proudly, with a wide grin, which displayed slightly crooked front teeth and some silver amalgam fillings.

"That's good, I'm Deena Potts, the one with the money," Deena announced, before introducing the rest of the team.

Tom noticed that Chenda had taken position on top of the central console, directly facing the rider, and was viewing her fellow countryman with suspicion.

"Why didn't you say so when speaking to me," Chenda said, in an authoritative tone, which sent a message to the rider that she was the Cambodian top dog in the vehicle.

Instantly, he changed his facial expression, from smile to neutral, before offering his hand to Deena.

"My name is Seng Sopheap. Sopheap is my given name. I am here on behalf of my sister; I am the only one in my family who can help her. Thank you for coming all the way here and seeing me," Sopheap said, slightly bowing his head, placing his left hand over his right wrist, before shaking hands.

"Well, let's hope it's all been worth it?" Deena replied.

Sopheap then went through the same handshake, and bowing process, with Tom.

"Pleased to meet you, Bong."

As he turned to Sarah, his eyes widened, and his smile started to return. Without looking, he sensed the flash of warning that came across Chenda's face and quickly bowed again.

"Pleased to meet you, Ohn-Srei."

Sopheap looked up, faced Chenda, and seemed as if he were going to make a formal greeting with her, but, seeing the look of defiance on her face, decided against it.

"Do you have the money?" Sopheap enquired in a respectful tone.

"Yes, I do. First of all, though, there are some rules on how this works. You tell me everything you know, and I decide if it is worth the money or not. If you tell me something that is worthless, or something I already know, then, no payment. If I think you are lying, then, no payment. Do you understand?"

"Yes, Bong-Srei."

"Good. In that case, away you go!"

"Go where?" Sopheap replied, with a startled look on his face.

Chenda let out a giggle, before saying something in Khmer, in a tone that seemed to scold Sopheap.

"Ok, I understand," Sopheap replied sheepishly, squirming in his seat. "My information comes from my sister. She is married to a very vicious gangster who will not let her out of his sight: or the sight of his guards. I am only able to visit occasionally. She wants to escape, but cannot, so she has given me information that I can use to secure her release."

"Have you been to the police with this information?" Deena asked.

"I cannot do this; they are all corrupt and receiving money from the gang. They are also involved with the trafficking. Even the police station has been used as a staging point. If I went to them, my sister would be killed, as I would, and my whole family. I cannot do that!"

"What information has your sister given you?" Deena asked, in a calm, but firm manner.

"She says there is a child trafficking team operating between here and Poipet. The team is a Chinese Malaysian, a European and a Thai national. They are the bosses. They then use my sister's gangster husband and his gangster team for protection and security. They kidnap children off the street, both boys and girls, for direct trafficking out of Cambodia to mainly Malaysian, Arab and North Korean markets.

"Very large sums of US dollars are being paid, with some clients even travelling to Cambodia to secure sex with a virgin first. My brother-in-law gangster and his team do the kidnapping, storing and transporting out of Cambodia into Thailand. From there she doesn't know what happens to the children. He also oversees paying the local senior police to do nothing if any reports come in. He told her that once he even used one of their buildings as a transit point.

"The gangster is being paid large amounts for his work. They guard the safe house and have been well armed by the bosses. He bragged to her one night, when drunk, he had a rocket launcher. She hasn't seen it but has seen many different weapons."

Deena, Tom, Sarah and Chenda sat shocked as Sopheap finished speaking. He had been looking directly at Deena the whole time he was talking and had now paused, waiting for a response.

Deena looked at Tom, with an expression that said, you first.

"What's your brother-in-law's name?" Tom asked, whilst getting out his counsel book and a pen.

"Pang, Chakra."

"Pang is the surname?"

"Yes, Bong."

"Age, or date of birth?"

"I do not know, he probably doesn't know, many of us don't."

Chenda sniffed loudly, causing Sarah to think that she was proud to know hers.

"Address?"

"Battambang."

"Actual address?"

"I don't mean to be disrespectful, Bong, but first I need to see how you progress this; I will tell you, but I need to know more what you can do for my sister first."

Tom glanced at Deena, who nodded.

"How many are in Chakra's gang?"

"I don't know, but my sister will."

"Do you know any names?"

"I don't. I have seen some when I have visited my sister. They are bad people. My sister will know their names, but maybe only nicknames— probably not full names."

"Have you seen weapons at your sister's house?"

"Yes, Bong."

"What types—do you know?"

"I have seen one rifle, and once I saw a handgun."

"Do they have ammunition for these guns?" Deena asked, interrupting.

"I have asked this same question, because many times people will have a gun but no ammunition, but they have plenty, my sister says. They have been armed by the Malaysian. She says that most of the weapons are at the safe house, along with US dollars."

"Where is this safe house?" Tom continued.

"My sister does not know, Bong. It is too dangerous for her to ask. She says it is heavily guarded by Chakra and his gangsters; he would beat her just for asking. She says, wherever it is, it is only 45 minutes maximum from Battambang. She overheard some of the gang saying that the Malaysian and the Thai are often there. They talk about them in a manner of respect. The European—they don't like, but he has been to the safe house, because she heard the men saying he makes video recordings of the children, before they are taken away."

"Is there anything else you know, anything else that your sister has told you that I haven't asked you about?"

"That is all I know, Bong."

"Tasking time?" Tom said to Deena.

"What is your sister's name?" Deena asked, who now had her own notepad and pen out.

"Nuon, Bong-Srei."

"What does your sister want out of this?"

"She wants Chakra in jail for a long time, so she can escape. She has a cousin in Phnom Penh that Chakra does not know. She can go there with her two children and start a new life. She wants some money to help her do that: that is all."

"What do you want out of this?"

"For my sister to escape that gangster and to be safe—plus I am taking great risk, so is my family by me doing this. I have to show them that we have been rewarded for this risk."

"How do you contact Nuon?"

"I have to go there. Chakra has a phone at the house, but Nuon is not allowed to use it."

"Do you know, or has your sister told you, about a foreign child being kidnapped by Chakra?"

"No, Bong-Srei. She thinks it is just street kids, because nobody cares if they go missing."

Deena removed an envelope from her chest pocket and handed her notepad and pen and the envelope to Sopheap.

"There's 50 US in there. Write down Nuon's address, then we can discuss what happens next."

Sopheap hesitated for a moment, then took the envelope, quickly put it in his pocket, then wrote down the address.

"Ok. We have to get these men arrested so your sister can escape and start a new life away from her husband. I agree to pay her some money to help her do this. For this to happen though, I will need to maintain communication with you, and for you to gain more information from Nuon. The main thing we need to do is identify the safe house, so, to help with that, I want you to ask Nuon to listen and remember everything she hears and sees from now on. Then she must tell you, and you tell me: no matter how small that information is."

Deena handed her notepad to Chenda. "Write down this list in Khmer for me, please."

"I want vehicles, makes, colours, descriptions, licence numbers, telephone numbers, emails, passports numbers, identity documents, descriptions of the weapons, names of the gang members, times they arrive and leave, any patterns to their arriving and leaving. In fact, just about everything she sees or hears from now on, I want to know. This list that Chenda will give you, you must memorise and then destroy. You will need to see your sister more often than you have been doing. This may cause Chakra to become suspicious, so you will have to come up with a cover story—a reason for being there. I suggest you think about that and let Chenda know tomorrow what your decision is, so I can consider it, then approve it."

"Yes, Bong-Srei."

"In the meantime, we will return to Phnom Penh and come up with a plan.

CHAPTER FOUR

If you have ever been lucky enough to sail under the White Ensign, as I have, then you will have been in possession of the very latest Admiralty charts. As any mariner will tell you, no chart is infallible, all charts can be incomplete and electronic charts are only as good as your fuse box. Policing is no different, in that all plans sometimes have their limitations.

— I. R. Tyler

The next day, Tom, Sarah and Deena travelled back to Phnom Penh, en route making plans for what to do next. No matter how many they made, it all hinged on the response from Cambodian Law Enforcement: something Deena couldn't foresee. By the time Chenda had pulled up outside the Sunflower Hotel, they had decided to start a second operation, keeping it completely separate from Operation Veritas; the new one dealing with the approach and initial meetings with the Immigration Police. The thought was that they were less likely to slip up and mention their real reason for being in the country if they concentrated on new aims and objectives. It would also benefit from looking and feeling more realistic to an inherently suspicious, non-Western organisation.

The plan was, that Deena would approach the police through formal channels in her capacity as Canadian Ambassador, seeking an urgent meeting that day to discuss an unexpected capacity building opportunity. Tom and Sarah would deliver their training as agreed, something that the Immigration Police could later validate, whilst Chenda would chase up Sopheap and his cover story for being at his sister's more often in order to capture further intelligence from her.

Back in his room, showered, and now in shorts and T-shirt, Tom sat down to Skype Maggie with the update.

"So, what news, Tom?"

"We're not long back from Battambang. It was worth the trip. In short, Deena has got an informant. His sister is married to a major crim in Battambang who has a gang. They are being paid to kidnap street kids from Phnom Penh, who are then trafficked – mostly out of the country – although there have been some cases of clients travelling here for sex first. The group behind the local crime gang are a Chinese Malay, a Thai national and a European. The local gang are being well paid and are well armed. Weapons have been seen."

"Who is the European?" Maggie interrupted, with concern in her voice.

"No names are known. The gang keep the children at a safe house, the location of which is unknown, but it's not that far from Battambang. Local police are implicated. Intelligence suggests they are being paid by the gang, and that on at least one occasion a police building was used as a transit point."

"Bloody hell! Is that informant telling the truth?"

"No way of corroborating anything he says because we can't go to the police, but yeah, I would say he is telling the truth. Deena paid him, she thought he was telling the truth."

"So, what's next?"

"Sarah and I will do the second training session tomorrow. Deena will make contact with a new Immigration Officer, who she thinks we can trust enough to at least meet. That will be under the guise of us being here for the training – it being a shame to miss a capacity building opportunity – and then try to set up a meeting with us. Deena thinks that won't raise too much suspicion. She will chair it and, if it all goes smoothly I will pop the question about joint working on a case if we had the occasion to do so. From there step by step."

"When will you have that meeting?"

"Deena will try to arrange it for tomorrow evening."

"Alright, that sounds workable to kick things off. This informant, what has been done around him?"

"He has been tasked with coming up with a reason for increased visits to his sister, and then through him his sister will be tasked to get as much information as possible about the husband and his gang, to pass back through the informant to us."

"Who's tasking the sister?"

"Informant one, the brother. Yes, it breaks all our rules on informant handling, but we aren't in the UK, we are in rural Cambodia."

"How do we know she won't tell the husband?" Maggie demanded in an incredulous tone.

"She wants him nicked. He beats her, she has kids, she wants a better life. She can't get away to meet us, says it's too dangerous for her to do that, or to ask about the safe house. All she can do is watch and listen, pass that to her brother; then he tells us."

Maggie paused. The thought of trying to impose their usual informant-handling procedures on this situation wasn't viable. It was something, however, she would need to overcome with others.

"What's their surveillance capability?"

"None."

"Did you take any camera equipment with you?'

"Work equipment? No, but my own will do."

"Have you got an open line with the informant?"

"Yes."

"When do you expect an update from him?"

"Tomorrow."

"OK, so what are your aims, now you have this intelligence? What do you see as your best outcome?"

"Meet with Immigration, offer joint working, get a rapport going. Hint that intel might be forthcoming, but local police are compromised. If that goes well, second meeting, offer up the intelligence; hold back the informant. Then look to locate the safe house; identify the three suspects behind it and the local gang members, then immigration swoop, arrest them all and we get to find out who the European really is."

"Easy then!"

"Would be back there!"

"I was being sarcastic."

"I know," Tom quipped, with a smile.

"What's the likelihood of the authorities there working the weekend?"

"Zero, I would have thought."

"In that case, your undercover officer performance better be a good one, so we can extend without raising suspicion. Update me once you've had the meeting. Timing should be good for me."

Maggie put the receiver down and immediately began the procedure for copying the Skype call, which, being different from telephone conversations, meant she needed to follow a printed and laminated set of instructions to ensure she didn't make a mistake. Completed, she retrieved the mobile phone from the safe and dialled.

"Yes?"

"I've just had a Skype call with Tom. The disc should be with you soon. I'm going to have to take some action surrounding what was said, so I will need a steer."

"I'll let him know. Thank you, Maggie."

Phnom Penh, Cambodia

Tom and Sarah took a tuk-tuk from outside the hotel to the FCC. Spotting two spare, tall bar stools available at the balcony, Sarah went ahead, whilst Tom bought their drinks and ordered food. They both sat watching the street scene below, it was a world apart from theirs: alien, yet mesmerising.

"We haven't had chance to speak. Are you OK?"

"Yeah, wasn't quite expecting what we got from the informant though!" Tom replied, not sure if Sarah was referring to last night's information.

"I meant what we discussed the night before."

Tom produced what he thought was his best genuine, warm smile, and decided to open up. He didn't know Sarah at all, but his inner instincts told him she was a good person, and that was enough for him.

"Ah . . . that. Not at first, no. I was angry as hell, but worked my way through it. We're all good."

Sarah weighed up whether to probe further. He certainly seemed as if he had let it go; it wasn't affecting his ability to work.

"I'm glad," she replied, taking another sip of her cocktail. "What do you think about the informant and the intelligence?"

"Explosive, and I believe him," Tom said confidently, glad they had moved on.

"Yeah, me too. Really hope Deena can pull a meeting on."

"I think she can. I mean, why wouldn't they come; they have nothing to lose. They will be naturally inquisitive, if not suspicious. The real question will be, are they willing to do anything, and if they are, what exactly can they do?"

Sarah was about to reply when the waiter appeared, informing them that their meal was ready, even though only a few minutes had passed. The food provided a welcome break from work and a chance to find out about each other, so much so that it was late by the time they left to fight their way through a wall of tuk-tuk drivers, all waiting to take them back to their hotel.

Thames Valley Police HQ, Kidlington, England

Margaret Thrinton had just finished typing up the Skype conversation between Maggie Burrows and Tom. She collected the document off the printer and entered the Chief's office.

"Here's the transcript you asked for."

"Thank you, Margaret. How long until my next meeting?"

"Thirty-five minutes."

"Should be enough. Can you close the door please?"

Alone, the Chief read the transcript, quickly making his way through it. He placed the document down, walked over to a small key safe that had been securely fixed to the wall and tapped in the numeric code. He removed a plastic key, then placed that key into the side of a Brent secure telephone. He slid out a laminated instruction sheet from underneath, followed the instructions and waited for the call to be answered.

"Good afternoon Chief Constable, it's Toby Spencer-Drummond. How are things in the land of policing?"

"Full of politics, ridiculous expenditure targets we have no hope of meeting and enough bureaucratic red tape to go around China three times with plenty to spare! And if you tell me you're faring any better, not only will I be jealous, but I might just consider a career change!"

"As you well know, James, I'm not in a position to confirm or deny the internal machinations of the United Kingdom's most secret organisation," Toby replied, with a hint of mirth in his tone.

"I thought the 'most secret' one was the SIS!" the Chief shot back, in a stern voice. He had no idea of Toby's equivalent rank in the police, but he wasn't accustomed to being called by his first name in such a familiar manner.

"From what I hear, my 'comrades' over the bridge find it hard to share a pencil, whether that's to do with resourcing or culture I have no idea, but I suspect the latter," Toby replied, in a flat, emotionless tone.

"God, I hate spooks," the Chief thought.

"Things have moved on a bit. Intelligence has been captured from a new informant, and there is a strong likelihood more will follow within 24 hours. My team may meet with Cambodian law enforcement as early as tomorrow afternoon their time. Maggie needs directing over the contents in the transcript I am about to send you."

"Send it. I will ring you straight back."

With the call concluded, the Chief opened his door, checked to see who was around, then whispered, "Margaret, can you send that to 'he who cannot be named'!"

Well ahead of her boss, she pressed her keyboard with one finger, before looking back up at the Chief, with a self-satisfied look, whispering, "Done!"

"I don't pay you enough Margaret," the Chief replied in a louder tone, returning to his office, closing the door behind him.

"I know," Margaret replied to herself and an empty room.

Within moments the Brent telephone rang.

"Well, this is looking good," Toby began. "I would suggest Maggie leads with Deena all the time. Just keep Tom out of the equation. No need to mention tasking informants, just that Deena now has an intelligence update, and that she is going to meet with law enforcement there to scope out the possibilities of sharing that intelligence. In line with our agreement, she is keeping Tom out of it; until there is a need to know. In the meantime, they are conducting the valuable capacity building exercise awaiting an update."

"That sounds good. Just enough then?"

"Yes, hopefully it will generate some product on our assets"

"I have a great deal on next week, Toby. I'm going to need that meeting firmed up soon."

"Let's see what the next 24 to 48 hours provides, then we should be able to plan."

"Can you arrange that meeting together at short notice—with those agencies involved?"

"Yes, that won't be a problem."

"In that case, I'll put things in motion now."

The Chief, back at his desk, removed a mobile phone from a locked bottom drawer of his desk and switched it on. He then used his desk phone to call Maggie Burrows.

"Yes Chief," Maggie answered smartly.

"Are you alone?"

"Yes, Sir."

"Is that phone switched on?"

"Yes, it is."

"Incoming," the Chief replied quickly, disconnecting the desk call, then ringing Maggie back using the mobile phone.

"I want you to say you've been updated by Tom. It relates to intelligence that Deena has, and which she alone is taking to Cambodian Law Enforcement. She has not divulged that intelligence, in order to maintain the agreement that Tom is not working on operational matters. Tom and Sarah are still undertaking training, which is going well, and we expect more once Deena has met with authorities tomorrow their time."

"OK—not sure I've told that many whoppers before!"

"You're covered, Maggie. Make it look good."

"Isn't there a risk that it could generate contact with Tom?"

"That's one we'll have to take. It's the chance it may generate activity and intelligence elsewhere that trumps the risk."

"We can negate that risk by bringing Tom into the fold now though?" Maggie said, in a questioning, respectful tone.

"He stays out in the cold Maggie. He will act more natural if he doesn't know at the moment. That's my call. Let me know when you've done it."

Sat in her office, she contemplated the best way to communicate her update. It was too big a deal for a text, yet the nature of the deployment really deserved a meeting, one which she wanted to avoid if possible. If she prevaricated following an email that might raise suspicion, meaning she would have to go in person in any case. She sent a text requesting a meeting, offering an email if the timing wasn't convenient and got an immediate reply. She walked over to her office safe and retrieved two black plastic Pelican boxes and opened them. Inside one was a small body recording device, two coiled wire microphones, spare batteries and miniature cassette tapes, all neatly packed into black foam cut-outs. The other contained two rolls of medical-grade sticky tape and an oversized, stretchy knee brace. Locking her office door, she took off her uniform shirt and removed her bra. Unzipping her skirt, she let it drop to the floor and stepped out of it. She slid the bracing on until it reached the top of her groin. Then, taking the recording device, she checked it contained a tape and placed it between her tights and the brace, ensuring the device was offset between her legs so it didn't rub as she walked. She then used the sticky tape and wound it around the device bulge to keep it in place. Satisfied with its position and feel, she inserted both recording wires, fed them under her briefs, and taped each miniature microphone tip into place, either side of her breasts. Dressed again, she grabbed her briefcase and left.

Arriving at the Police Headquarters, Maggie found a remote parking place and took a minute to calm herself. Scanning the area to make sure no one was coming, she hitched up her skirt, pulled back the top edge of the bracing, located the plastic recording cover shield, slid it downwards, pressed 'record', then reset the shield before pulling her skirt back into place. Finally, she took hold of the rear-view mirror, angled it so she could check her hair and what little make-up she had on, then went inside for her meeting.

Arriving at her destination and finding no one present, she took a seat and began to wait as she had done many times before, only this time she could feel her heart racing and wondered if it could be seen pulsing in her neck. Just as she began to feel her neckline for the carotid artery, John Troy walked in and sat down in front of her.

"Where are we?" he said, in a disinterested but demanding tone, whilst unlocking his desk top PC via the keyboard.

"The training is going well, one down, two to go. Deena has some intelligence from a new source, which she intends to take to the Immigration Police tomorrow, their time. We don't know what that intelligence is, but once she's had that meeting, we will know more."

"What do you mean, 'We don't know what that intelligence is'!" John almost shouted back.

"She hasn't told Tom, because she feels informing him at this stage would place him in the operational decision-making chain, which you have given specific instructions not to do. They are just following your orders, John."

"That's bullshit, and you know it. Have I got grown-ups over there or children? This is a joint operation and I demand to know what that intelligence is. So, you had better get back onto Tom, and Deena, and tell them I want it on my desk as soon as they're up. Understand!"

"OK, I can ask, but if Deena says no, I can't make her."

"Don't get smart with me, Maggie. I might not be able to control what Deena does, or doesn't do, but I can with my staff. If that intelligence isn't on my desk in the morning, I'm pulling them out and returning them home: understood?"

"I'll get that relayed."

"You better had, otherwise Veritas is finished. Now, who are these

Immigration Police?"

"I've got no idea. Deena says there is a new officer who she thinks will be the best bet to place the intelligence with. He is the most likely one to take action and he is in the Immigration Police."

"Maggie, what do you exactly know? Do you know anything? Why are you wasting my time?"

"You're the one that wanted this meeting," Maggie said, in a defensive tone.

"That's because I thought you would actually have something worthwhile to discuss! Get me that intelligence, and I want the names of the immigration officers," he replied, by way of a final statement.

Maggie, just happy to get away, went straight to the toilets, entered a cubicle and locked the door. She hitched up her skirt, unwound the sticky tape, removed the recording device, switched it off and removed the tape cassette. She neatly wound the sticky tape in on itself to make a roll, placed that and the device into her briefcase, then texted Margaret Thrinton, who arrived within minutes.

"I understand you might have something for me?" Margaret said seriously, wearing an expression that clearly indicated she was really enjoying all the cloak and dagger.

"Yes I do," replied Maggie, grinning, as she handed over the tape.

"Are you OK?" she enquired with concern, placing a hand on Maggie's arm.

"Elementary, Margaret. Elementary," replied Maggie confidently.

CHAPTER FIVE

Phnom Penh, Cambodia

As Chenda turned right opposite the airport and towards a line of government buildings, Deena could see two uniform officers quickly come to attention outside the main entrance, whilst a third disappeared up a set of stairs behind them. As the vehicle drew up, one of the officers opened her door and stood back, holding it open for her to get out. Simultaneously, the officer who had disappeared came back following a fourth officer who, from his insignia, she could see was a Major. She immediately noted that his uniform fitted him well compared to the other officers, looked new, was freshly laundered and his name badge was written in English. The young officer who had been standing back moved closer to Deena before speaking.

"This is Major Pich Narith. He is very pleased to welcome you to the Immigration Police Headquarters."

"This is my interpreter, Sok Thy," Major Pich said, in well-spoken English, shaking hands.

"I haven't had the occasion to use my English much, so I will use the interpreter when I get stuck. These are two of my colleagues, Captain Chey Leap and Lieutenant Dith Samlain." Both officers, who were already standing to attention, stayed where they were, bowing their heads. Deena noted their uniforms had clearly not come from the same tailor as Major Pich's.

"They will be joining us for our meeting. Follow me please."

As Chenda drove off in search of a parking space with a view of the entrance, Deena entered the building following the Cambodians into a conference room. It was sparse by Western standards, containing only a table and chairs: three on one side and two on the other. Familiar with diplomatic seating arrangements and the use of interpreters, she knew which side she should be on. Seated with Thy positioned slightly behind her, Major Pich sat opposite flanked by his staff.

Her intelligence brief on Pich, limited as it was, was accurate. He was a confident, well-dressed, good-looking Cambodian, clearly comfortable with meeting Western diplomats. That was rare, and it wasn't just his persona that impressed her. The two other officers, albeit subordinate in rank, seemed almost in awe of him, and by comparison did not seem comfortable at all being there.

"You can call me Pich, or Narith, whichever you prefer?" Major Pich said, in a questioning tone.

"Narith it is then, call me Deena."

"Good. What is it you wish to discuss?"

'Straight to business, I like that,' Deena thought.

"I am currently working on a capacity building project, with a new law enforcement agency from the United Kingdom." Deena paused, to see if the interpreter was going to talk or not. Because he was remaining mute, she continued. "They are delivering some training modules to NGOs here in Phnom Penh. It's something I have been working on for quite a while. I thought it would be good if they met with local officials involved in enforcement operations. I asked around and your name was the most recommended across all the embassies, so I was wondering if you might be interested in meeting with them?"

Major Pich had been looking directly at Deena as she spoke and, although he held a half smile, his eyes were steady, steely and suspicious. She thought it bore all the hallmarks of having been through some form of special government training.

"What is this new agency?"

"They specialise in online child protection, child trafficking and sex crimes involving children. They are based in the UK, but are working in partnership with agencies from other countries."

"What is its name?" Major Pich asked, his tone indifferent.

"Global Online Police: GOPOL for short."

"You're from Canada, right?"

"Correct."

"So, why are you here, and not the British Ambassador?"

"Because Canada is one of the GOPOL partners; this is my project, and I am paying for it. That means I have to account for it being a success. Plus, I always lead from the front!"

Major Pich managed a full smile, then briefly spoke in Khmer to the two officers either side of him.

Although Deena could speak some Khmer, he spoke quickly, making it hard for her to understand what he was saying, and it was clear the interpreter wasn't going to translate for her.

"What would the purpose of this meeting be?"

"Sharing experiences, ideas, police practices and methods—that sort of thing. It's a real opportunity."

"How many are there?"

"Just two: one male, one female."

"What rank are they?"

Deena knew where this line of questioning was going.

"One is a Detective Chief Inspector – I would say the equivalent rank to a Major – the other is a civilian communications officer – in the diplomatic service her rank would be similar to that of a Lieutenant."

Major Pich again spoke to his officers, before turning back to her.

"Where would this meeting take place and when?"

"As they aren't here for very long, I thought tonight. I am prepared to secure an area and refreshments at the hotel they are staying at, which is the Sunflower," Deena replied, in her best upbeat and happy tone.

Major Pich turned to both officers and began speaking. On the previous two occasions only one of them had spoken. This time though, both spoke animatedly; just enough for her to understand that at least one of them, Chey Leap, the Captain, was not happy with the venue.

Deena had been in Cambodia long enough to know that Captain Chey was probably the designated Political Officer, with Lieutenant Dith, performing the role of Intelligence. The three were the classic team deployment used by the authorities when they met with embassy officials; and, certainly when it was at short notice. Although she couldn't understand exactly what was being said, the body language of Captain Chey told her all she needed to know: it wouldn't be that it was against protocols to go there, it was just that he probably wasn't used to the Western-style venue and therefore not comfortable with it. Major Pich, however, had no such reservations.

"We will be there. I will bring Thy as well. This will be an official meeting. What time?"

"Would 5pm suit?"

"Yes, who will be there?"

"Tom Ross, Sarah Dorsey and I, that is all."

Captain Chey Leap immediately spoke to Major Pich, this time with a happy look on his face, which caused both the Major and the Lieutenant to smile at him. Deena suspected it was probably something to do with Sarah.

"OK, where do we meet you?"

"I will meet you personally in the lobby, Narith."

Major Pich stood up, shook Deena's hand again, then walked her out to the entrance. Chenda, who was parked not far away, spotted her Boss and quickly pulled up to collect her.

The training delivery went smoothly for both Tom and Sarah, mainly because it was their second time of doing it. Even so, their minds were elsewhere, wondering how things were going with Deena. Time went quickly, and they didn't have to wait long to find out as Chenda had information for them when she arrived to take them back to the Sunflower Hotel.

"You will be meeting Major Pich Narith at 5pm tonight at your hotel. I am to drop you back there now, then go and collect Deena, who is at another meeting. We will meet for late lunch at the Sunflower. She has asked that you obtain the same conference room and to order food for us all."

"Great news!" Sarah said, turning to Tom and raising her eyebrows.

"Yes, this is indeed very good news, Sarah. This means I get to eat one of those club sandwiches. I have never eaten one of those before. I am really looking forward to it!" Chenda grinned.

Tom was relieved to hear the news. They were a long way from their goal, but without this small step they would not have been able to continue.

"This is very good, Chenda. How long will you be so I can order the food?"

"Once we get to the Sunflower, it will be 15 minutes to Deena's location. Then I will be 15 minutes early, so I will have to wait. Then, it will be another 15 minutes back, so all together 45 minutes. At this time of day there is heavy traffic, but don't worry, Tom, I have expert knowledge of the city. I will use some back streets that I know of to make sure I am back with you in 45 minutes exactly. This is for sure. If you don't believe me, set your watch when I leave!"

Tom and Sarah were waiting in the conference room when the food arrived, delivered on trays by two staff. Immediately behind them were Deena and Chenda.

"Did you set your watch, Tom?" Chenda cried in a proud voice— which gave away the fact that she knew the answer to the question.

Tom, who was now silently wishing he had, could hardly believe that Chenda was able to navigate the Phnom Penh traffic and arrive at the exact time she claimed she would.

Sarah though, who had secretly taken her up on the challenge, checked her watch.

"Forty-five minutes exactly, Chenda, well done! I'm officially impressed."

Tom looked incredulous, first at Sarah for outwitting him, then at Chenda for pulling it off.

"It's her party trick. I don't know how she manages it either," Deena said, looking admiringly at Chenda. "Some food first, I'm hungry," she said, with Chenda wasting no time, jumping into a chair and taking a bite— seemingly all in one motion.

Sandwiches demolished, Deena began.

"I suggest we use the seated area outside the bar. It's still inside the hotel area but closed off from the end of the lobby and quiet. It has a round table that we can use. The bar staff will serve customers from there, and the police shouldn't feel too uncomfortable with being in that environment. It's not air-conditioned, so factor that in.

"We should put a few nibbles on, not too much, both Khmer and European. I will take care of that and the drinks. It will be interesting to see how they manage in this situation. I'm expecting Major Pich will be comfortable with it—not so sure about the others."

"Do they all speak English?" Sarah enquired.

"Don't know. I am expecting they can all speak a bit; we will have to wait and see. They will be like fish out of water to start with, so we want to make this as informal as possible, even if they have difficulty with that. So, use first names. They won't be used to shaking hands Western style: be prepared for that, but still do it. They will come with their own game plan, and it should be apparent what that is pretty early on. We mustn't break that down, leave them to deploy it."

"What do you know about these three? Is there anything I can use to engage with them?" Tom interrupted.

"Nothing that you don't already know. However, my assessment is that Leap is the Political Officer; he was wearing a green uniform, whereas both Samlain and Narith were wearing the khaki uniform of the Immigration Police. Samlain has the look and feel of the Intelligence Officer. They will be at the meeting with those heads on, so don't be fooled by their smile. Sok Thy, the interpreter, will be fluent, so treat him as a 'hot mic' if you're talking with one another."

"This sounds like it's straight out of a Bond movie!" Sarah said, with a gaping expression.

"You're a born spy, Sarah, you'll be fine!"

"Should I just stick to engaging Narith then?" Tom asked.

"You will need your own strategy. I suggest sticking with just him, but, as I have said, I suspect they will come to the table with their own plan. They aren't subtle: it will be obvious, so if they do, go with it."

"How long will it last?" asked Sarah.

"We shouldn't let this go on for more than an hour. We should aim for 45 minutes. I'll manage that side, so you don't have to. This all about giving Tom the maximum amount of exposure and time to make the offer of joint working, so, Sarah, if the conversation centres on you, subtly get it back to Tom, OK?"

"Got it!"

"Our overall intelligence is that the police here, especially senior officers and the ones that have travelled outside of Cambodia, like golf, karaoke and drinking Black Label. If they make any offer like that, have an excuse ready Tom. A good one, that doesn't offend. It's designed to get you into embarrassing situations, that they can later use. It's their communist training, so don't take it personally."

"Are you ready for this, Miss Moneypenny?" Tom asked, leaning forward, looking at Sarah with a smile.

"I'll have you know, I'm not just a pretty face, Mr Ross!"

"Absolutely for sure, Sarah," Chenda chimed in, who up until now had been clearing every single crumb off her plate.

"My guess is they will do most of the initial questioning, then, when they dry up, it will be game on for you Tom. Any questions?"

"Nope."

"Sarah?"

"No."

"In that case I will see you here, 16:45, in the lobby. Before I go though, we must call the informant. Chenda?"

Chenda, who had been eyeing up some crusts left by Sarah, snapped out of her gaze.

"For sure Deena, on to it," and rang Sopheap.

When the call was answered, she spoke Khmer, then quickly switched the speaker facility on and placed the phone closer to Deena.

"Sopheap, this is Deena speaking: what are your plans?"

"Hello, Bong-Srei. My plans are very good, thank you."

Chenda dropped her head, shook it from side to side, before slapping her forehead with the palm of her hand, and tutted.

"Good, I'm pleased for you. What exactly are they?"

"My very good plan is to say that our mother is sick. I have told her she must be sicker now than she normally is, and that I have to see my sister, who requires regular updates in case our mother might die without her knowing, and that I am also needing to moan to my sister because of all the extra duties I am having to perform for my mother. I have already used this reason today. It worked well."

Deena wasn't pleased. She wanted to approve the plan first, but it seemed to have worked.

"How was this received?"

"Very well. Gangster Chakra was there. He challenged Nuon when he saw I was with her. But he seemed happy about it, once it was explained, and he left us to talk. Nuon says she will do what you ask. I will get my first update from her tomorrow, when I visit."

"Good work, Sopheap! What time will you visit her?"

"About 1pm."

"Expect a call from Chenda tomorrow, say 3pm?"

"Yes, Bong-Srei."

MI5, Thames House, London, England

Meanwhile in London, Toby Spencer-Drummond had just arrived at his desk, when his pager alerted him of a message to call Intelligence Group 'L'. It was his daily update for non-urgent intelligence involving telecommunication warrants relating to national security: the suspects involved were a worldwide secret network of senior politicians and police officers. He mentally prepared himself for dealing with the intelligence group staff. It didn't matter who you got, the intelligence was theirs, and you always felt that you had to beg to get it. The fact it belonged to no one and was never going to be used as evidence nor see the light of day in an English courtroom, meant nothing to them.

"How's the 'L' room this morning?"

"Busy as always, Toby!"

"Good to hear, otherwise we would all be out of a job!"

"You maybe. I'm not on a short-term contract."

"Well, aren't you the lucky one!"

"Are you ready?"

"Of course," he replied, having prepared his communication log before calling.

"There was quite a bit of activity across all three of your subjects, but only one call is covered by the warrant. That was to subject one, 7.34pm last night: incoming call from a UK mobile, details in a mo, only words spoken were 'Alpha Five', said twice. The caller was a male, but the call was muffled. The operator suggests cloth or clothing bunched up: enough to thwart voice recognition in any case. Also, there was no reply or acknowledgement, so we don't actually know who answered the call."

"No activity from subject one following that call?" Toby asked, in more of a statement to himself, knowing the answer already, having been told there was only one call for him.

"Some good news for you though. The caller number was resolved to a burner phone, financed through cash cards: nothing there for you. Intelligence log coming through now, so you can check for CCTV at point of purchase, for the phone and SIM. The operator managed to secure cell site data; it seems the phone was left on for about ten minutes—SIM is now dead though. Guess that will be the last time we see that number come into our sphere."

"And the good news?" Toby asked, having to stop himself from sounding condescending.

"Outer Oxford; mast location and GPS coordinates are in the log."

Toby checked his email account and could see that it contained the intelligence document.

"Thanks, the log is here. Toodle-pip, old chap!"

Toby Spencer-Drummond opened the email, copied the coordinates onto a slip of paper then went to another computer and placed the details into Google Earth. Zooming in, he quickly identified that the mast was about ten miles from the home address of one of the suspects not covered by the warrant. Probably too far from the home address— there would be closer ones in that sort of built-up area. However, it was close enough, especially in light of his recent call with Jim Galloway. He needed more intelligence, so rang the investigations team leader.

"Mr Pink, how the devil are we this fine morning?"

"Awaiting orders, squadron leader!"

"Excellent! Sending you a log from the resolution team. CCTV search, from point of purchase."

"How urgent?"

"Today."

"Wilco."

Toby sat back in his chair and mulled what to do next. He had no idea what 'Alpha Five' meant, but the Oxford connection was interesting. He texted Chief Constable James Galloway and got an immediate response. He then went to the canteen, got himself a flat white, returned to his office and rang the Chief on the Brent phone.

"You're up early," said the Chief.

"Well, Queen and country, you know how it is!"

"Yes, I do. What's up?"

"Subject one took a call last night: speaker was a male, voice disguised, said, 'Alpha Five' twice, then hung up. UK mobile, burner, no trace. We are checking CCTV. I'm always hopeful, but realistic at the same time. Cell site analysis had it coming off a mast ten miles from your man."

"That's a long way in his neck of the woods," interjected the Chief defensively.

"I agree, but, considering the timing, I can't ignore it. Do you have any idea what 'Alpha Five' might mean?"

"None."

"Could it be a code that the police use, one that you wouldn't know?"

"I came up through the ranks, Toby. I'm not a parachutist, and I remember exactly where I've come from. No!"

"Well, in that case, this leaves us with a problem. Either you go, or I'll have to. Your call."

"It's on my watch, I'll go. That meeting we talked about: it would be good to have that first."

"I agree. Let me know your date, and I will work around that. More notice the better."

CHAPTER SIX

The public often ask what happens when the Police need to police the Police; how does that work? Having worked in Professional Standards – albeit for a short period, enough to ensure my halo was still intact – I found many think it is incestuous in nature. The reality is though: it works and works well, saving more careers than it ends. The process, limited mainly to code of conduct breaches or petty crime, can be hampered when it involves serious crime, specialist officers and conspiracy. That's where things become tricky.

The first thing the Chief wanted to do after the call with Toby Spencer-Drummond was to read the transcript Margaret had typed up. He knew, and had long known, about the possibility of a powerful cabal within the UK Police; one that supposedly had its tentacles within every force in the country—his included. He had been one of the Chiefs of Police who had banned membership of the Masons, and he was also the one who left it to Professional Standards to decide, if they came into information, what to do about it. So far, not a single case had come before him. Despite the intelligence from the Security Service, he was still finding it hard to believe that they were looking at the right person in JT.

He unlocked his drawer, removed the sealed envelope, read the transcript and then rang Maggie using their covert phones: ones that weren't attributable in any way to the police.

"Morning, Sir."

"Good morning, Maggie. I've just read the transcript. Firstly, well done. Secondly, I've just had a conversation with Box. They tell me one of their facilities had an incoming call within a couple of hours of your meeting. Code only, voice disguised, burner phone, cell site had it coming off a mast ten miles from JT's home address."

"I know where he lives, that's a long way in terms of technology. There will be plenty of other masts between him and that one, Sir."

"My thoughts as well. We have two problems though: it's enough for Box to take it further, and from this transcript I can see that you are on a deadline!"

"My plan was to keep my head down and not respond to my phone until I'd heard back from Tom. A couple more hours and we should know."

"Stick to that for now. However, I will have to go to the Home Office in any case, so I'll call a meeting with JT. You don't need to be there. I will tell him I'm taking personal ownership of the deployment, due to it having corporate impact on GOPOL. That way, you won't have to avoid him all day. Let me know as soon as you hear from Tom."

"Will do."

The Chief found the number he was looking for in his contacts list, checked his watch, then rang it, knowing it was probably a bit early.

"Minister for Security's office, Ayesha speaking."

"Morning Ayesha, it's James Galloway, Thames Valley Police, how are you?"

"Jim! I'm fine. Thank you for asking. What can I do for you?"

"I need to make an appointment with the Minister, it's about Project Phobos."

"Ah, Phobos. Is it urgent?"

"Yes."

"In that case, can you hold the line please."

The Chief was checking his emails when Ayesha came back to him.

"Wednesday next week, 3pm, is the earliest that he can do, unless it's a matter of national security. Is it?"

"Not yet, no."

"In that case, does that date suit you?"

"Yes, it does."

"Excellent. The Minister has asked me to inform you that the Home Secretary may also attend. Will the Security Service be in attendance?"

"Not unless things change between now and the meeting."

"I will let him know that."

The Chief then texted Toby Spencer-Drummond, updating him about the meeting.

Maggie sat in her car, contemplating what she had just heard. The ramifications were huge, and yet she felt a strange mixture of foreboding and excitement. Was this really happening now, after all these years. She dragged herself away from those thoughts, entered the COCET building, then made her way to the conference room. Entering, she found ADS Jane King about to start an operational briefing to a room full of staff, who, upon seeing her, began to stand up.

"As you were please. Carry on, Jane."

As Jane sat down, waiting for the noise of shuffling chairs to dissipate, she caught sight of Maggie, who seemed miles away staring at the walls. She thought her body was rigid; her arms folded tight across her chest. Her gut made its presence felt again. Once, maybe her instincts could be wrong. Twice though, the dangers signs cannot be ignored. If her experience told her anything, it was that Tom was somewhere, somehow, involved. Which meant, so was she.

"Everybody currently seated on my left side of the table will be responsible for Operation Laverton. Here are your Op Orders," Jane began, handing out numbered operational orders.

"Everybody on the right side, here are yours. You are responsible for Operation Blackwood. You can read those later in your own time. You will all get another briefing by the home force involved tomorrow. Today's briefing is about getting our house in order, so that we all know what each other is doing and what it will look like once Dale, Owen and Anna Wilson start the covert phase.

"Archie, you, Owen and Dr Nick, from SDE, have Laverton, and your briefing starts at 0600hrs at Bitterne Police Station, Southampton. Archie, you are to stay there for the duration and relay the information into the intelligence cell here. Owen, once you have what you need, and Archie can do without you, you are to return and join up with Dale in Covert Ops."

"Yes, Sarge," both Archie and Owen replied simultaneously, with Owen giving Archie a sly wink.

"Nick, once you have made an appraisal of the scene can you let me know here? Otherwise, you have your own strategy, work to that."

"Of course," replied Dr Sharpe.

"The intelligence cell will consist of Anna Farley and Patrick Smith. I will be Ops Comm and all things logistical support is Sam Terry. Dale is OIC Covert Ops. Any questions so far from the Laverton Team?"

With none coming, Jane continued.

"Mitchell, Anna W and Dr Sue Tay from SDE have Blackwood. Your briefing starts at 0615hrs at Exeter Police Station. Mitchell, your task is to stay there and perform the same role as Archie. Anna W, once you have what you need, and are no longer required by Mitchell, return here to Covert Ops."

"Yes, Sarge," replied both officers.

"Sue, same as Nick. You are our expert on the ground there and have your own approved strategy. Once you have made a scene appraisal, please let me know your assessment of the situation."

"Will do."

"You all know the aims of tomorrow, but for clarity sake: arrest, search, interview and prosecution of the offender at each location is being dealt with by the locals. Your role there is to assist Covert Ops in assuming the identity of the two offenders. It has been assessed in this instance that the best chance for this to happen is for the warrant to be executed on a knock only; the presence of the family being used as leverage to obtain the passwords. SDE will advise you at the scene on how to stay within the guidelines if there is a need to access any digital device at the scene.

"Owen and Anna, you will need to stay for the interview phase to get online style habits and methodology. If you get it early on, then that's a bonus. Dale will stay here, unless there is a need to travel to one or both of the search locations, so he can cater for urgent online work. Urgent disseminations will be handled through us, as will all international cases. First team debrief to happen once we're all back here. Sam has all your accommodation and hire car details, so see her after the briefing.

"You've all been here before and know what to do. To make this a success we need the search to go well, with the interview stage revealing passwords and online methods. We then need the offenders to be isolated from the internet by any means after charge and their online identities assumed by us, with us remaining covert until all the evidence and intelligence has been gathered, resolved and disseminated. Are there any questions?"

"We had our initial set of instructions from the Boss before he left. As things progress, we will need more—has that been catered for?" Detective Sergeant Dale Walters asked.

"Yes, it has. Superintendent Burrows will be doing them," Jane replied, looking up at Maggie, enquiringly.

"If DCI Ross can't do them, I will. You should indicate to Jane early on if the instructions need updating. Don't leave them to the last minute!" Maggie said, with what Jane thought was, uncommon stern authority for her.

"Can we expect to be working long hours like we did on Resolve?" Archie asked.

"If all goes well, yes," Jane replied, in an upbeat positive tone.

"I haven't heard back from Adrian Smith, from the Australian Federal Police. Is there a problem?" Anna Farley enquired in her polite, articulate and diplomatic manner. "I'm going to need to know if he is our SPOC before tomorrow, just in case we have an urgent case that we want to send their way."

"I will get that confirmed for you tonight," Jane said, writing the query in her notebook. By the time she looked up the room was silent.

"In that case, the rest of the day is yours. Use it wisely. Away teams, factor in travel times from your accommodation to the briefing point. I don't want to hear that any of you were late! Good luck team."

As the room emptied, Maggie stayed exactly where she was, waiting for the last person to get to the door.

"Close the door on the way out please."

As Maggie sat down, Jane felt uneasy.

"That was a good briefing. Well done. With Tom away, you will need to be on top of your game, especially around urgent disseminations and decision-making with the UCs. I want you to keep me informed every step of the way until Tom gets back."

"Yes, Ma'am. Just a few more days I guess."

"Maybe, but you should prepare for a possible extension of his deployment."

Jane wasn't sure what to say, so decided to stay silent. But she now knew for sure that something was up, and it involved Maggie.

"Keep me informed by email please, headlines only will do."

"Yes, Ma'am."

Maggie got up, flattened her skirt with the palms of her hand and walked out without another word or backward glance.

Phnom Penh, Cambodia

Tom and Sarah were waiting at the meeting area, whilst Deena was in the lobby with Chenda as the delegation arrived. Deena immediately noticed that Major Pich had changed into a fresh ceremonial-looking uniform and was carrying an official flat cap under his arm. The others were wearing the same clothing they had on earlier, only it was far more creased.

"Pleased to meet you again, Major," Deena said, by way of a greeting. "Would you please follow me."

Tom watched as the delegation made its way through the central lobby towards them, Deena and Major Pich walking in front, the rest following behind. The Cambodian staff appeared stunned by the presence of the uniformed officers and stood stock-still in the hotel lobby, watching them as they made their way through to the area where Tom and Sarah were waiting.

"Major Pich, may I present Detective Chief Inspector Tom Ross from the Combined Online Child Exploitation Taskforce, UK."

"It's an honour to meet you Major Pich. Thank you for meeting us," Tom said quickly, wanting to get in first. He looked him the eye and felt the firm handshake. The Major didn't reply, but just nodded slightly.

"This is Sarah Dorsey, Corporate Communications Officer, also from the Combined Online Child Exploitation Taskforce."

"Pleased to meet you, Sarah," Major Pich said in perfect English, whilst shaking her hand.

The Major took a step back before speaking.

"This is my team: Captain Chey Leap," Major Pich said, holding his arm out in the direction of the Captain, who looked stunned as everyone's gaze fell upon him, keeping his hands clasped together, then quickly nodding as if remembering that it was something he had been told to do.

"Pleased to meet you," Tom said, just before Sarah.

"This is Lieutenant Dith Samlain."

Tom, seeing that the Lieutenant was going to follow the Captain in his approach to the introductions, took one step forward and held his hand out. "Pleased to meet you, Lieutenant."

The Lieutenant didn't move but smiled and tentatively held out a hand. Tom grasped it and was surprised by the cool limpness of the handshake.

Sarah took Tom's lead and did the same. She too felt the limpness in the Lieutenant's welcome, noticing also that as his gaze fell upon her, his eyes widened before nodding.

"And Thy is my interpreter," the Major said quickly in a dismissive tone, turning back towards Deena.

Deena, who had been watching the introductions, was pleased that the meeting was following her predictions.

"This way please," she said, leading the Cambodian delegation, Tom and Sarah around the folding glass doors to their table.

Two waiters quickly arrived to take orders. They looked nervously at the uniformed officers sitting before them, appearing unsure about whom they should address first. Deena stepped in to save them from their dilemma.

"I have already ordered some food; the kitchen should know about it. Please take our drink orders and bring the food at the same time," she said, pointing in the direction of Major Pich and the others.

Tom watched as the Major ordered for the group; the conversation being in Khmer he didn't know what was being said, but he got the feeling that there was a discussion around whether they should have a drink, and if so, what. Both the Captain and the Lieutenant looked unsettled. With the Cambodian officers' orders taken, Deena ordered their own drinks, and then it was game time for him.

"How long have you been in the business of policing Major?" Tom asked slowly, in his best pronounced English.

"Not that long. I've been with the Immigration Police for just over a year and a half. Please call me Narith. And you?"

"Please call me Tom. Over twenty years—not all doing this job; you must start as a recruit, then work your way into the C.I.D," Tom said, deliberately giving the abbreviation.

"What is this C.I.D?"

"Plain clothes work, stands for Criminal Investigation Department."

"Twenty years, that's a long time. Why are you not a Colonel by now?"

Tom had been assessing Narith as they spoke. He appeared open; his body language told him he was comfortable in the surroundings and meeting foreigners—unlike his colleagues. Although he wore a near-constant smile, his dark eyes betrayed him. Tom had interviewed probably thousands of offenders in his career: some were straightforward admissions taking no longer than ten minutes; some were minor cases, some serious; some were complicated crimes with conspiracies and multiple offenders, where following solicitor's advice, the well-practised reply of, no comment was the norm. There were far too many to remember them all, but a few did stick in his mind; they were ones where the offender had a deep, dark, devious mind with the mouth saying one thing, the eyes saying another. This was the same, and he felt a chill travel down his spine, even though he was still struggling with the heat.

"Promotion in the UK Police isn't based along the lines of the military. It's complicated to explain, but it can be very political at times."

"Ah! I understand the political side, that is one we have to overcome here as well. Tell me, what do you think of our country?" Narith said, his smile and eyes widening, eager to know what the reply would be.

Tom had spent time making a list of what the Major might ask. This one was not on it. He suddenly found himself wondering if Pich knew they had travelled to Battambang. Maybe they did have some surveillance capability, just not the sort anybody knew about.

"We haven't done much sightseeing yet, business first. But from what I've seen, I'm a huge fan. Everybody is happy, it's lovely and warm and the food is fantastic!"

Narith's response assuaged any fears Tom had about Battambang. He looked genuinely pleased with the reply.

"So, tell me, Tom, what is this new job of yours? This internet crime is not one we have here. Yes, occasionally we catch a paedophile, but, when we do, we boot him out of the country."

Tom was about to reply, when the food and drinks arrived. He could see that the Cambodian team had opted for orange juice or water. The food, a mixture of Khmer and Western, caught their attention immediately, both of them saying something in Khmer to Narith, before hesitantly reaching out for the Western offerings of mini hamburgers and sausage rolls.

'Good ploy, Deena.' Tom thought.

"It isn't just about the internet, Narith. Everything that is seen, viewed, exchanged or sold on the internet, has happened in real life somewhere in the world. It is a mistake to think that the digital and real worlds are separate—they're not. They are one and the same: the digital one is just an extension of our real lives."

"Maybe yours. Many people here don't have access to the internet and, even if they did, very few can afford a laptop or a computer to use it with," Narith interjected, picking up a mini hamburger, popping the whole thing into his mouth, savouring the taste, then awkwardly saying something in Khmer out of the side of his mouth to the others who, with their own mouths being full, nodded vigorously in agreement.

Tom looked quizzically at Narith, who by this time had swallowed his burger and had taken a mouthful of orange juice.

"Real beef, Aussie beef."

"Most of the beef here comes from Australia," Deena said, providing an answer to Tom.

"Australian beef is much better than what we normally eat. Good taste!"

"But foreigners from other countries have the means and the money. Their risk comes from grooming and then accessing the child. The risk is less here than in say, their own country."

"This is true. This is why we have that billboard at the airport—did you see it?" Narith asked keenly.

"Yes, I did," Tom replied, pausing, looking at Sarah, to see if she wanted to speak.

Sarah didn't need any prompting, "That's a great piece of communication. Impactive, sends a huge message and good value over the long term."

Tom watched as Narith's gaze, and that of the others, fell on her. The Captain and the Lieutenant stopped chewing, Thy the interpreter fidgeted in his seat with a worried expression, and Narith looked like he was either assessing how to handle the statement from a Western female who had the temerity to speak, or how much the advertisement would cost them in the long run.

"We got the Americans to pay for that," Narith replied, before looking back at Tom. "We haven't had any cases here. The ones we do catch we boot out. If statements are taken, then they can be prosecuted in their home country; they can in America. I am interested to know how you catch these people?"

"There are a number of ways, but mostly through tracing their footprint on the internet; that footprint can lead us to their front door. Or by a combination of undercover infiltration and traditional means, as well as their footprint."

"When you say trace, do you mean in the UK?"

"Not just the UK, anywhere. In fact, we recently worked with the Royal Thai Police to trace someone to their home."

"Did you catch him?" Narith asked, with noticeable excitement.

"He'd left a few hours before we got there."

"Tip-off?" Narith asked, with his eyebrows raised.

"Maybe, who knows. But when you conduct investigations on the internet it can lead you anywhere!"

"Why is there so much concern about this type of crime, Tom? I understand it is a bad crime, but these things happen in life. It's a crime here too, but there are far more serious things to worry about. Don't you agree?"

Tom wasn't really surprised by the question, one he had thought might come up. After all, he had been a young Royal Marine Commando not that long after Cambodia was slaughtering its professional population and their families in an attempt to take the country back to the Stone Age: ridding it of its past influence, starting again with a new form of Communism.

"I guess it comes down to our heritage, where we come from. I believe when a person is sexually abused as a child, they have mental health issues later on in life or throughout it. Some to a greater extent, some lesser. I have seen a great many lives ruined because of it, so for me it's as serious as murder. Some have their whole lives taken away from them—lives they should have been able to live normally: grow up, be healthy, get married, have children."

Narith looked at Tom for a long time before speaking, reflecting on what he had heard.

"You really believe that?" Narith said, incredulously.

"Yes, yes I do."

Narith again reflected for a period.

"Have you ever traced anyone to this country?"

"No, we haven't, but I am sure if we specifically tried, we could. Would you be interested in working on a case like this?"

"You mean a joint project?"

"Yes."

"I would. We don't have any capability in this area though, so it would have to be completely financed by you and I would have to get permission, but yes, this can be arranged. However, I understand you are only here for the week?" Narith said, looking at Deena.

Tom was assessing Narith's tone and body language. If he believed there might be a barrier, he wasn't displaying any concern.

"If you're able to get agreement in principle by tomorrow," Deena began, "I'm prepared to negotiate with Tom's Chief to jointly resource it. I would welcome an extension; I have had a number of requests for further training from local NGOs who have since heard about what I'm doing, so it would be a win, win for me. But Tom, would you be able to provide an intelligence lead in this short space of time?"

Looking across at Deena, he formed the opinion she would make a fine undercover officer, if she wasn't already a consummate diplomatic professional.

"I'm confident I can provide something we can work on. Yes!"

CHAPTER SEVEN

"That went as well as could be expected," Deena said, as soon as Chenda shut the door to Tom's hotel room.

"He seemed friendly enough, but there was unmistakeable mistrust in his eyes I thought," Tom replied.

"Me too," said Sarah.

"They ate all the Aussie beef as well! Did you see them? They were like my mother's 'chrouks', their faces went into the trough and never came out until all that lovely, tender beef was gone," Chenda growled, collapsing into a seat, arms folded, with an expression that was a mixture of sadness and annoyance.

Sarah was touched by Chenda's anguish.

"When this is all over, Chenda, I will buy you some of those burgers and sausage rolls."

"Thank you, Sarah. We women warriors need to keep ourselves fit for the fight ahead. When I eat Aussie beef, I become strong and healthy!"

"That's enough, Chenda," Deena said, in a firm, motherly tone.

Chenda abruptly stopped, nodding in acceptance of the request.

"So, Tom. What now?"

"I need to update Maggie first and agree an extension."

"How long do you think you will need?"

"With the weekend not that far away, I would suggest two weeks from next Monday."

"My thoughts as well. Anything more, and they will get suspicious."

"Will we be able to extend here?" Sarah enquired.

"That won't be a problem, and I'll arrange it. The timing needs to be after we have informed Narith, so if they enquire here, it fits the timeline."

"You were listening to him: what do you think?"

"He's a real mixture of cultures, Tom. He has been influenced by his Western experiences, but he will have a master who won't be. I can't guess how much command he has until the next meeting. From an operational point: how do you want to play this?"

The sudden offer of operational leadership to Tom was a surprise to Sarah, and she carefully watched Tom's demeanour in reaction to it.

"We need to secure the next phase asap. And that is with Narith's agreement. From there we extend here and have the weekend or beginning of next week to gather new intelligence from our informant. Then work out a way to feed it in as if it has come from the UK, put it across and hope they act on it."

"Sounds like a plan. For now, get authorisation from Maggie but don't book any flights. I will contact or meet with Narith tomorrow and see if he's got approval. Then we extend and go to work on Sopheap and his sister."

"I can see the key to this being the identification of the safe house," Sarah interjected with concern in her voice.

"Yes, it will be. Both Nuon and Sopheap will be working extra hard on it. They have very real reasons for making this work. That's in our favour. Good work team. Chenda will collect you and take you to the training in the morning and bring you back here afterwards. I should have spoken to Narith by then. I suggest meeting back here 3pm tomorrow. That will be a good time to pull the trigger on the flights, the bookings here and ring Sopheap."

Sarah and Tom nodded in agreement.

As Deena made her way out of the room, Chenda held herself back.

"Tom, I see you are taking the Embassy advice and only drinking Evian. This is a very good decision. You won't be needing your free bottles of water supplied by the hotel. I can use them at home."

"Yeah sure," Tom replied, surprised by his own lack of appreciation for Chenda's personal circumstances.

"Not to worry now. Bring them tomorrow, along with Sarah's, and any of the free biscuits if you don't eat them. Put it all in a plastic bag so the staff don't see it going out."

"OK, sure thing."

"Sarah be careful around that Captain Chey. He's not trustworthy. He ate more than the other two put together. Greedy at the dinner table is greedy in life, is what my mother always taught me."

Chenda promptly left, shutting the door behind her.

"Do you need me here whilst you call Maggie?"

"Not unless you want to be."

"I think a quick dip in the pool wouldn't go amiss before it gets too dark. You can fill me in at dinner."

With the room suddenly silent, Tom opened his laptop, called Maggie and after three attempts got through.

"How did it go?"

"As well as could be expected. They were naturally suspicious, I think. Don't have any capability in this area of work. Seems like if they do come across offenders, they just boot them out of the country."

"What about the offer of working?"

"Narith, the Major in charge of the group, has said yes. But he has to get agreement from his boss. We should know the result of that sometime tomorrow morning. Looks positive."

"So, extension, or is that too early?"

"Deena has suggested we hold off flights and room extensions until tomorrow. Extending the rooms here needs to wait until after Narith has given the green light tomorrow just in case they check up on us. She has asked that the extension be authorised at your end though. Can you get that from JT today? It's early evening here."

Maggie took a second to think about the reply. She didn't want to alert Tom to anything he didn't need to know. Plus, if JT did ring him for any reason he would act more naturally if he didn't know what was happening back home.

"I'll text it through once I have it. What's the plan going forward? Do you know how long the extension will be?"

"I suggested, and Deena has agreed, it will need two weeks from Monday."

"And the plan?"

"First get the green light from Narith. If he says yes, then we have the weekend and the beginning of next week to get more intelligence out of the informant; hopefully that includes identifying the safe house. Then we pass that across as if it has come from our own sources and in a form that he can take action on."

"Seems good. You say they don't have any capability. How is this all going to work when it gets to the pointy end?"

"First off they will need funding. Deena says she will fund half of it, but we will need to find the other half."

"What do you mean by funding?"

"I don't know, but I'm guessing, everything from petrol, food, accommodation and probably even a daily allowance for the Cambodians involved."

"You had better bottom that out with Deena. If it means hard cash, we will need to be creative how that's shown here. And, how we get it to you."

"I'll find out. Whilst we're on the subject of the pointy end, I get the feeling Deena will want me to take the operational lead once this gets going. She doesn't know the true extent of the constraints on me that you do, so this could very quickly come on top."

"How do you mean?"

"Well, if we get good intel which I say is ours, hand it over gently, suggesting that, as we are paying, we would like their actions to be undertaken to our very specific, very non-Cambodian way, then refuse to get involved, it won't go down well. This bunch are a suspicious lot. If I make that play, their suspicions will be off the Richter scale."

Maggie knew this time would come. And she knew what had to be done. Even if she hated herself for doing it.

"Look, Tom, when and if that time comes you need to do what you need to do. I'm not there, you are. You will do the right thing. I have every confidence that you will make the right call."

Maggie kept a deadpan face. Her own small video box providing her with immediate knowledge of her performance.

At Tom's end her picture was grainy and not that clear. He searched the screen for help to interpret what he was hearing. He never had any idea how he was going to keep himself out of the evidential chain, and listening to Maggie made him wonder if she was telling him to just go on and do it, even though it could be career suicide. The image and the words were not exactly adding up, but asking questions might give him answers he did not want to hear.

"Good to know I have your support. Next update about this time or a bit earlier tomorrow?"

"That would be good. Send my regards to Sarah please."

"Will do."

With the call complete, Tom sat and pondered the last section of the conversation with Maggie. He had effectively been given a green light, or had he? Was Maggie just passing the buck or giving him enough rope to hang himself with? The fact was he had been trying to convince himself to do just what JT had demanded; not get involved operationally. The enormity of the reality hit him front and centre. One, there would be no way to avoid it, and two, no matter how many times he told himself not to do it, if there was a choice between saving himself or saving a child, he knew which one he would choose. The weight and worry from JT's threats lifted. He couldn't deny who he was. If they tried to sack him, he would fight it. If they demoted him, he would accept it. If nothing else, that realisation gave him a boost.

Thames Valley Police HQ, Kidlington, England

Maggie completed the copying procedure, then rang Margaret Thrinton.

"Maggie, how are you?"

"Excellent, thank you. Another call is on its way. There is something in it I will need authorisation for."

"I will let him know."

The moment the copy of the call arrived, Margaret typed up the transcript and took it into the Chief.

"Maggie has asked for authorisation for a matter contained in the transcript."

"OK, can you locate the whereabouts of JT, please. I want him here within the hour. If he's further away than that, I'll call him."

"Will do."

The Chief quickly read the transcript, then texted Maggie with the single word, 'Authorised'. As he placed the transcript in his drawer, locking it, his direct line to and from Margaret rang.

"I have JT here now, Sir, if that's convenient?"

"Send him in."

"That was quick, JT, were you skulking around the corner waiting?" the Chief asked in a tone of annoyance with a hint of satire. A skill he had perfected over many years, designed specifically to put someone on the back foot, create fear and give him the edge.

"Just happened to be here," JT replied, defensively, taken aback by the severity of the Chief's tone.

"Really, what for?" This time the Chief softened his delivery, instead letting his gaze fall on JT.

"I'd just finished a meeting with the ACC," JT replied flatly, wondering why he was being grilled.

The Chief, picking up on JT's body language, was satisfied he had the advantage.

"We all need to be leading by example. If I can't check up on you, nobody can, and that wouldn't be good corporate governance, would it?" The Chief had no intention of allowing JT to answer the question.

"I have made a decision: I will be the SIO of Veritas as of now," the Chief paused a fraction, just enough to see JT flinch in his seat and frustration start to show in his face. "I'll require your SIO log, do you have it with you?"

"No."

"In that case, I want it here no later than this afternoon."

"Can I ask why?"

"There is too much riding on it from a GOPOL perspective. If this goes south, then it needs to be down to me and not others. It's as simple as that." The Chief delivered his words without any emotion and in a tone that said the conversation was over. JT, however, wasn't ready to give in quite so soon.

"That is why it is best left with me. If this does go wrong, then there will be space between you and it. The least you know, the better in those situations. I really must ask that you reconsider your position."

"Don't take this personally, JT. I know you have done a good job, and would continue to do so, but GOPOL is my pet project, and on this occasion, albeit very rare, I am assuming direct command. This is about survival and brand. Now, don't make me dismiss you." The Chief seeing that JT was stunned, smiled and let out a small laugh.

"We all wake up on the wrong side of the bed sometimes. Today is my day, so unless there is anything else my next appointment should be here."

"If you insist. You should know that I was waiting for an update from Maggie over some intelligence. I'll get that, complete my log and have it sent across."

"No need. I have to speak to Maggie over another matter. I'll get it then. Just sign the log over to me. I'm looking forward to doing some real police work again. Maybe tomorrow I won't be so grumpy!"

Later that afternoon Margaret handed John Troy's log for Operation Veritas to the Chief. He read it thoroughly. There wasn't anything untoward in it. In fact, it was an accurate reflection of where they were. He thought about the meeting, how JT had behaved and his body language, and couldn't square it with what the spooks were thinking. He went through the log a second time, searching for anything that might provide a clue. There simply wasn't anything. The rationale for decision-making was accurately recorded and justified. He accessed the Brent key and rang Toby Spencer-Drummond.

"Chief Constable, I was just thinking about calling you. Good timing. You first though."

'Bloody spooks!' The Chief thought—not for the first time.

"I've assumed command of Veritas. The first meeting went well in

Cambodia. We have to wait until tomorrow to see if it is authorised higher up the chain. Feedback though, is that it's looking good. I've authorised an extension of two weeks, which will be triggered tomorrow once we get the green light. With the weekend not far away, what news on our meeting?"

"Tuesday, here, 11am."

"Who will be in attendance?"

"My 'comrades' from over the bridge and our cousins."

"Good."

"How did your man react?"

"Nothing untoward at all. I'm still not convinced."

"Point of purchase for the phone and SIM have drawn a blank. The vendor is a small communications hub on Banbury Road, in Summertown. As the crow flies, not that far from your man."

"The point of purchase for the phone and SIM, and the close proximity of its eventual use could be seen as normal. It doesn't mean to say it was him!" the Chief said harshly.

"There is more. One of our teams was on another job, not connected to this. They were intelligence gathering, had an automated number plate recognition car placed in Banbury Road, about a mile north of the purchase point. Seems a car registered to your man went past it."

The Chief was taken aback by this news.

"On what day?"

"The day in question."

"What day was that exactly!" the Chief almost shouted.

"Last Wednesday."

"Any other day?"

"No, but then the car was pulled off to another job the next day."

The Chief knew JT lived in the Headington area but didn't know the exact address.

"What time?"

"8.20am."

"Just the one time?"

"Yes, and the car had been there for six straight days."

The Chief didn't trust Box to tell him the truth. They would play him along if it suited them. He wouldn't put it past them to know a great deal more and not tell him. Maybe they even had JT under surveillance and weren't telling him.

"What type of car?"

"Vauxhall Astra. It would be a good idea if you could do some work around that before Tuesday. I'm sure you will get some questions on it, and they won't necessarily be friendly ones."

The Chief ended the Brent call, went to his desk and immediately rang Stuart Simmons in Professional Standards.

Stuart, who was in his office concluding a meeting, could see the incoming number flash up, waited until his door was shut before answering the call.

"Good afternoon, Sir?"

"Not sure what's good about it, but afternoon to you too. I'm ringing about 'Phobos'. You alone?"

"Yes."

"Excellent. I want two things on my desk first thing. Firstly, I want to know what car JT uses to get to and from work. What police parking permit he has allocated to what vehicle. Next, I want to know what the login times are on his PC, and that's to include any external access he has from home. I know he has a Blackberry: if he can access work emails then that too. I am only interested in the hours between 0600 and 10am on Wednesday of last week."

"Are you after content?"

"No. I just want to know his online profile, if he was active between those hours."

"How far do you want to go?"

"Isn't that far enough?"

"Well, he could be at his desk, log on, leave it on, lock his office door and go and do something. I could ask Jerry to dig deeper but that would be a much larger piece of work."

The Chief paused to think. He didn't want Jerry doing unnecessary work, but he was probably going to get a grilling next week.

"As deep as he can go then."

"What about internet usage?"

"What about it?" replied the Chief, starting to feel he had been out of the investigative loop for way too long.

"I know he's got dual capability on his desktop, but he didn't like to use it, so requested a second stand-alone, on another small desk in his office."

"How do you know that?"

"I make it my business to know. It comes with the job description."

"You were the best candidate for the job by a country mile, Stuart."

"I was the only candidate if my memory serves me, Sir."

"Hard to get people to see the plus side of your job. Yes, internet history please, for the seven days leading up to last Wednesday across any work-related devices, searching for anything relating to mobile communications such as retail outlets selling phones and SIMs in the Oxford area."

"Will do."

At the COCET office, Jane was working late and alone. She enjoyed the peace and quiet. No phone calls, texts, meetings, authorisations, decisions requiring micro meetings—all stopping her from getting her own work done. She occasionally saved up some of her work to do at the end of the day. During these lone working periods, she was able to think about other matters that she wanted private time to consider. Items that she tried to leave at the office door when she left, then pick up again on her return; but her job didn't always allow for that. She often felt there were not enough hours in the day, and not enough overtime in the budget.

As she put the finishing touches to an annual appraisal for Owen Marks, her mind focussed on Maggie and decided she needed to find out more about her, so rang her father.

"Hi cupcake, how's the battle against crime today?"

"You know what it's like, Dad."

"I do, but I was always in uniform and able to walk out the door as soon as the shift ended. It has also become a different job these days."

"You haven't been gone that long. Hey, I wanted to pick your brains."

"If it's about your line of work, forget it, you're light years ahead of me."

"Corporate memory stuff."

"Gossip! Now you're talking. Fire away, cupcake."

"Something is troubling me, or more to the point, someone. I know you don't like me working with Tom, but I trust him. He has taught me to trust my instincts and when to act on them, and something is troubling me about Maggie Burrows."

The line went silent for a couple of seconds.

"I had about three or four years in when Maggie joined. We served together at a few stations. Only once on the same shift. She's a professional, fair, honest and doesn't have any axe to grind from my knowledge.

"There was gossip floating about in the early days. She didn't seem to date, so at the beginning we all had her down as playing for the hockey team. I guess she must have had about ten years in, just been promoted to Sergeant when she got caught in the snooker room, or across it, with the duty Inspector from another shift. That went around like wildfire. He was married, so that didn't last long. In those days one of the two was posted overnight and he got it.

"Then there was the scandal with her and this time a Superintendent. They had both been on a course and had booked different hotel rooms in the same hotel. The management at the hotel, wanting to help the police budget, refunded the police credit card because one of the rooms hadn't been used. Somebody in admin leaked it, it got out, he was married as well. This time she got the posting and somehow a bloody promotion. From there she has kept her nose clean, or should I say, pants on."

"It takes two to tango, Dad," Jane interjected.

"I know. Anyway, we both got promoted to Chief Inspector on the same board. As you know I wasn't interested in any further promotion. Maggie was, and eventually got herself the next rank."

"Did she stay in uniform all her career?"

"Yes, she did. Although there was that one time, when she did a spell on Internal Discipline, now Professional Standards. So, what's your instinct telling you about her?"

"If I knew that, I wouldn't be speaking to you about it. She has been off, acting strange since Tom left."

"Where's he gone?"

"Cambodia."

"Why?"

"Chasing down a lead we have for 'Lost Boy'."

"Does that go all the way back to Operation Benson?" Jane King's father asked in a flat tone.

"Yes. Why do you ask?"

"Just asking, remember the name, that's all."

"Anything more?"

"She has made a few poor operational decisions over the years, nothing major, something most of us have done, or will do. That sort of thing does the rounds. Can't even remember what they were now."

"Would you trust her?"

"This is a strange line of questioning, what's bugging you?"

"Just a question. Would you trust her?"

"As far as I would trust anyone else, apart from you and your mother, who I would trust my life with."

"Ok, thanks, Dad."

"Any time, cupcake."

Her father put the phone down and stood staring at it for a while. He walked out of the kitchen and into his study, opened the drinks cabinet, poured himself a large single malt whisky, took a big gulp, then sat down in his leather chair staring at the garden outside; his face white, as if he had just seen a ghost.

CHAPTER EIGHT

Any person who has authored a serious case review, whether it be in policing or a civil case, will tell you there is always a point in the review timeline where, had another path been taken, the events that followed would have varied; altering the eventual outcome. This is known as the 'case threshold' and is invaluable to the review officer, as it is from this point that lessons are learnt and the finger-pointing starts.

—I. R. Tyler

Phnom Penh, Cambodia

Tom spotted Chenda waiting at the back of the conference room as Sarah closed the final training module. He was hungry and tired. He hadn't slept well, nagging memories of the Skype call with Maggie keeping him awake. In the stillness of the night – with just the air-conditioning humming in the background – he had gone through every scenario that he thought the next few days might bring. Whereas earlier he had been relieved to know the shackles had been lifted, 'though not implicit,' his current thoughts had moved him forward from that position. If Narith gave them the green light, he would step into the operational chain of command, and there would be no going back.

"Good work, Sarah! Another day, another dollar, another 1.76 to the UK pound it is today, for sure. I checked," Chenda beamed, immediately helping Sarah to dismantle her equipment.

"Any news from Deena?" Tom asked, wishfully.

"Not yet, not that I know of, but she sent me a text to say if you finished early, I should take you to S-21, Tuol Sleng. But you are not early, so we will have to do it another day. You cannot come to Phnom Penh and not visit S-21. You know this, Tom, the Germans did terrible things to people from other nations, but we did the same, but it was to our own people, our own babies, children, parents. Our own. Can you even believe we did such a thing? I have memories of this time, Tom. I was a child. One day I will tell you about it."

"We have both read the story surrounding the school; it's on our list to visit," replied Sarah.

"It would be my honour to guide you, Sarah. Now though, we must pack up and return to the hotel. We can stop on the way. I know a sandwich bar on the Riverside. You can get a sandwich and sit on the grass and eat lunch."

"Great idea, I'm starving," Tom said, rubbing his tummy in a circular motion.

"That's very funny. To me that means I have a pain in my belly!" Chenda retorted with a laugh.

All three managed to find some shade to sit under and eat their lunch. Tom had gone for his normal ham salad and can of Coke. Sarah chose an avocado and tuna wrap and bought Chenda a baguette stuffed with nothing but cold beef. The shade provided welcome respite from the sun's 32° heat.

"Tell me about your childhood, Chenda," Sarah asked, looking at her, silently wishing she were able to sit cross-legged, as well and as comfortably as Chenda was now doing.

"I remember nothing but pain, Sarah. Pain from hunger and swollen legs from walking. When I think of it now, it makes me angry."

"If you would rather not speak about it, please just say?"

"No, Sarah. I want to talk about it. It is good for me to talk about it, especially to people from the UK, you understand. If I speak here with Khmer people you don't know who they are related to and what they still think. You still have to be very careful. If you speak too loudly the police will come and arrest you."

"Does that happen?" Tom enquired.

"For sure. We had demonstrations not that long ago. The main people involved were saying exactly what we all thought, but weren't brave enough to say it. They all got arrested."

"I didn't realise it was still that bad here. Why did you have swollen legs?"

"When the order came, we had to leave the city. We had just a few days to leave. I was a small child. We had no money, no possessions that we could trade with. My father said we had to walk to Thailand from Phnom Penh. Which is what we did."

"All the way there?" Sarah asked, with incredulity in her voice.

"Yes, Sarah. All the way. Nearly 500 kilometres in this heat, no food, no money, one small container of water which ran out very quickly, and every night the mosquitoes would bite me."

"Did you make it?"

"Yes, Sarah, eventually we did. But it took a great many months and I still remember the pain very well in my memory. Some days the pain in my tummy hurt so much I cried. When I did, my father would tell me off or beat me. Some days all I had to eat was the grass from the side of the road. The grass, Sarah. I became a cow!"

"I'm so sorry, that is just awful."

"It is not your fault. It was Number One Brother. It was his fault."

"You have a brother?"

"No, I mean Khmer Brother Number One, that is what we all call Pol Pot. He was Number One. Then came the rest in order of command. Number Two Brother was Nuon Chea, but he was not born with that name. Number Three Brother was Ieng Sary, and then it goes on. The one in charge of Tuol Sleng, he was Comrade Duch, but that wasn't his real name either."

"I see."

"The walk was very far and painful, not just because of the pain in my tummy, which got big, but my legs were hurting at my ankles and my knees. They got as big, as you say, as a balloon!"

"Are you alright now?" Sarah asked urgently, with concern in her voice.

"Yes, I am OK now, but the memories will always be there for me."

"What did you do when you got to Thailand?" Tom asked, wondering if Chenda had lived in Thailand as a child.

"They wouldn't let us in. So, we lived there, by the border, for a time. Then we heard the news that the Vietnamese had taken Phnom Penh, so we walked all the way back again. This time though we had more to eat, as people were happy."

"My God!"

"Your God, and my God, both put together Sarah!"

Sarah, watched Chenda, sitting in a manner that she had not been able to do since a child, calmly recounting the horror story whilst devouring the beef and bread—clearly relishing every morsel. Dressed in her black trousers, pale cream blouse and white lacy hat: occasionally lifting her head from her food to reveal an infectious, warming smile, clashing violently with the story she was telling.

"You've done fabulously well to have gone through all that, learn English to the level you have, and then secure this job; huge credit to you," Tom said, in recognition for what he had been hearing.

"I agree with Tom. Is your father alive still?"

"No, he is not."

"Are you married?"

Chenda, who had popped the last piece of the baguette into her mouth, savouring it as long as she could before swallowing, first looked at Sarah, then Tom and then back to Sarah again. She paused, taking her time before speaking.

"No, I'm not. I've heard an expression before from other people from the UK. The phrase used is 'hockey player.' We Cambodians don't play hockey, I don't know it or understand the game; but, nevertheless, apparently, I'm a 'hockey player.'"

"Well done you for saying so. I know a number of girls in the UK who still can't admit it in public."

"We don't have that problem in my country. But I don't have a girlfriend either. I spend all my time now caring for my mother and my older brother who is disabled."

Tom and Sarah fell silent, neither of them really knowing what to say next. Both, though, were saved from their dilemma by Chenda's phone ringing.

"Yes, we're not far Deena. OK, for sure. No, they didn't get time, they ran late. Yes, see you soon."

Chenda jumped up from her cross-legged position in one motion. "We have to go. I must drop you back to the hotel and then go and collect Deena. She has another meeting and then she will join you at the hotel as arranged.

Battambang, Cambodia

Sopheap arrived at his sister's home, pulled his moto onto its stand and walked inside to find her cooking rice in the kitchen.

"You're early. He's still here with his men," Nuon said, startled by her brother's arrival.

"I had to come now. Mother wants me to do the laundry."

"You are becoming a housemaid, brother. You'll be wearing the uniform soon; your knobbly knees will be seen by everyone!"

"Don't tease me, sister!"

"I have to. You need to grow a pair, otherwise Mother will have you tied to her until she dies, by which time you will be wearing a dress!"

"But I already have a pair. I have told you this before. If I grow another pair, I will have four. Two sets. And the world is not ready for that!"

Nuon giggled at her brother's words, walked over and hugged him.

"Think about all the children you could sire, brother, with all that power between your legs!"

This time it was Sopheap's turn to giggle.

"Where is he?" he asked, his tone immediately changing.

"He's out the back with his gang. They are getting ready to leave."

"How many of his gang are here?"

"All of them."

"Are they all going?"

"He always leaves one behind to keep an eye on me, so I don't expect so."

"Have you found out anything for me, to tell the Barang?"

"I have news, brother," Nuon replied, walking over to the window, then looking and listening intently towards the rear yard of her house, before returning to Sopheap.

"We have to be careful, only whisper. If we hear them coming, we must switch to the health of our mother."

"I understand."

"Two of his gang, the two he trusts more than the others, I overheard them speaking yesterday. They thought I was in the bedroom, well away from them, but I wasn't."

"Which two?" Sopheap asked in a manner that suggested he was someone of importance, asking a very important question.

"Keo and Utey."

"You must be more careful, sister! What if they had seen you!"

"I overheard them, dear brother," Nuon replied with a sigh.

"Yes, but if they . . ." Sopheap began, before he was halted by Nuon putting her hand on the side of his face affectionately.

"Sweet brother, they didn't see me. Now listen to what I have to say and don't interrupt me, otherwise you won't get any rice."

Sopheap looked over to the pot that was bubbling away nicely. It would be new season rice—his sister always got it first. Just the smell was making his mouth water in anticipation. He nodded in agreement.

"Before you ask again in that important voice of yours, I don't know either of their family names. They both come from Phnom Penh. They were talking about how pleased they were with Chakra's choice of safe house, now that the moat was full of water again. Those words gave me the first clue, so I did move from the bedroom, that way I could hear everything they were saying, but they never saw me.

"They had concerns over one person, who they didn't name, who they had to kick out of the house so Chakra could take possession of it. They thought he was a danger to them, even though they had paid him off to keep silent. They were proposing to speak to Chakra, to suggest that he was done away with, as a necessary precaution to protect their ongoing interests.

"I know that when Chakra first started his gang, he came into some money. I don't know how much. I never saw a single dollar. But it wasn't enough to buy his cousin's house. He didn't have enough money to buy it, he got terribly angry about that. He got drunk one night and beat me just because he was short. To save myself from yet more injury, I suggested he rent it and use the rent money to pay back what he was short, until it was paid off. That is what he did."

"Do you think the safe house is the same house he bought off his cousin?" Sopheap asked urgently, trying not to use his important voice.

"Yes, because that house had a moat, that only fills with water at certain times."

"And do you know where that house is?" Sopheap asked, leaning forward, whispering the words, hardly able to contain his excitement."

"Of course, I do, brother. Do you fancy some rice? It's fresh season!" Nuon replied, whispering back in his ear, in a superior, important tone.

Nuon and Sopheap were eating fresh jasmine rice and greens when they heard the sound of Chakra's old Hilux drive past the house without stopping. Nuon jumped up and raced over to a side window, peering through large teak slats.

"The whole gang is with him."

"Are you sure?"

"Yes, quick. Finish your food. Then go around the back and check. If you find anybody, say you were going for walk after eating. Ask if they want any rice. Quickly!"

Sopheap gulped down the rest of his rice and did what he was told, but soon returned.

"They have all gone. There is no one here!"

"I have an idea, 'dear' brother!"

"What idea is that?" Sopheap asked warily, knowing that his sister only ever called him 'dear' when she wanted something. That something nearly always being good for her and not for him.

"You must change your clothes and use my safety helmet. I will explain where the address is and how to get there. You must then drive past the address that I suspect is the safe house on your moto. I haven't been there, but I remember where that Choi Mai said it was. If it is there, you should be able to see the Choi Mai's Hilux, as you drive by. If not, maybe you can see something else."

"This an exceptionally good idea, sister. Why don't you go?"

"Because I have to stay here, in case they haven't gone there and come back. You know I'm forbidden to leave. And I can't ride your moto well: it is so dangerous to drive!"

"Yes, I suppose you're right," Sopheap replied forlornly.

"The safety helmet is in the box by the back door. You get that, and I will find an old jacket. If you manage this, brother, it will give you great power!"

"I have enough power for all the young women of Battambang. I've never had any complaints!"

With Sopheap now wearing an old, worn, dirty, grey jacket and a safety helmet, Nuon began to explain the location of what she suspected might be the safe house, writing directions on a scrap of paper, in case he forgot. As she finished, Sopheap took the helmet back off.

"What are you doing! Put it back on and get going!"

"That is a very long way. I will run out of fuel!"

"Well, get some on the way, brother. Now hurry up!"

"I don't have enough money!"

"What?"

"I don't have enough money to buy fuel!"

"I gave you some of the money from the Barang. Where has all that gone?" Nuon almost screamed at him.

"Mother was making me do so many chores that I couldn't keep up. I paid for some of them to be done, so I could come to see you," Sopheap replied, pleadingly.

Nuon wasn't convinced one bit, causing her to scream in anger, then storm off into her bedroom. When she returned she thrust two one-dollar notes into her brother's waiting hand.

"Don't fill the tank all the way up. You won't need it . . . and I want the change!"

Sopheap sighed and left.

Forty minutes later he came to a halt, just before a deserted, wooden shack that had lost its woven palm roof. He got the note out with the directions that Nuon had given him and was about to take off his helmet to read it, when suddenly, he thought better of it and left it on. From the description, the next track on the right would lead to the house that his sister thought was the safe house. He put the note away and drove off along the dusty road, cursing the fact that his highly polished shoes were now completely covered in brown dust.

Within about half a kilometre he began to see the early signs of a track emerging from his right. There were two wooden posts that looked as if they had once had signs attached to them. As he got closer, he slowed down and could see that the small, single-lane dirt track made its way through a mixture of coconut, banana and rubber trees. As he passed the entrance, he could see the track disappear around a bend as it reached dense bush, about 200 metres in from the road he was on; this stopped him from being able to see anything from his position. He travelled further along before turning back. He then drove past the track, this time from the opposite direction, to see if he could see something from a different angle. Not noticing anything, he drove back to the shack, parking up behind it. He got off his moto, removed his helmet and lit up a cigarette, contemplating what to do next. It was too risky to drive up the dirt track. He could not see anybody in the dense bush, but the sound of his moto would alert them if they were there.

He checked his watch. There was plenty of time before he had to speak to the Barang's. He was halfway through his cigarette when he told himself he had two options. Either he went back and told Nuon he couldn't see anything, risking her wrath. Or he went up the track on foot, keeping to one side, hoping nobody would see him. If he could do that successfully, he should be able to confirm if there was a house on the other side, and if there was, if Chakra's car was present. Both options were dangerous: both had their risks. One however was short-term: the other, his sister, long-term. She would never let him forget it. The many years of taunting about the lack of power between his legs would be too much for him to bear. There was also the extra, incredibly large carrot that he could feel being dangled in front of him: the carrot that had a big, fat, US dollar sign sitting on top of it. Sopheap dropped the cigarette on the floor, putting it out with his foot.

Placing his helmet back on, he walked the distance back to the track. As he approached it, he became nervous, and felt himself shaking with fear. If Chakra or any of his gang drove down the track, they would find him in the middle of nowhere, wearing a crash helmet and no moto. He would stand out so much, they would be sure to stop him and force him to take off his helmet. Once they saw him, they would kill him for sure and then his sister. The fear was so much, that he stopped. He turned around and began to walk back to his moto and safety, but the combination of the carrot and Nuon caused him to turn back once more.

This time, having made it all the way, Sopheap turned down the dirt track, quickly making his way to the left, through the sparse coconut trees until it became a thicker mixture of banana and rubber. He pushed his way into it a short distance, squatted down, and waited to see if his presence had been detected. Whilst he waited, he scanned the land ahead. After a few minutes, he made his way towards the thicker bushy tree line in small increments until he finally arrived at it. Up close, he could see there was no quiet way of pushing through it, so made his way quickly towards the dirt track again, preparing himself to dive into the thick bush if there was a sudden need. As he moved forward, he could hear a male voice, but could not make out the words. As he reached the track, the trees became thinner, so he pushed himself inside it, making his way as quietly as he could towards the direction of the voice. He had only taken two steps when one of his shoes scuffed itself hard up against a tree root. He stopped dead. The noise was significant and not in keeping with the environment. He saw that his right shoe now had a dent and scratch marks on the leather which he knew, would never come out, no matter how much polish he put on it. He was angry and scared at the same time. He found himself sweating profusely inside the helmet, causing his whole body to overheat. He wanted to remove the helmet, but had to keep it on, lest anyone spot and immediately recognise him.

After a few nervous minutes, a clearing appeared. He saw the track led past a building on the right, before going over a bridge towards a courtyard area and more buildings on the left. Sopheap's full view was obstructed by a single banana tree. As quietly as he could, he moved around it to gain a better view. With the obstacle removed, he peered through searching for anyone or anything. What he saw sent a chill down his spine: the chill, in a split second, neutralising his previously hot body.

CHAPTER NINE

MI5, Thames House, London, England

Toby Spencer-Drummond stood waiting to alight the Waterloo-bound train, the queue having formed some minutes before the train reached its destination. Standing passengers lurched violently, as the carriage rumbled and rolled in its final moments leading into the arrivals platform. Toby was grasping hold of a hand strap attached to the roof of the carriage, anticipating the lurch, when he felt the soft vibration of his pager. He glanced down, immediately recognising the number.

The moment he entered his office he prepared a communication log, then rang the 'L' room.

"Good morning, Toby, are you ready?"

"Sure am!"

"There was heightened activity across all your subjects from 6pm last night. Again though, only one is covered by the warrant. 7.02pm: incoming mobile, details in the log. We checked your operational reports: it relates to one of the SIMs that was purchased along with the phone. As you know, there were five. Two down, three to go.

"Muffled voice, as before, only words spoken were 'Alpha 7', said twice. Again, we don't know if it was the subject who picked up the phone, but the operators say the wife and children hardly ever use the landline phone. Static intelligence tells us the children weren't at home.

"Cell site: the same as last time. The SIM and phone remained active for a few minutes before going dead. No cell site movement within those few minutes; the same as before, which could be significant. I see you're due a renewal update. I would suggest you factor that into your pitch to keep these going. I would expect to see it on there! Pip Pip."

Toby put the phone down. It was early, he'd overslept, not had time for breakfast, and if he had a voodoo doll right at that moment, he would requisition a large box of pins to stick in it.

He was required to undertake a renewal. The fact the phone did not move for those few minutes might be significant, on the other hand it might mean nothing. He would make it enough to extend the current warrants. What the 'L' room didn't have sight of, at least until they got his renewal application, was the recent police activity. That did make the most recent call even more significant, especially as they were trying to piece together an intelligence picture of who was, and who wasn't, part of the deep state cabal. He picked up his desk phone and rang Mr Pink.

"Greetings, this fine morning. How are we all?"

"We are indeed splendid, Squadron Leader."

"That is very pleasing to hear, Mr Pink. Do you have any capability?"

"What do you have in mind?"

"At least two ANPR cars, arterial routes between the mast location and our possible caller. I'll send you the number I want scanned and a suggestion for the placement of the vehicles."

"Start and end time?"

"To be advised, but within the next seven days."

"Should be able to do that. Anything else?"

"Mobile surveillance?"

"Not unless it's urgent or 'L' room driven."

"It's neither of those today," Toby replied, forlornly.

"I can do a data logger if you think you have the intelligence case and the vehicle to put it on? That would work nicely in tandem with the ANPRs?"

"Excellent, Mr Pink! I'll get you the authority!"

Chief Constable James Galloway was also in his office, reading the intelligence he had requested the day before. JT did have a Vauxhall

Astra: it was registered to him. He had a parking permit for that car. His swipe entry card for the building indicated he had arrived at 8.40am that day, had logged onto the intranet five minutes later and two minutes after that the standalone internet PC. There were no hits for communications retailers or anything remotely similar. There was also nothing untoward noted in his online intranet usage. The only thing that did stand out was the swipe login for that day. Virtually every other day, JT would arrive at 8am, plus or minus a couple of minutes.

The Chief slapped the intelligence log onto his desk. There could be any number of reasons why he was late that day. The spooks, however, would seize on it for sure. He was pondering what to do next when his Brent phone rang a couple of times and then stopped. Sighing, he got up, inserted the key and waited, considering what his next moves were. His thoughts were interrupted by the phone ringing again.

"Morning, Toby. I take it you have news?"

"I do, I do indeed. Another call last night. Muffled. 'Alpha 7' said twice. Call was made on one of the SIMs purchased along with the phone. Cell site the same, as was the fact we don't know who answered the call. Other intelligence indicates that it must be my subject. Things of note here though. One, how is it these calls don't have anybody speaking at the subject end? What alerts them not to speak? Two, the phone SIM was not terminated for a few minutes following the call and did not travel during that time. And three, the alpha scale is going upwards. Is that call and the scale related to the conversation with your man?"

The Chief made an instant decision to not reveal the little intelligence he had on JT: not until he had undertaken more research.

"As for point three, who knows? It certainly is of concern. I would suggest we try and trigger another call—by me releasing some information to JT. What do you think?"

"My thoughts exactly!"

"I want to do some further research first. I'll let you know when I feed the disinformation into the system."

"Don't take long to think about it. I would strongly recommend you have this done before the meeting."

"I agree. You available over the weekend?"

"Yes."

With the call completed, he immediately rang Stuart Simmons.

"Thanks for getting this to me quickly, Stuart, but I now need more work done."

"Fire away, Sir."

"I want to know JT's intranet log off and exit swipe times. I'm looking for a pattern generally. Then focus on the two calls Box have captured. Was he still at work? Did he stay on and leave late? That would allow for him to be in the right place at the right time."

"I can do that. Anything else?"

"Yes. The SIMs: the user seems to be using them once. I can get you their details and the three that haven't been used yet. Can we get an alert from the provider the moment the SIM goes live?"

"Yes, if you authorise the application. Why haven't Box done it?

"The second call was only last night. So, it might be on their radar. If you say it can be done, then I want us to do it first."

"I'll get it arranged."

Phnom Penh, Cambodia

Tom, Sarah, Deena and Chenda all met up at the Sunflower Hotel. Deena began.

"Narith wasn't available for a meeting. Which is a shame, as I wanted to measure his demeanour when he spoke. He has been given the go-ahead. It will be the same team that came to the meeting yesterday, including the interpreter."

"That's great news, Deena," Tom interrupted: unable to contain his excitement.

"It is, but I wasn't pleased with the tone of his voice. He seemed wary, on guard. It might have been nothing, but I suspect they are suspicious at our sudden, flexible offer."

"They would be correct in their suspicions!" Sarah said, stating the obvious.

"We must expect and accept this will be their style going forward. From our side, the strategy must be to keep their suspicions to no more than that. They cannot be allowed to transform them into reality. Suspecting is one thing, knowing is another," Deena stated, looking at everybody in the room.

They all nodded in agreement.

"Excellent. Chenda, ring Sopheap please and put him on speaker."

Chenda did as requested, the room falling silent, waiting for the call to be answered.

"This is Sopheap, how may I help you?"

"That's how to answer a phone if you were working for the Embassy, don't be stupid," Chenda retorted in her best 'put down' voice.

"But I am working for the Embassy, dear sister, we are both now working for the Embassy. We are in fact, I think the term is, 'colleagues'!"

Chenda was about to launch into Sopheap, but Deena intercepted her.

"Sopheap, this is Deena. You are providing us with information, and we are calling you for an update. Do you have any?"

"Yes, Bong Srei. I have an especially important update for you. You must travel to see me as before, so we can discuss this important update. We must also discuss payment for it. The update is particularly important, so the payment for it, must also be very important!"

Sopheap's tone was respectful but overly grand, as if he had suddenly been made the King of Cambodia, and it came across like that, even over the phone.

Chenda squirmed in her seat, the expression of an angry fighting tiger flashing across her face, hardly able to stop herself from roaring in anger.

Spotting it, Deena considered letting her loose, but, waving the palm of her hand in Chenda's direction, decided to play along for the time being. When she had Chenda's nodded compliance, she proceeded.

"Sounds like you have been doing some particularly important work, Sopheap. I am, however, the judge on whether work is classed as important or not, so, if you tell me what work you've been doing, I will decide if it is important or not."

There was a distinct pause before Sopheap replied.

"I would very much like to reveal it to you, Bong Srei. But this information is so important that it must be relayed face to face. This is so payment can be immediately made. Our arrangement is based on I give you something, and I get US dollar for it. I cannot get my US dollar if you are not here."

Deena had no intention of haggling over the phone.

"Sopheap, stay on the line. I'm going to put you on hold whilst I discuss your demands. Do you understand that?"

"Yes, Bong Srei. My sister often puts me on hold."

Chenda leant over to the phone and activated the hold facility. She was desperate to speak her mind, but knew it wasn't her place to do so.

"Look, I'm happy to work this weekend. That's not the issue here," Deena began, "the issue is risk. We shouldn't make the trip to Battambang now we have an agreement with the police. I don't think for one minute they have mobile surveillance capacity, but there are other means of achieving essentially the same thing. It will be extremely easy for them to get reports on your movements from hotel staff here."

"This is all about money," Tom interjected.

"Yes, it is. But your movements need to fit the story we've given, so we can't go."

"How about telling him that, maybe that would change his mind?" Sarah enquired.

"I'm not going to bargain with him, Sarah. He has something, something he knows, or thinks is worth money and he wants that money straight away."

"What options are there?" Tom asked.

"We go and get him. Chenda, are you free this weekend?"

"I can be, yes. You want me to go and get him?"

"Yes. You can either go today and stay overnight there and be back here midday tomorrow. That means leaving to go back with him later that afternoon, then stay overnight there again before returning on Sunday. Or, go early tomorrow. That will entail you either going back up there and overnighting tomorrow or doing a long day on Sunday. Your choice."

"I'll leave today, take him back Saturday or the Sunday."

"OK. Put him back on."

"Can you hear me, Sopheap?"

"Yes."

"Good. We cannot leave Phnom Penh. There are very good reasons for this. I'll send Chenda for you and I'll pay for your overnight stay here tomorrow. Chenda will take you back the same day or Sunday. Are we in agreement?"

"Yes, Bong Srei."

"Good. However, you must tell me the nature of your information, otherwise the whole deal is off, and your sister can find other means of getting herself out of the situation she's in. That means, no more dollars. Let me make this perfectly clear, we will be going ahead with our investigation: with or without you. So, speak now, choose your words carefully and do not ever pull this type of demand on me again!"

Deena's tone carried such severity that it took Sarah by surprise. Chenda though, was silently giggling.

"I didn't mean to offend you, Bong Srei," Sopheap began, quickly losing his imperial tone, replacing it with one of respectful sorrow.

"This will not happen again. I can swear on my mother's life to you; this will not happen again. This information relates to the location of the safe house. That is all I can say for now."

"Are you saying you know it?" Deena shot back, maintaining her stern voice, while looking at Tom, Sarah and Chenda, with a hopeful look of surprise on her face.

"Yes, Bong Srei. I know it."

COCET, Aylesbury, England

Back at COCET, Jane was settling in for a long day. Both warrants had gone smoothly, with the searches well underway. Early reports indicated the two offenders were cooperating. That meant the prospect of their identities being successfully assumed by COCET was high.

Whether they could maintain it, and over what period, remained to be seen. But she was keen to know what progress, if any, had already been made, so she went to see Dale Walters in Covert Ops and found him busy typing at his laptop.

"Hi, Dale. Early days I know, but is there anything to report?"

"Yes, there is. I was just coming to find you. Take a seat."

The managerial situation between her and Dale was a strange one. He was a substantive sergeant and had been for years. She was still 'acting up' and yet in charge of COCET whilst Tom was away. Even if he hadn't gone away, she was seen as second in command. It was probably because of Operations Benson and Hope, the first two of which had led to COCET, which in turn, had led to Operations Ascent and Resolve. Dale had been brought in to be head of Covert Ops, had the skill set, and she didn't interfere or question the operational deployments. There was no undercurrent between her and Dale, and she respected him for that. Many officers would not have been able to manage the situation as well as he did.

"I've already assumed both identities. I made the decision based on the intelligence coming out at point of arrest. They are both senior admins, so the intel was correct, which is both good and bad."

"Why is that?"

"Because one of them 'eyes2die4' is lazy. Hardly ever engages or enforces the rules of the group he's in. From what I can see, he's not actually on a great deal, just takes what he wants and leaves. Which is good for us. I've made an initial assessment: there is nothing there that's urgent. In fact, there were only two on when I assumed his identity. They didn't appear to spot the break or the attached comm data change and they left without saying a word. All of that is good."

"And the bad?"

"That's what I was coming to see you about. The other subject: his group is quite busy, although there are only three online now. Nobody seemed to be at their keyboard either when I took control, as I didn't get any incoming contact, but that might be normal. Our subject, 'youngsweetlips' is quite an active enforcer. So, we will need to replicate that. That's not what I'm worried about. We can manage, especially when Owen and Anna get back here. There is one thing that is worrying me though, and that's this internal group of four here."

Dale pointed at the screen for Jane to see what he was referring to.

"'youngsweetlips' is a member of that group. They call, or refer to themselves, as 'Alphas'. That could just be because they all have some sort of hierarchy within the main room. I'll need more time to work that out, or it could be that it's just the name of the group. On the face of it, only our subject is an admin of the main room.

"The red flag, though, is I think they've only been in existence for about a month. I can see all the chats and it goes back about a month. They speak in a clipped code. I'll get you a printout so you can read the chat logs. They refer to recipes. My view is that they are substituting ingredients for children. The recipes are Asian, and the 'meals' they refer to will be ready to be tasted soon. My analysis is that someone in that group will be getting hands on an Asian child very soon, so we will need to take some form of action to stop that."

"Why soon? Maybe they already have the child!" Jane said, in an urgent tone.

"Read the chat logs when I bring them through. They are missing the main ingredient and that hasn't changed. I've already spoken to Owen and Archie. I've asked Owen to stay there until the interviews have taken place, and, if possible, to either be part of the interview team or, at the very least, downstream monitor."

"Can I have the chat logs now?"

Dale turned back to his laptop. "Do you know your printer code?"

"Yes. CT2008TVP."

Dale tapped quickly at his keyboard before pressing a final key.

"Printing out there now!"

Jane returned to her desk, having collected the chat logs from the printer as she went by. There were only four pages, and she rapidly read through them. Dale was right. It was all about recipes—Asian stir fry. There were three recipes spoken about. All with the main ingredient, beef, missing. One chat log came from user, 'pureisbest'. Whoever that was, and it was likely to be a him, would be the one to source the beef ingredient. That was dated yesterday and was the latest log. She rang Dale.

"Dale, I've read them. What exactly have you tasked Owen with?"

"Sit and listen to start with, nothing more."

"Is he aware of the chat logs and their contents."

"In brief, yes."

"Is he aware of the recipes?"

"Yes."

"I think it best he doesn't tell the local interview team of this. Not yet. Can you let me know the result of the first interview? We can take it incrementally from there."

"Sure, I'll let Owen know. It might be an idea he updates us both at the same time."

"I agree."

Jane immediately walked through to the Intelligence Cell and handed the chat logs to team leader Anna Farley.

"Dale has already assumed the two identities. We should get a better idea of where we are later, but this, as of now, seems to be the only urgent matter. Once the first interview has been completed, Owen will ring in for a conference call. I'd like you there."

Anna began to scan through the first page.

"Dale was quick off the mark!"

"Yes, that part has gone well. Couldn't have hoped for better!"

"Well, this is interesting," Anna replied, moving onto the second and then the third page of the chat logs. "Is this all recipes?"

"Yes, it is."

Anna quickly scanned the fourth page, before placing them down.

"I'll get this logged in. Just so we're ready if it comes to urgent dissemination."

"Thanks, Anna," Jane said, walking back to her desk.

"Do you want me to give Interpol and Niall the heads up?"

Jane stopped abruptly, turning back with a surprised look on her face.

"Why Niall?"

"The attached comms data. From working on Operation Resolve, some of this looks like Thailand. I will have to country code it, even though I'm sure Interpol will do it again."

CHAPTER TEN

Ban Mai Nong Sai, Thailand

Umar joined a border trader who was in the queue, waiting to re-enter Thailand. The trader had spent the day in Poipet, Cambodia, selling clothing and cooking utensils. It had been an average sales day. The huge cart he had hauled in that morning felt as heavy at the end of the day as it had at the beginning. The one good thing to come out of it: he had been joined by Umar. That meant a personal bonus, one which went straight into his pocket, with no middleman to reduce it. It was also the easiest 1,000 baht he had ever made. All he had to do was make it look like they were partners. As soon as they got through the border gateway and out of sight, Umar handed over the money and left. No questions. No threats. No nothing. The only downside was that it didn't happen every day. Umar flagged down a passing tuk-tuk and he headed away from the border to Ban Mai Nong Sai, his base of operations.

Once inside his villa, he stripped, leaving the peasant clothes neatly folded on a shelf and went to the bathroom. Waiting for the shower to warm up, he checked his physique in the mirror. Two old knife wounds had long since turned light brown, matching his skin. The single bullet wound, however, was still dark brown. He admired his muscles, tensing his torso to accentuate them. He was strong enough to kill with his bare hands, if he needed to, which pleased him.

At sixteen Umar had left behind his poor, Malaysian east coast roots for Kuala Lumpur. The move had been tough at first. He had spent many weeks sleeping rough, going hungry, fighting over scraps of food. One of those fights, though, got him recognised by one of the local gangs, who recruited him. From there, his life changed: slowly at first—just a tin roof and food once a day. In return he ran small parcels of drugs between addresses in KL. As time went by, he was trusted with larger consignments and then money. By the time he was twenty, he had control over other gang members, had even killed on the order of his boss, and had begun to make real money. Five years later, he was now second in command and had his own trafficking arm, a splinter group of Gang-09.

The six golden commandments of Gang-09 started with: you can retire, but you can never leave. Two more years, and he would be able to retire to Pulau Pinang, leaving others to manage operations and take the risk. The next few weeks, though, would make him enough money to pay for a six-bedroom, detached property overlooking Batu Feringgi Beach and the Melaka Strait. It was going to be a very busy couple of weeks.

As he stepped into the shower, he began to think about the 'Khn b̂ā.' He was the only real risk to operations running smoothly. When Chet arrived, he needed to discuss that risk with him.

COCET, Aylesbury, England

Jane and her team were gathered around her desk when Owen rang.

"Owen, you are speaking to Dale and Anna as well," Jane said quickly. Just so Owen knew he had an audience. She suspected Dale would have told him. But it wouldn't have been the first time an officer spoke out of turn, not knowing the person they were talking about could hear everything.

"Cool. My warrant's gone really well. No problems at the home. Made admissions quickly. Offered to help whilst still at the address. Back at the nick he got a touch of the seconds, asked for a solicitor to start with, but then changed his mind."

"Was that all covered at the beginning of the interview?" Jane asked, with concern in her voice.

"Yes, it was. I also got him out and in front of the custody officer. So, it's all on tape there as well, and that's before the interview started.

We'll cover it again at the beginning of every tape."

"What changed his mind?" Dale asked inquisitively.

"He says he knows what we're going to find, wants to help us."

Jane, Anna and Dale smiled at each other.

"Excellent. How many interviews have you had?" Jane asked.

"We did two tapes. Had a break, then did another two. He's now on a longer break, getting a meal and a bit of rest, then we will be back into it. To be honest, we probably only have another one, maximum two tapes left. He's been talking non-stop."

"Are you able to give us a synopsis of what you've got so far?" Dale asked Owen, knowing that he had told him to be ready to do so.

"Yes, Sarge!"

"Enlighten us, then."

"He says he's only offended online. Hasn't touched his own kids. Or any others. They're being interviewed today. My guess is, he hasn't. The wife didn't seem to know either. She went for him when he admitted to her what he'd been up to. His own interest is prepubescent boys, although he started with girls, 'Lolita' type age group. He says he's got a large collection amassed from when he started, which was about four years ago. It covers the whole age range of both boys and girls. Admits he has some baby collections but says that he only has them for trading with others; to get certain images he wants in return. He sees them as a form of money."

"Was his PC encrypted?" Dale asked, not showing any emotion from Owen's comments about the baby collection.

"Yes, TrueCrypt. He handed the password over straight away."

"Go on," Jane said, pleased with the way things were going and eager to know more.

"He says he only collects level four where he can. He has admitted to receiving and supplying for the last four years, and that whatever we find on his hard drive is solely down to him. He's admitted he has one folder that holds only home-grown images and videos in it. Which is why he became a member of the group of 'Alphas.' He got invited by the owner of that group because he had supplied a lot of home-grown. These are images and videos which he's collected over the years.

"He says if we hadn't turned up, he would have gone hands on soon. The purpose of the group is to obtain access to young boys through the owner of the group. They have to pay, and they have to travel to Thailand to do it. But it had been agreed by the group they would all travel and meet up there. He's already paid for his flight.

"He doesn't think any of the other members have gone hands on either. He thinks they would have boasted about it, if they had. He thinks the group founder may live in Thailand, as he seems to be online only during that time zone."

"Has he booked his accommodation for Thailand yet?" Dale asked, arching his eyebrows in excitement.

"No. He says one of the others in the group was going to research it, once the founder, 'pureisbest', tells them what area they need to base themselves in."

"Price?"

"They've all asked about it, but they don't know that yet. What they do know is, it has to be paid in US Dollars and whoever goes first has to pay the most."

Anna lowered her head and shook it from side to side in a shuddering motion. When she looked up, Jane could see anger and disgust on her face.

"Owen, it's Anna speaking: this founder, is there anything to suggest he might be the one actually sourcing the children within Thailand?"

"My offender doesn't think so, because, he's had plenty of chat with 'pureisbest', and he's never indicated that it was him. He's always spoken in a way that it was someone else. But of course, that could be just disinformation!"

"When is the flight?"

"Next week."

"Do you have the details?"

"Not to hand. Thai Airways from London Heathrow. I'll get it to you."

"How far have you got with his online style?" Dale asked, shifting in his seat, moving closer to the speaker.

"We haven't covered that yet. He's brought it up himself, as part of wanting to help us track down the other offenders. So, it should be easy to get it, without alerting him to what our intentions are."

"Is he telling the truth? He could be making it up. Maybe they have some code word, that, if used, means police have infiltrated them," Jane said, sternly.

"That's true. He's on hyperdrive at the moment, can't stop talking. I think it's all true. Later though, once he's banged up on remand, he may get second thoughts."

"By that time, it will be too late," Dale said, looking at Jane as if to say he had heard enough for now.

"Well done, Owen. Finish off there but call Dale before you leave. I'll give this some thought and come back to you."

"Yes, Sarge."

Jane looked at Dale. There was more than enough for him to get moving on, but she wanted to cover some basics first. She redialled her phone, put it on speaker and placed it back on the table.

"Nick Sharpe speaking."

"Dr Nick, it's Jane here. I have Dale and Anna with me. How are things with you?"

"Good. I'm at the station, and the exhibits are all logged in. I'm sort of done, unless you want me to do anything more?"

"Yes, there is something else. Are you able to speak?"

"No, give me a minute."

They could hear Nick making his way outside, through doors and corridors. Suddenly, they heard the sound of wind.

"I can talk now."

"The forensic team there: how competent are they?" Jane asked.

"I can't say. They'll be trained to the same standard. Whether that makes them good, I can't tell. They did exactly what I would have expected them to do at the scene. Why?"

Jane ignored the question.

"How long will it be before the forensics get done?"

"No idea. But I did overhear one of them saying that this case was being entered into their system as a priority. One of the officers laughed and said, 'Six weeks rather than twelve then,' which I thought was probably about average for most Police forensic units these days."

Jane shook her head.

"That won't do," Dale said gruffly.

Anna nodded her agreement.

"Six weeks isn't what I agreed with their head of forensics. I had an agreement they would start on this straight away. I'm going to give him a call. If the agreement has changed, I won't have the clout to make them change it back. What capability have you and Sue got right now?"

"I haven't spoken to her this morning. I guess we can do it. Look, I can just ask now if you want me to. The guys have been really friendly."

Jane thought about it for a second. She was annoyed. It was likely just a throwaway comment, but she couldn't take anything for granted. They needed the forensics done urgently.

"Find out, Nick. If they aren't starting on it today, I need to know."

"I'll be straight back."

"This is your ballpark, Dale. What do you advise?"

"They have the capability and the expertise. Every force has. It will be down to workload, money and personal motivation. If they have bounced it down the list, you could go to the Chief, who could go to their Chief, and then back down to them. But that would piss them off. It's way better having SDE do it. They are committed to us and have bought into COCET.

"I can start online, researching past chats, ones that I can access to get going. I can enhance our capability with the intelligence of his online style, once Owen gets it. That will help enormously. But we need to see what's on his PC. What chat logs are held there. What his words, phrases, pet nicknames, slang usage and past conversations are. We need that to corroborate what he's saying in interview, matches what is held on his own PC."

"That's going to be especially true with the 'Alphas'," Anna said, the anger still showing.

"Yes, that's correct. The language used will have been very personal to them. It surrounds one topic. It's high risk. One wrong word. One wrong phrase or comment. Something really innocuous could raise alarms."

Dale and Anna looked towards Jane.

"If the agreement has changed, then SDE will do it. It will blow most of the forensic budget, but this is worth it. In the meantime, you'd better tread softly, Dale."

"Understood. Once we're armed and ready to go, I'll need fresh instructions, probably by tomorrow at the latest."

"OK," replied Jane.

"What about this flight," Anna enquired. "You want me to start making some enquiries around that. Just as confirmation?"

"Yes," Jane replied, checking her watch. It would be evening time in Cambodia. "I'll need to check in with Tom, so he can do your instructions, Dale. At the same time, though, I'll scope the possibilities of deploying an undercover officer into Thailand in place of our offender." Before she could continue, her phone rang.

"You're speaking to ADS King."

"Hi Jane, it's Nick. Not good news. They knew it was due to be the next job, but we have been bumped down the list. It will be three days at the earliest before they can get to it."

"OK. Sign it all back out. Is Archie with you?"

"Yes."

"Get him to help you. Do you want to set up there, come here, or go to your own base?"

"It would be best if I came to you. That way I can speak to Dale and better understand his needs as they crop up. I will need accommodation though."

"I'll get Sam to sort that and phone you direct."

"Done."

Jane turned to Dale to relay the conversation, but being close, he could hear both sides of the conversation and spoke first.

"I got all that. Barring any disasters, we should be in a position to begin full infiltration tomorrow or the day after at the latest."

Ban Mai Nong Sai, Thailand

Chet pulled onto the short drive in front of the villa in Bang Mai Nong Sai and entered to find Umar naked on the floor with a Thai girl, also naked, sitting astride him.

Umar, hearing the door open, looked up to see Chet smiling down at him.

"Do you want to join me, brother?"

Chet looked at the girl. She was Thai, like him. She wasn't one of Umar's regulars or one he had seen before.

"What's your name, girl?"

"Mink," she replied, smiling coyly at Chet.

She wasn't new, Chet thought. She hadn't stopped moving even though he had suddenly walked in on them. He considered the offer, studying her face closely, deciding if he wanted to or not.

Mink spotted the consideration in an instant, arched her back, threw her head backwards allowing the long, silky, black hair to fall freely. She placed both hands flat on the floor behind her, slipping with her right hand, regaining her position clumsily.

"Two, no problem for me, if you like. But 2,000 baht, only short time," smiling again at Chet.

He saw there were beads of sweat on her top lip. She was either drunk or on drugs. He suspected the latter. They were all on drugs, using it to help them get through what they had to do to earn a living.

"All yours," Chet replied, leaving them and making his way with his suitcase into a bedroom where he shut the door.

He lifted the heavy case onto his bed and opened it. Inside were boxes of ammunition which he removed, placing them under his bed. The last item was a green wooden box which he opened to check the contents again. Inside were four POMZ-2M anti-personnel mines and trip wires. They would finish off the security for the Cambodian safe house. They had been difficult to purchase. He had to meet people he would rather not have met; there had been no option. The sellers wouldn't deal with anybody but him. Ammunition wasn't the problem: it was the mines. He understood. But all the same, his face had now been seen. He placed the box containing the mines under the bed, put the suitcase against the wall, lay down and fell asleep.

Phnom Penh, Cambodia

Tom and Sarah were at their hotel, both sipping Singapore slings through a straw, when Tom's phone rang.

"Tom speaking."

"Boss, it's Jane, how are you?"

"Good—Sarah and I were just talking about you, wondering how Blackwood and Laverton were going?"

"That's why I'm ringing. What time is it there?"

"Bit before seven."

"Not too late then. They're both going very well. Searches are done and interviews almost finished. Both offenders are cooperating. Dale will need further instructions from you tomorrow morning our time. He's already assumed both identities, just getting used to the site, grabbing as much intel as he can. We have one urgent matter though. One of the offenders, Harris, is part of a small group of four who were planning to travel to Thailand, to go hands on. They haven't done it yet, but they're close. Harris had bought his ticket, due to fly out next week. Don't have the full details yet."

"Is he the organiser?" Tom interjected.

"No, another member of the group is, and initial intelligence indicates he's the leader of this group who call themselves the 'Alphas'. Harris thinks that he may live in Thailand, and Anna thinks so too, as some of the chat logs have Thai communication data attached. This has got me wondering about two things, Boss."

"What's that?"

"One, is the Thai angle connected to Michael? And two, what are the possibilities of deploying an undercover officer into Thailand posing as Harris?"

Tom's mind began to race. It was exactly what he would want to do and did want to do. Reality though, was something else. Real world was, if he was just starting the idea now in the UK, he would be writing, arguing and pleading for months. All for it to go nowhere.

"Great idea, Jane. And the right one. But, we'd never get it off the ground inside a month let alone a few days. Does Maggie know yet?"

"No," Jane replied, wondering whether to tell Tom about her concerns surrounding Maggie.

"Alright. I have to ring her anyway, to update her about developments here, so I'll let her know."

"What developments?"

"There is an informant here who thinks he knows the location of a safe house children are being taken to once they've been kidnapped. The three major players behind it are Malaysian, Thai and European. They use a local gang to do the kidnapping and keep them at the safe house until they're trafficked."

"Where to?"

"China, Malaysia, further afield."

"Do you think this group, the 'Alphas', might have something to do with this? I mean it all fits, right?" Jane said, astonished.

Tom started to take in the question and analyse the possibilities. Jane, hearing the pause, couldn't wait for an answer.

"If that European is LB, and we know from the intelligence there is good reason to think he is, and the 'Alphas' are travelling to Thailand to go hands on, with one of them located in Thailand, what are the chances that the person in Thailand, is either LB or someone connected to him?"

Tom could hear the virtual cogs whirring in Jane's head through the telephone line. They meshed with his own, matched his pitch, delivering an explosion of ideas. He felt that familiar rush of excitement.

"The chances are high. We should arrange our response as if they are all connected. That way, if they aren't, we won't have lost anything. Get hold of Niall. Send the intelligence to him. The resolution on the communication data is absolute top priority. Tell him I want all stops pulled on this one, do whatever it takes to get it. I know it's the weekend, but we must make moves over it now, not leave it until Monday, otherwise it will be mid-week before anything gets moving on it. We know the RTP won't work the weekend and, even if they did, the companies we need to hand the intelligence over to, either aren't working or won't do it on a weekend."

"I'll speak to him. Are you sure we can't do anything around deploying an undercover there?"

There was no chance of it in the time frame, Tom thought. He looked over at Sarah, wondering how much of both sides of the conversation she could hear, or decipher, from just his side of the conversation. He didn't really know her. Whether it was the Yorkshire lass in her, her general demeanour or her capability, he couldn't put a finger on it; however, he had this unshakeable feeling she would have his back. That was good. He suspected he would need it in the coming days. He was already in the operational command chain, where he shouldn't be. That chain would increase very quickly in the next few days with serious repercussions for him.

In for a penny, in for a pound. Thailand was only a small plane ride away. If push came to shove, he was an undercover officer. He knew what to do. He could just do it on the side, under the guise of needing a break, get out of Cambodia—the nearest country being Thailand. One which Deena knew as well. Maybe he could come to a side agreement with her.

Tom shivered at his thoughts. They were career ending.

"No there isn't. We can deal with this through the data once it's resolved."

"It might not get resolved."

"But we don't know that yet. And we do have the advantage of posing as one of them online."

"What about disruption tactics, using Dale."

"That's a possibility, we could try to delay it. We could take out the two outside of Thailand. Have them arrested before they travel. It all depends what comes back. Where are you on that?"

"Anna is on to it."

"What grading is she using. Are we treating this as life or death?"

"No."

"Change that. A European boy has been snatched off the street along with young Cambodian street kids. I'm deployed here on the basis that 'Michael,' LB, might be behind that. You have the operation there, with intelligence saying they are preparing to fly to Thailand, to go hands on. We can say one of the 'Alphas' lives in Thailand. One of the members running the safe house in Cambodia is a Thai. Write it up Jane, you know how to phrase this."

"I do, you taught me well!"

"Doesn't matter what time it is, call me if you get any movement on the data comms."

"Will do."

Jane didn't know why she wanted to say what she was about to say, she just felt the need to say it, and wasn't prepared to put the phone down until she did.

"Tom, you must be careful."

The sudden change in tone caught him off guard. Tom was the other side of the world, but, in that split second, he might as well have been back in his office with Jane beside him. He knew she meant it; she was also right.

"I'll do my best."

"How much of that did you get?" Tom asked Sarah, wondering how the next few minutes would go and still taking in the enormity of his conversation with Jane.

"Most of it, but not all."

He was about to speak, when the door to the bar opened and a group of customers walked in.

"Maybe we should go outside," he replied.

Having found a table overlooking the Mekong River, the pair sat in silence for a while, taking in the sight of the flowing river which could be seen shimmering in the moonlight which had already appeared.

"Save me repeating, what bits do you think you missed?"

"I'm not sure. You'd better repeat it."

"I have to update Maggie. Will that cover it?"

"Yep, try that."

As Tom waited for Maggie to answer, he tried to assemble what he wanted to say in his head.

"Hi, Tom, I was wondering when I might hear from you. Anything to report?"

"Yes. Cambodia first. The informant thinks he knows the location of the safe house."

"Where is it?"

"He's being collected and brought to Phnom Penh, we'll know tomorrow when we debrief him," Tom replied, thinking Maggie had interrupted him unduly abruptly.

"Why didn't you get the location off him when you spoke to him?"

Tom paused. There was a definite note of demand in Maggie's tone, one he hadn't ever received from her before.

"He wants payment on delivery. Deena also thinks it's too risky to go to him."

"What time is the debrief?"

"Midday, early afternoon. There isn't a time set yet. When Chenda, the embassy driver, gets back with him, then it will go ahead."

Tom heard a definite pause. Maggie was thinking. Why?

"So, what's the second side, if Cambodia was the first?"

"Laverton and Blackwood. Jane's updated me and there's a connection here, I told her I would update you."

"Go on, then."

"Both warrants are positive, and both offenders are cooperating. Dale has already assumed their identities. One is a member of an internal group calling themselves the 'Alphas'. They are all planning to travel to Thailand to offend in the real world. One of the them appears – but we haven't yet confirmed – to live in Thailand. The 'Alpha' offender has his flight booked. Dale has secured some data that Anna will be submitting under a life or death grading. Some of the data looks like Thailand, but until we start the process, we won't know how far it leads us. They could be behind a proxy."

"How is that connected to Cambodia?"

Tom was surprised by Maggie's reply. She already had the intelligence. She was busy, had many other duties and meetings. His would just be another case she had to deal with. So, he ignored it.

"One of the three men behind the safe house is a Thai. One of the others is a European we think is LB; the 'Alphas' are due to travel in a few days; our offender is into young boys; we have a boy missing here. I mean, if it looks like a bomb, ticks like one . . ."

"Don't get flippant, Tom. The other side to that is Thailand a sex destination?"

Maggie's comeback was a fair one, but it was delivered like a machine gun. Tom decided to hand over the reins.

"Would you consider an application to deploy an undercover here?"

"No, I wouldn't."

"In that case, I will call you once we've debriefed the informant."

"We haven't finished yet. What's the plan, once you know the location of the safe house?"

"That hasn't been finalised, because we don't know what we'll be told. But it will be handed over to Major Pich. He will go there, search the place, bottom it all out."

"Are you happy that Jane's got it all covered at this end?"

"Yes, I am," Tom replied, thinking that Maggie's tone had suddenly changed to its normal self.

"Good. Get those applications in. I'm duty AO. Call me as soon as you've had the debrief."

"Of course."

Tom placed the phone on the table in front of them. Staring at it, trying to assimilate the undertone of the conversation with Maggie.

"Everything alright?" Sarah asked.

"I guess so. Maggie seemed off. Can't put a finger on it. Doesn't matter. Was that enough? Did you get the gist of it all?"

"Yes. What about the UC?"

"Nope. It's a great idea. I'm sure the Americans would authorise one in a blink of an eye. But we're so stuck up our risk assessment arse, the application wouldn't even pass Maggie."

Sarah sipped the last of her Singapore sling. They really were good.

Pondering Tom, as he contemplated the Mekong River, she again recalled her briefing on him. He was an undercover officer. She had worked with police officers most of her career, in her role as corporate communications officer. She knew cops, understood their humour, what made them tick. Had seen their good and bad sides. Their mistakes, triumphs and tragedies. They were on the cusp of locating a safe house, in the middle of rural Cambodia, where children were being held captive. One of the traffickers was said to be a Thai national. Narith probably wouldn't do a thing unless Tom went with him. Tom's instructions were, he couldn't. Now there was information a UK citizen was going to fly to Thailand, to meet up with someone living there who had access to children.

The UK media were still struggling to get their heads around this line of work. She was knocking back requests for an interview, inside story, fly-on-the-wall documentaries almost daily. She could see a result coming out of this, with live pressers both here and the UK. Those expectations did not concern her. That was a challenge, one she was up to. What did concern her was that there was no way on hell's earth this was going to be achieved under the current operational mandate.

Tom, she had no doubt, would go rogue. Leaving her, right in the middle of it.

CHAPTER ELEVEN

Ban Mai Nong Sai, Thailand

Chet woke to the loud sound of a television. He rolled out of bed and stretched, rubbing his face hard to clear his eyes. There were going to be some busy and risky days ahead. The profit at the end would be enormous. The risk involved in getting to that payment would be great. If he got caught in Thailand or Cambodia, it would mean a lengthy jail term. If he got caught in Malaysia, it could mean the death penalty. If there was a plus side, it was that money talked, and it didn't matter who you were or what job you did in the Justice ministry: corruption was a way of life. In his country, he knew that virtually all the police were on the take. The higher you were, the more you got. As for the courts, there were some judges that could not be bought. They were well known and mostly in Bangkok. Further south or in the far north, it was a different story; it all depended on the case, how much money you had and what your connections were.

His personal risk, though, would be mainly limited to Cambodia. He had worked hard to ensure that when he was at the safe house, he would be well protected. Law enforcement there was virtually non-existent, any police that were around were unarmed. It was a communist run state, secretly managed, poorly funded, and unable to act with fluidity. All he needed was good protection and loyal men. He had both.

When he was in Thailand, he had others to take the risks. People who would never hand over his identity. If he had a problem, he paid for it to go away: sometimes handsomely. There was, however, one risk that neither he nor Umar had been able to fully manage or mitigate.

"Are you deaf, brother?"

"Chet! You should have joined me, you missed out."

"I don't think so. She looked riddled."

"She was drugged up for sure. I saw her papers. She was clean!"

"How old?"

"Never asked."

"Papers, Umar. How old were they?"

"Last week. I took precautions."

Chet grabbed the TV remote, muting it.

"We need to talk about the Khn b̂ā."

"I agree, Chet. My view is we should just kill him, but after this trade."

"That would cut our profits by over half. Is that what you really want?"

"Of course not, but he's crazy. How about we replace him?"

"Who with?"

"I've been thinking about that. He has that contact here in Thailand—him."

"But that's his side, we have no idea about that. Who's involved? Who they are?"

"I know. Which is why we need a plan to find out who they are, brother. This boy is really hot at the moment. I think we should say we aren't going to process the boy unless we know more about the security around him once the boy leaves our control. He will object. We then say it's for the good of ongoing operations. He will likely tell us that he has it covered. We give him an ultimatum: that one of us confirms ongoing security, to protect our own operation, or the boy doesn't get processed."

"You mean, kill the boy?"

"Yes, and him!"

Chet sat next to Umar. It was good plan, unless the 'Khn b̂ā' stuck to his position. Without him, the operation would not be anywhere near as profitable. But he agreed with Chet: there was too much risk, and it needed to be dealt with. The operation had to be secure to be profitable.

"I agree. Once we have access to his contacts though, we kill him. If the contacts aren't good enough, we kill him and the boy straight away. Then we decide if it's worth carrying on with the risk or not."

"Agreed, brother. Now turn the sound back up!"

Chenda glanced at her watch to double-check the time. The car clock was always set five minutes ahead of her own; she was on course to get back to the hotel for lunchtime. She was hungry and could almost taste the club sandwich. Having had one, she really wanted a second. The French fries at the hotel were also mouth-wateringly good. She checked her near and offside mirrors and then her rear-view mirror for following traffic. With nothing near, she glanced over her shoulder to check on Sopheap. He was still asleep, curled up like a small child across two seats. She had made him go there. His incessant bragging and talking about what he had seen but wouldn't tell her, had worn her down. After 15 minutes she banished him to the rear of the car, just to put some space between them. Initially that didn't stop him, and it took another 15 minutes of ignoring his whining before he eventually curled up and fell asleep. What annoyed her most was that he would be paid handsomely for what he knew, when she believed it was his moral duty to hand it over for free. As she pulled into the Sunflower car park and switched the engine off, she noticed Sopheap had not stirred. She got out, closing her door gently, walked around to the door nearest Sopheap's head, opened the door, then quickly slammed it shut, before opening it again.

"Why did you do that?" he screamed, jumping with fright.

Chenda looked at Sopheap's face. His eyes were encrusted, squinting in the sunlight that now poured into the rear of the car.

"We are here. Get yourself together, act like a man—if you can. You better not be wasting their time, Sopheap. Because, if you are, I won't be driving you back. You can walk!"

Sopheap gave Chenda his biggest grin. His mother had once told him that if a girl was mean to him, it probably meant she liked him, and Chenda was being very mean.

"Make way for a very important person, driver!" Sopheap replied, jumping out, closing the door himself. "I have very important information; you would do well to treat me differently. I would be a good catch for someone like you."

Chenda kept a blank face, opened the driver's door, retrieved her lacy white hat, slowly placing it upon her head. She then used the side mirror to check its position. She took her sunglasses from the sun visor, placing them on, before closing the door and locking the car using the vehicle's remote. She stood back in front of Sopheap, with the same blank expression on her face, the fire in her eyes hidden behind the black glass. She suddenly, without any warning, slapped Sopheap around the back of his head and immediately walked off.

"Follow me, fool!"

Sopheap, stunned by the response, felt the back of his head, which stung from the strike. It must surely be confirmation of his mother's words. When Chenda heard what he had to say, she would throw herself at his feet for sure. He quickly chased after her, still rubbing his head.

As Tom's hotel room door opened, Chenda pushed Sopheap through the doorway with enough force that he stumbled slightly.

"Straight through," Sarah said, smiling at Sopheap, who was looking stunned.

Sarah sensed the tension. "How was the trip?"

Chenda stepped in and closed the door behind her, before removing her sunglasses.

"That was painful, Sarah, really painful. He's bragged so much, that I had to put him in the back. Have you had lunch yet?"

"No, we agreed to wait until you got here. Have you eaten?"

"We haven't, thank you for asking. Give him only rice and water!"

Sarah struggled not to laugh.

With all but Chenda seated – she stood furthest away from Sopheap, but in a position she could maintain unobstructed eye contact with him – Deena began.

"Chenda, thank you for undertaking all the driving to get Sopheap here today."

Chenda just nodded. It was her job. Sopheap sat upright. The sound of his own name being mentioned caused him to smile, and he glanced at Chenda.

"Right then, Sopheap, what is it that you know?"

"I know very much," Sopheap began, turning to face Deena, "I know very important things. Things that are very valuable to you, Bong Srei. These things are so important, that when I tell you, you will feel that it is your honour to pay me very handsomely. I want you to know that I did very heroic things to get this information. I put my life in danger. Very great danger. I also put the lives of my family in danger to get this information. All I ask is that you consider that danger and reward me and my family. You can just pay me, and I will ensure that they get their share."

Chenda coughed loudly in disgust.

"Did you just say, 'Arsenal'?" Sarah asked, in huge surprise.

"Who, me!" Chenda replied, beaming at her, then winking.

The exchange between Chenda and Sarah wasn't lost on Tom, or Deena, but not for the same reasons.

"We have been here before, Sopheap. You really don't want to test me. You will come off the worse," Deena replied, in a very stern voice, "I will pay you what the information is worth. I cannot do that until I hear the information. If you don't like it, then you can get out and make your own way back!" Deena stared defiantly at Sopheap, who immediately recoiled back into his seat in alarm.

"Yes, Bong Srei. Yes, of course. Please do not take offence. I will tell you immediately," he replied, suddenly feeling uncomfortable. He paused, looking around at his audience. They were all staring at him. This was his moment. He regained his composure, straightened his back and lifted his chin slightly.

"As you know, I told my sister to listen carefully for anything, no matter how small. Well, she did this and when I last visited her, she told me that she overheard Keo and Utey talking . . ."

"Are those first names?" Tom asked, interrupting Sopheap.

"Yes, Bong. Nuon does not know any last names. These two, though, come from Phnom Penh. She overheard them talking about the safe house, that they were glad the moat had filled with water again, which is when she remembered that Chakra had a property that he bought from his cousin and rented out. This property had a moat around it, which filled with water at certain times."

"Why certain times?" Deena asked.

"I'm not sure, Bong Srei."

"There will be rice fields somewhere nearby. When they are flooded, the moat will fill up. Once the rice has been harvested, they will drain the fields, and the moat will lose its water," Chenda said, glaring at Sopheap.

"Yes, this is most likely. Anyway, I was talking," Sopheap said, facing Deena again, glad to get away from Chenda's glare. "She also overheard them talking about someone who they had kicked out of the property. They had paid him off. But Keo and Utey thought that he should be got rid of permanently. This gave her the idea that the safe house might be this property."

"Does she know the location of this property?" Deena asked.

"She does, and I do too. We were eating fresh season rice when Chakra and his gang left. All of them, in his old Hilux. I checked to make sure they had all gone, and they had. This put me in great peril. My sister then gave me instructions on where the house was. I drove out there to see if I could spot Chakra's car. When I got there, the house was set back from the road, behind tree growth, so I was unable to see anything.

"I hid my moto, then secretly made my way through the jungle to get to the thick tree line. This was at huge risk to me, because, if I was spotted, they would have seen I was in the middle of nowhere with a safety helmet and no bike."

"Why did you have a helmet on?" Sarah asked.

"So they couldn't see who I was," Sopheap replied, with surprise on his face.

"Go on."

"Yes, Bong Srei. I had to take great risk. I made my way up to where the jungle became very dense. Once there, I had to make my way along it, until it was light enough for me to push through. I damaged my shoe." Sopheap pulled up his leg and revealed a shoe with torn leather. "I then pushed through until I could see. What I saw made me stop breathing, Bong Srei. It was all I could do not to run away. It was my bravery that kept me there and brought me to you here, today."

"OK, almost there, Sopheap. And what did you see?" Deena asked, calmly.

"I saw a big house on the other side of a small bridge. The big house was on the right. The bridge went over a moat that was full of water. On the other side, there were other buildings, storage-type buildings on the left. I saw Chakra's Hilux, Chakra and most of his men. Many of them had rifles. Three of them were on the back of another truck— it might have been an old Toyota with a flat wooden tray. Anyway, they were all fixing a very large gun onto the back of it.

"I was watching them do this when I saw a Barang come into view. He was holding the hand of a small white boy. The small boy had ankle chains on. He walked the boy around the yard a few times, then he disappeared back into the house."

The room fell silent, all eyes on Sopheap.

"Would you recognise the boy if you saw a picture of him?" Tom asked cautiously, the first one to respond to the news.

"Yes, I think so."

Deena delved into her cavernous handbag and produced a paper flyer with the image of the child who had gone missing from the Riverside area. She handed it to Sopheap, who stared at it for a long time before answering.

"I would say this is the child that I saw at the house, with the moat around it."

"Are you telling the truth, Sopheap?" Chenda said in a harsh voice.

"I am sure, Chenda. Yes, this is the boy."

"What did the Barang look like?" Tom asked excitedly.

"Hard to say. You Barangs all look the same to us."

"Try," Deena said.

"He had jeans and a grey T-shirt on, with some sort of sign on the back. He had dark, collar length hair. He was of average build, no belly. He was brown from the sun."

"Age?"

"About 30 to 40 years, Bong Srei."

"Could you hear any talking?"

"I did hear some shouting, Bong, before I saw them all. But I couldn't hear what was being said. I think it was Khmer though. They were too far away to hear what they were saying."

"How many weapons?" Deena asked, the concern in her voice obvious to everyone.

"I think they all had one."

"Do you know what sort?"

"No."

"What else did you see?" Tom asked.

"Nothing. I was so scared, I left immediately."

"Who else have you spoken to?"

"Nobody, Bong."

"What about, Nuon?"

"Yes, I told her."

Chenda let out an exasperated huff and spoke a flurry of Khmer words to Sopheap which made him recoil in his seat. He slowly turned back to face Tom.

"Only Nuon. Nobody else. I had to tell her something. I had to tell somebody what I saw. I was frightened."

"What did you tell her?"

"Exactly what I told you."

"Are you sure it is exactly the same?" Chenda asked, this time in English, suspicion clearly showing on her face.

Sopheap looked down at his feet before answering. "I may have painted my bravery differently."

Deena had heard enough. She gave Chenda a look, which she clearly understood, as she nodded back.

"What's the address?"

"I have written it down here," Sopheap replied, handing over a piece of paper to Deena.

"Tom?"

"I'd like some time with him, to get a sketch plan of the buildings and the land around it. Maybe show him some images off the internet of known rifles, to see if we can build up some intelligence around that."

"Now?"

"Before he goes back, but we need our own meeting first."

Deena removed an envelope from her handbag and handed it over to Sopheap. She then opened her purse and removed more US dollar bills, which she also handed over.

"That's for what you and your sister have done. I will give you both more and hold up my end of the bargain with regards to Nuon once this is over. Chenda will take you back this afternoon. Well done, Sopheap. I am very pleased."

"Thank you, Bong Srei. I am at your service."

"Chenda will take you down to the lobby. Take a stroll to the Riverside, have some lunch and be back downstairs in an hour. You will then speak to Tom before Chenda takes you back."

"Yes, Bong Srei."

When Chenda returned, Deena looked at her watch.

"Club sandwiches all round?"

"Absolutely," said Sarah, ringing room service.

"Right, Tom. Over to you. How're we going to play this operationally?"

Tom found himself looking at Sarah first, before he turned to Deena.

"What sort of capabilities do the police have to take a well-armed stronghold?"

"None."

"What do they do, when something like this occurs?"

"It never has."

"What about terrorism or some sort of plot to overthrow the country: who would they use?"

"The Army. Trusted soldiers from Hun Sen's army barracks. The soldiers that protect him."

"Can we use them?"

"No."

"That limits our options then!"

"Yep, this is Cambodia."

"Taking a step back, I think we need to resolve how we're going to pass this intelligence on?"

"I'm all ears!"

"The way I see it, we have two options. One, hand over the informant and all his information directly to Major Pich, stand back, hoping it turns out well, or . . ."

"Or?" replied, Deena, arching her eyebrows.

Tom felt Sarah sit back down. There was nowhere to hide now. His orders were to stick to option one. Sarah would become exhibit 'A' against him, whether she liked it or not.

"Or . . . we put the intelligence down to some action back home and hand it across."

There was silence in the room.

Chenda, who could see Sarah's face, stared at her.

"It wouldn't be, 'we', Tom. It would be you," Deena said.

Silence pervaded the room, while Tom decided what to say next.

"Yes, me. I have some intelligence forms here on my laptop. I could write it up as coming from an intelligence source. For example, I could call the source a number, then classify the intelligence according to our grading system, which would be high, and hand it over to them."

"They will want to know more than what they read in a sanitised intelligence document. I see those from time to time. They get so sanitised that you end up ringing the originator to ask what it really means!"

Deena stared at Tom, letting her comment sink in.

"They will question you on the content, Tom. They will become suspicious, unless they can see, and, more importantly, understand how you have come by this intelligence."

"I can say it came from online chat between two offenders, one of whom is in Thailand and the other in the UK. That offender having been arrested and replaced by an undercover officer. That much is true. I can tack on the address, the gang numbers, firearms, the children. The European child alone should make them just act. That would keep the informant out of it."

Deena was about to reply when there a was a knock at the door, heralding the arrival of lunch.

Chenda wasted no time, rolled up her sleeves and took a huge bite of the triple- decker toasted sandwich. By the time the others had arranged themselves for eating, Chenda had already finished her first mouthful.

"Hand him over, Deena. He's not worth trying to protect."

"It's not that, Chenda. Although, if I treated informants poorly, word would get around and my sources would dry up. Once we hand it all over, we can't control it. The way it works here, as you know, calls would be made to local police up there, and they would tip off the gang. By the time police eventually went in, the whole place would be empty and scrubbed clean with disinfectant, the children will be lost forever."

"Yes, I understand this. This is true, Tom and Sarah. What Deena says is correct," Chenda said, biting into another large chunk.

"How about we try to control what they do through the intelligence, as well as the unofficial interpretation of it?" Tom said, before taking his first bite. An idea was starting to form in his mind.

"Go on?"

"The intelligence sheet will give the location, numbers and firearms, children there now. Local police bribed, so they cannot be trusted, indicating that the strike needs to be done from here. If they take the Army, then fine. As long as they don't tell the local police then it should be good. If I'm questioned on how we know all this, I'll stick to online chat."

Deena had cut her sandwich into triangles. She had eaten enough layered sandwiches to know it was the easiest way to consume them, whilst maintaining a degree of dignity.

"It will have to be the performance of a lifetime, Tom."

"How do you mean?"

"They already don't understand your work. You might half convince the Major. He seems open and has lived outside Cambodia. Above him, though, will be older, much older, cronies, who can be tracked straight back to the slaughter. They never went away, Tom. They're still here. They are all around us. Many of them are in uniform, some will have hotlines straight into Hun Sen's intelligence-gathering group."

Tom, suddenly, wasn't feeling very hungry.

"Pich has been given the green light. Let's give him the intelligence. None of it is untrue. It's just the source I'm bending the rules on. I can live with that. The question is, can both of you?"

Tom didn't know what to expect. The fact was they had to do something, and Deena wasn't prepared to hand over the informant lock, stock, and barrel.

"I was always prepared for it, just needed you to get to this point!" Deena replied, flatly.

"Sarah?"

"My job is Comms. You have your brief, I have mine."

Tom wanted to ask more, but doing so in front of Deena wasn't the time.

"In that case, I'll write it up after lunch."

Oxford, England

The Chief rarely worked weekends. He had others able to do that. He made it a rule not to contact his ACPO team, and they not to contact him, unless it was absolutely necessary. That didn't mean to say he never undertook any work. The fact was he spent nearly every weekend, at least four hours a day, reading up on Home Office circulars, professional reports, and confidential briefings from other Police Chiefs around the world. Today was going to be an exception, as he listened to the ring tone in his ear.

"Sir," JT said, with surprise in his voice.

The Chief found himself trying to gauge whether the surprise was real, faked or generated through fear.

"Yes, it is. I'm surprised by it as well. But – as you know – GOPOL is a personal project, and this really can't wait until Monday. There has been an intelligence update that I want to make a decision on today. What I want to know is, if I asked for a small dedicated team, say a sergeant and three, hush-hush type of set up, have you got them? And can they be totally trusted?"

There was a long pause before JT spoke. Too long for the Chief.

"I can get them off division, no problem there. How long do you need them for?"

That was, and wasn't, the answer the Chief was looking for.

"Two weeks, tops."

"When do you need them by?"

"If I want them, it will be on 24 hours notice or less. You need to identify who, but I don't want them knowing until they are required. They must also work out of COCET."

"I can have that arranged within the next few hours. Can I ask what they will be doing? Just so I can ensure you get the right skill set."

"Probably 50% detective work, 50% intelligence."

"Will you need an analyst, or a communication data single-point-of-contact-type person?" JT asked, in a tone that the Chief felt was too enquiring: one designed to quickly paint a picture of what he was trying to do, even though he had no intention of doing it.

"Yes, that would be very helpful. I have to rush. Fenella wants me to empty some flowerpots for her. They are too heavy for her to turn over alone. Can you text me as soon as you have the staff identified?"

"Of course, Sir."

CHAPTER TWELVE

Without strong watchdog institutions, impunity becomes the very foundation upon which systems of corruption are built.

—Rigoberta Menchú Tum, Nobel Prize Laureate

Phnom Penh, Cambodia

Tom read the content of the intelligence document he had created for Major Pich. It was the fifth time he had read it, making small changes each time. The changes weren't the issue. The intelligence read well and true—mostly. What was now causing his unease was the act of handing over the address at all. With it, Major Pich had to do something. That something could set off a chain reaction that Deena would not be able to stop. If they held off providing the address for a day, they would be able to assess the Major's thought processes and intentions. What Tom was about to do wasn't sitting well with his moral compass either. He was considering bending his own rule, a rule that put the child first and justice second. The missing boy was there or was, when Sopheap last saw him. He could already be gone. There could be other children there in his place, or none. Policy and best practice were there for a reason. That policy was: child first. An end, justifying the means, had one foot firmly in the corruption camp, and he knew it.

But he was in Cambodia, not in England, and English best practice, policy and procedures could not just be overlaid here, even if they were later used against him back at home. He reconciled his unease by producing two documents, one with the location of the safe house in it and one without, deciding to reflect on it for a few hours before discussing it with Deena. In the meantime, he had to update Maggie and quickly found himself wondering how much to tell her. As he listened to the familiar call tone, he decided that a problem shared was a problem halved.

"Morning, Tom. How'd the meeting go?"

"Explosive!"

"Really, tell me more . . . wait a sec," Maggie replied, disappearing from the screen, reappearing a moment later with a large mug in her hand.

"Coffee. I have a new machine, still getting used to it, but it's awesome! OK, I have a pad and pen. Explosive you say. Fire away then: no pun intended!"

"Good mood this morning?"

"I am indeed. Do I need to be?"

"In short, yes. The informant has located the safe house. He has identified the missing European boy, the one that was snatched in Phnom Penh, as being there. He saw him in the company of another white male. We don't know who that is, but we suspect it to be Michael. The property had most, if not all, of the gang members present, and all or most of them were armed. He saw a large gun being mounted on the back of a small truck. The boy disappeared back inside the house. The informant got away, and we spoke to him today."

"Wow. How does he know it was the boy?"

"We showed him one of the flyers that have been posted around. He said it was him."

"What have the authorities done about it?"

"Nothing, as I, or we, haven't told them yet."

"Why on earth not?"

"Because this isn't the UK. It's the weekend, and even if they knew right now, they still wouldn't do anything straight away. They simply don't have that capability. The information would go into the regime structure, bounce around, with the locals in the area being tipped off. We know they are in on it, so by the time they got there, the place would be empty. We might as well consign the boy to his fate."

"You have to tell them, Tom!"

"I know, which is why I have spent the time immediately following the meeting writing the intelligence log. Then I called you."

"OK, so when are you handing it over?"

"Once I have spoken to Deena."

"Why? You're the law enforcement officer."

"But, it's her informant. That's where the problem lies. If she hands over the informant, his life and his sister's life could all be at risk. That isn't an exaggeration, Maggie. The intelligence has to be sanitised to protect them. It also needs to go through her; she has to be satisfied it won't come back on them."

"Sanitise it as you need, but it must go across today!"

"She will get it today, but, in all likelihood, she won't disseminate it until tomorrow. As for sanitising, the intelligence will look as if it has come from unnamed COCET sources."

Tom looked at the screen, searching for the first sign of an eruption. Maggie, though, just took a long drink of her coffee before answering.

"You'd better email me that log. Don't move. I'll call you back once I have read it," Maggie replied, disconnecting the call.

Tom emailed one log, the one that contained the location of the safe house, then made himself a cup of tea and waited.

Minutes later, Maggie called him back. "You've taken sanitisation to a whole new level. There is nothing in here to suggest the intelligence has come from COCET. In fact, there is nothing in here to suggest where it comes from. So, what are you going to tell them when they ask you?"

"They already think we will be working on intelligence that I provide. They know what we do for a living, how we operate. I won't stop them thinking that."

Tom watched the screen. Maggie had been writing down what he had been saying and didn't look back up until she had finished.

"You are sailing very close to the wind. Too close. Were you a politician in another life? They can make lies seem like the truth. You are doing just that!"

"The log will go into their intelligence apparatus. It has to say something, yet at the same time nothing. They do get the location."

"They get a description of the location, and, from what I can see, not a very good one. You will be under the spotlight once they get it. They will be straight back at you!"

"I know."

"I'll have to speak to the Chief on this. When are you seeing Deena?"

"Not until you get back to me?"

"Correct answer. Don't leave the room. As Arnie said, 'I'll be back.'"

Tom pondered his actions. He hadn't told the full story to Maggie, and it nagged him. What he was doing in Cambodia, albeit with the right intentions, had led him to being economic with the truth back home to a senior officer. Within a few short hours he had gone from having one foot inside the corruption camp, to now standing right in it. He was also making plans to go even deeper. The thoughts made him restless, which just aggravated him more, because he had to sit and wait for the return call. It was a long ten minutes until Maggie called back.

"Right, this isn't up for discussion. Don't hand the intelligence over until Monday, at the earliest. The Chief wants to have a meeting with the lawyer you met that day in his office. Do you remember him?"

"Yes."

"Good. We are basically a working day behind you. The child protection side of things from a UK standpoint is covered, in that we don't have eyes on the premises, so it could be empty now or later. The Chief must have his meeting with the lawyer before you take action there. Understood?"

"Yes."

"In the meantime, you'd better get some rest, because it will all come to a head next week."

Relieved, he made himself a second cup of tea, having not finished the first one. He checked his watch, which had two clocks on one face one set on UK time, and rang Jane.

"Morning, or should I say afternoon, Boss?"

"Good morning to you as well. Any update?"

"Yes, quite a bit. Ops first though. Both suspects remain in custody for court on Monday morning. In the end, there were no problems with the local custody sergeants, and the remand files are very strong."

"Excellent!"

"Nick is working out of here and with Dale, who now has his UCs back with him. Best you get an update from him. They need more instructions."

"OK. Are they all there now?"

"Yes."

"I'll do that straight after this chat then."

"Niall has managed to pull off a near miracle."

"How so?"

"He got straight onto the same contacts he made when he was working on Operation Resolve. Appears they have since made their own contacts within the providers there, who put something formal in place with the Royal Thai Police, should they ever need urgent intelligence."

"And . . ." Tom excitedly interrupted.

"The 'Alpha', calling himself 'pureisbest', has been traced to a warehouse address near the Cambodian border. I'll forward the email from Niall. He wants to know what the plan is."

"Tell him, the plan is to get on a plane asap and hook up with the team he met before. I want him on a plane no later than Sunday."

"Will do. That's about it. Dale can fill you in from the covert side, which is all shaping up nicely. By the way, the duty Commander at Taunton sends his regards."

"Who's that?"

"Chief Inspector Maggs?"

"Maggsy! Great guy. Will you be speaking to him again?"

"Possibly. Why?"

"Just pass on my regards to him as well. And 'well done' for his promotion. Is that it?"

"You going to call Dale now?"

"Yes."

"That's it then."

Tom dialled Dale, thinking about Tony Maggs, the West Country cop he had met in Taunton. It seemed like it was ages ago, but it wasn't.

"Boss!"

"Hi Dale, how's it going?"

"Going really well. We all need fresh instructions. Particularly around the 'Alphas'."

"Are you all there?"

"Yes."

"Update me first. Then get one of the team to open a Skype connection to me."

"Will do. Starting with Blackwood, as it's the easy one. The offender in custody, Small, is a lazy admin. He is a senior one, though. He isn't an active enforcer, and to be honest his online activity will be easy to replicate, especially as he has helped so much in interview. Nick has corroborated that for us as well. I will be working with Anna on it. We are now in a position to fully infiltrate his P2P group, and so our instructions will need to reflect that."

"Great news. Next."

"Laverton is a bit more challenging. I will be working on this one with Owen. The offender, Harris, is far more active as an admin and is also a member of the 'Alphas'. Owen did a great job gathering online behavioural characteristics, while Harris was in custody, which Nick has been able to confirm from the work he is doing, so we are ready to go on him."

"I would like a two-pronged strategy with Laverton, Dale."

"That's what I was hoping you would say!"

"Good. Starting with the 'Alphas': the objective is to make it look as if you are travelling. Whatever arrangements you make should be good for all of them. What is known on the others?"

"I haven't got into them yet; they are behind proxies. I have a plan to get them out from behind it though. Ultimately, they may not be identifiable until they are on the ground in Thailand."

"We can't say for certain that the user who's been traced to Thailand has anything to do with Michael or what I am doing here, but we are working on the assumption that it's connected."

"It would be good to get a UC out there, so we can go from keyboard to pavement. I'm authorised."

"I'd love it. I've raised it, but it's a non-starter."

"Pity."

"You happy with that side then?"

"Yes, Boss."

"The other prong is to infiltrate and capture evidence that accurately shows the level of criminality of the users in the group. Seek to identify any user who either has, or purports to have access to children as a priority. Taking action with Jane to safeguard those children."

"Understood. The team is ready when you are for the agent provocateur and case law warnings."

Oxford, England

The Chief took a gardening glove off to answer his phone.

"Morning, James. I got your cryptic text message. All systems go at my end. Is there a change of plan?"

"No, that side is all done with no change there. But there is a change elsewhere. Are we safe to talk on these?"

"Can't reveal trade secrets, James, best stick to that code."

The Chief let out a sigh, 'Freaking spooks. Never again', he said to himself, wondering how many more times he would say that.

"Number six, has found number two, if memory serves me."

"Can this wait until Monday, James?"

"Yes, first thing though."

"In that case, Monday. I have the ability to let our associates know, but that should wait until then."

"Are we finished?" the Chief asked, not bothering to hide his annoyance.

"Pip, pip, James."

As the line went dead, it was as much as the Chief could do not to throw the phone into his fishpond.

Phnom Penh, Cambodia

In Cambodia, Tom rang Deena.

"I have those intelligence log sheets for you. I've done two versions. How can I get them to you?"

"Can you put them on a stick?"

"Yes."

"Good. I will get someone to pick it up. Chenda has already left, so I will have to make some calls to find a driver that I can borrow to collect it. Give me a few minutes, and I'll get back to you."

"Before you go, Deena. You'd better know my Chief wants the handover delayed until Monday at the earliest."

"Really? Why so specific?"

"Apparently, he needs to speak to the government lawyer before we do it."

"What, the same one I spoke to over the phone at the beginning of all this?"

"Yes, him."

"I'll get back to you shortly," replied Deena, who closed that call and scrolled through her directory before ringing another number.

"Hi, Gerry, it's Deena. Chenda is on another job and I urgently need a small package collected from the Sunflower and brought to me. Could your driver do it? Would you mind?"

"Thanks, Gerry. I owe you one."

Deena immediately re-called Tom.

"There will be a driver downstairs in the lobby in 15 minutes. You'll recognise the car when it pulls up.

"Thanks, Deena. One more thing: the Thai connection that Sarah told you about on Operation Laverton—you had an email on it, about one of the 'Alphas?'"

"Yes."

"Not sure how, but Interpol have traced the IP to a warehouse near the Cambodian border."

"Where, what's the address?"

"It's on its way."

"OK, ring me as soon as you get it, but I'll call you once I've read the intelligence logs."

It was too early to ring Canada. In any case, the out of hours service would not be able to deal with what she wanted. She could, though, ring the duty officer at the Security Service. As she waited for the call to be picked up, she wondered if she was being too sensitive.

"Code word, please."

Deena duly provided it.

"Go ahead, Ambassador, how are you this afternoon?"

"I am fine, thank you for asking."

"What can we do for you?"

"Can you find out, or do you have an inventory of people who are currently working with the British Security Service?"

"Do you have a name?"

"First one only."

"What's that?"

"Toby?"

"Bear with me," the duty officer replied, before the phone went dead.

A few minutes later, he was back on the line.

"We don't have a full register, there's so many on short-term contracts it's hard to keep up with the turnover. However, we have three Tobys. Toby Bryant, Toby Jenkins and Toby Spencer-Drummond. We don't have much contact with the SIS, so if he is one of theirs, we wouldn't know."

"I'm just texting someone, as we speak, to see if I can confirm the last name. If the Brits were up to something over here, would we be sighted as a Five Eyes partner?"

"Maybe, but my guess would be no. If they are operating away from home, then it can only be through their SIS. As you know, we can only operate internally, so they wouldn't see the need."

"What about if they knew I was in the mix somewhere?"

"Probably still no, not unless they thought it was absolutely necessary."

"Could I make a request?"

"You could, but that would just show your hand, and there would be no guarantee they would confirm it anyway. We would have to ask the Security Service, and they can't operate there either, so they must be doing it through their SIS, who can. They, by the way, would probably rely heavily on the CIA. As you well know, the US have a big station there."

"OK, I just got confirmation. It is Spencer-Drummond."

"In that case, I think you have your answer, they are up to something. I would suggest you give it some thought. If you want to pop the question, we can do it for you, but once it is out, and they don't include you, then you will be seen as a possible liability."

"I'll sleep on it. Thanks for your help."

When the driver arrived with the data stick, Deena was preparing a short speech for a dinner she was attending that night. She plugged it in, found the folder and opened version one, reading it quickly. She then opened version two, scanning through it carefully, locating the difference. She rang Tom.

"Got them. Perfect. Yes, I agree. Hold off the address. If your Chief has the need to speak to the lawyer, then there will be a very good reason for it. Even if the request to hold off wasn't there, I think it's a good idea anyway. It gives us the opportunity to see what the Major does first. Can you Brits live with the child protection issues you have?"

"Apparently."

"In that case, have a good rest of the weekend."

Tom was about to ask Deena why she needed the lawyer's last name, when, for some reason he just let it go. As Deena ended the call, she wondered why Tom hadn't raised the text message.

Tom checked his email and saw one from Anna Farley. He opened it, read the contents, and immediately rang Deena.

"Hi Tom, having a problem with the weekend?"

"Not at all. I have an update on the IP: it's a warehouse at Ban Mai Nong Sai. Do you know it?"

"Yes, it's just the other side of the border at Poipet. That's significant, because we know Chakra is using the Poipet border crossing. It must be connected. Send me the address, and I will get some work done on it before Monday."

"Will do."

Oxford, England

The Chief was just about to take a bite, of his now very late lunch, when his phone rang. Seeing it was a Professional Standards number, his mood lightened.

"Stuart?"

"Yes, afternoon, Sir."

"Good news, I need good news!"

"You'd better be the judge of that one, Sir. Log off times and exit swipe times: we don't have any pattern there at all; for both calls he was still at work. His only pattern is, he always works late."

"Hmm, getting my money's worth then I suppose."

"The remaining SIMs: we were beaten to it by Box, although only just."

"Those bloody spooks!"

"It will get fed back to them that we asked. So, if they were thinking about not sharing, they can't do so now."

"Anything else?"

"No, that's it."

Deena was about to leave her official residence, when she stopped, removed her phone from her handbag and rang Chenda.

"Susaday soksaby, Chenda?"

"I'm fine, Deena."

"Do you have your passport with you?"

"Of course, Deena. For sure."

"What arrangements have you made for being away?"

"My cousin is staying until this big job is finished. I thought it better to be prepared."

"Good thinking, Chenda. Would you mind leaving early tomorrow, for Poipet? I want you to go across the border to Ban Mai Nong Sai and have a look at an address."

"Sure, I can do that for you."

"Good, I will text you the address."

"This car, Deena: it's not the best for secret work with the diplomatic plates."

"Yes, I know. Just be careful, drive by only. Make a sketch plan, try and get a photo if you can. You can overnight at Battambang on the way back if you want. I can make other arrangements for Monday."

"OK. I will see how I feel on the return journey. Shall I have some different plates made up at the garage? I can swap them over once I've crossed the border."

"Do you have enough cash with you?"

"Yes."

"Can you get Thai plates in Battambang?"

"For sure."

"OK, get them anyway, but don't use them unless you feel there is a real need, and not unless you have rung me first!"

CHAPTER THIRTEEN

Anlong Run, Cambodia

Chet and Umar arrived at the safe house in the district of Anlong Run, having passed through the border at Poipet nearly three hours earlier. They came empty-handed on this occasion, which was a disappointment for the two guards who belonged to Chakra's gang. The guards sensed that something was up, the moment Umar asked for a handgun. It was not the first thing he normally asked for. They watched him unload and check the magazine. He then racked the gun, catching the round. He pressed the round back into the magazine, replaced the magazine back into the butt, letting the chamber slide forward which placed the same round back in the chamber. Umar looked at both guards.

"Stay here, no matter what you hear. Understood?"

Both of them nodded.

Chet and Umar went into the main house and found the Khn b̂ā awake sitting in his office, next to his many screens, cameras and computer equipment.

"Didn't expect to see you both at this time of day," the Khn b̂ā said, with concern in his tone.

Chet sat down in a chair, whilst Umar stood over the Khn b̂ā not bothering to hide the gun he was holding.

"How are you?" Chet asked.

"This looks ominous!"

Chet stared back, letting his eyes and look provide the answer.

"We need to make some changes."

"Not advisable at this late stage."

"We disagree, and if you don't have our support, the current trade will not be going ahead."

"Why the sudden worry? You said you were fine with the plan."

"We've changed our minds. This isn't open for discussion. We don't operate like you do in Canada, or Holland, or wherever you're from—all talk and mind games. We need to satisfy ourselves of the ongoing security around the white boy, or Umar will kill him now. Your decision."

The Khn bā looked at Umar and didn't like what he saw. He was in a tight spot, but he wasn't quite ready to roll over yet.

"What is it you want? More money?"

Chet stared back at him, with hatred in his face.

"I've not driven all the way down here, when I didn't have to, to get into your stupid discussions. Now, I want to see for myself the ongoing security, or this trade ends here and now. Frankly, the whole operation can end as far as I'm concerned!"

There was silence in the room as he weighed up the threat. It was a surprise to him personally that it had taken them this amount of time to get to this point. He looked at Umar who moved the gun to the front of his body. Umar knew physically that the Khn bā wasn't a threat to him or Chet, on a 'one-on-one,' basis. But that wasn't how he worked. He checked for signs of nearby weapons. There was one rifle, but not within reach. With little or no clothing on, due to the heat, the only weapon he could possibly have secreted would be a small knife.

"The fact you haven't replied sort of solves a number of problems for me. Umar?"

Umar drew the weapon up and placed it next to the Khn bā's head.

If Chet was expecting some sort of reaction, he didn't get it. Instead, all he got was laughter.

"If you do this, kill me, you don't get your money!"

"If it all goes wrong, we don't get the money. But don't worry. The gun is to keep you seated while I kill the boy."

Chet got up and began to leave the room.

"Wait!"

Chet turned around, raising his eyebrows. Umar's grim-faced

expression turned into a grin.

"No need to get violent with the boy! What will satisfy your concerns?"

Chet sat back down again. He could see there was absolutely no expression or worry on the face of the foreigner. In the face of the danger he was currently in, you either had to have the biggest ever pair of balls or be totally mad. He suspected the latter.

"We need to be happy with ongoing arrangements with the boy. All of them."

"OK. I'll need to make a call to clear that. You can go and check all the arrangements, but you're wasting your time."

"Make the call then," Chet replied, threateningly.

"I will, once you've left. He's going to the same location as your base in Thailand. You can speak to my contact there. He will convince you that all will be well. I'm not making the call to my person in front of you. If you don't like that, then kill the boy. I'll leave, we can all call it a day."

The reply was devoid of any threat to them and displayed no concern for himself. It all just added to their assessment: that he was truly a 'Khn b̂ā.' They had what they wanted.

Ban Mai Nong Sai, Thailand

Chenda pulled over to the side of Thana Way Street, in Ban Mai Nong Sai. She checked her map twice, before surveying the area around her. She could read and speak a little Thai. With everything she had at her disposal, she felt sure she was at the right location. The only warehouse-type building was a large commercial car part store, opposite her. It extended back off the road some way, and she suspected the location that she needed to identify must be at the back, out of view from the road. The only way to see what was down there would be to drive down the dusty dirt track to the left of the store. There would be no reason on earth why a diplomatic car from the Canadian Embassy in Phnom Penh would need to be down there.

She texted Deena, asking for permission to use the false, Thai plates, giving her reasons. She got an affirmative reply within seconds.

Chenda drove off, found a quiet area out of view from prying eyes, then quickly and efficiently changed the real number plates over to the false ones. When they were being made, she had ensured that the holes for the screws were in the right places to match the holes on the car. The process went smoothly, and in no time, she turned left down the dirt road and made her way slowly along. She pulled her lacy hat down, hunched up her shoulders and wore another set of sunglasses which she kept in the car as a spare. They were oversized for her and broke up her facial appearance.

As she passed what appeared to be the end of the store building, it immediately gave way to a large canvas-covered area. She could see through gaps in the fence line and saw hundreds of rusting old cars. It was a scrap yard. She made her way further along, until just before the end a single-storey warehouse building came into view. It joined onto the end of the scrap yard but looked independent. She saw that the road ran out just past the building, meaning she would have to turn around just past it and would, almost certainly, be in full view when she did. She stopped, got her small embassy-issued camera out, turned it on and held it in her left hand, ready to take pictures as she drove by. With everything set, she moved off. As she passed the building, she noted it had one main glass door on the far left, with a roller garage entrance on the far right. It looked deserted. As she passed the end of the building she came to a stop and began a two-point turn. As she did this, the left side of the building came into view; it had no windows or doors in it. It appeared to be built out of cement or concrete building blocks, which had been painted light blue. There was no signage, names or number on the building and no cars parked nearby. She took lots of photos as she manoeuvred around. Just before moving off past the building for a second time, she quickly put the camera into her right hand, nimbly holding both the wheel and the camera so that she could also press the camera's shoot button. She then put her phone to her ear with her left hand, slowly driving past the warehouse, moving her lips as if she was talking on the phone. Chenda maintained this back up to the junction with Thana Way Street. Once there, she returned to where she had put on the Thai registration plates. Checking to see that the coast was clear, she replaced the Cambodian plates, then drove into the centre of Ban Mai Nong Sai, pulling over to make a sketch of what she had seen. Once complete, she texted Deena to say she was on her way back.

Deena received the text, just before arriving at the Sunflower Hotel, where she had arranged to meet Major Pich, Tom and Sarah. She had arrived early so she could update them about Chenda's activities and to go over the plan again before handing over the intelligence document. She found Tom and Sarah sitting in the foyer at a central table. It was far enough away from other hotel guests and its public nature would not encourage in-depth discussion, which is what she wanted. If Major Pich did go down that route, they could always go to a conference room.

"Morning team!" Deena announced brightly.

"Good morning, Deena. How's your weekend going?" Sarah replied, smiling vibrantly.

"Mine are often made up of functions that tend to have some work element attached. In this job, in a place like Cambodia, you are never really off duty. What did you two get up to?"

"We spent some time by the pool, eating and drinking. We wanted to go and see S21, but Chenda has asked to take us there, and we'd both like that."

"Good idea, Sarah. Right . . . to work, before the Major gets here. I suggest I hand it over here and tell him, once he has read it, to call me for another meeting to discuss it. I have no idea how good his English is when it comes to reading the language. If he gets it out, reads it and wants to discuss it straight away, then it's over to you Tom. If this location becomes too crowded, I will ask for a conference room for a few minutes. Happy?"

"Yes, of course," Tom replied.

"Excellent. I have an update from Chenda. As you know, she took Sopheap home. I then asked her to take a quick trip to the address you sent me. She has done that and is on her way back. I have given her the option to overnight again at Battambang, but, knowing Chenda, she won't. We should meet here again once I hear back from the Major, unless something changes that."

"What did she find there?"

"Don't know, haven't asked her, Tom . . ." Deena replied, trailing off as she saw Major Pich arrive and make his way towards them.

"Good morning, Major."

"It is a good day," the Major stated, with his now familiar, set grin. He clearly wasn't going to say anything more.

Deena quickly picked up on the Major's pause, delved into her large handbag, produced an official envelope and handed it to the Major.

"Intelligence is often sanitised. This is no exception. Call me once you have read it so we can meet again to discuss it."

"I will. I cannot stop, I have a busy schedule today. I will ring you, but it will be after the weekend."

The Major deliberately looked at Tom and Sarah, nodded, turned and left.

"That was short and sweet," Tom announced, once Major Pich had left the building.

"That's good. It plays into our hands, with your Chief wanting a delay. Looks like the rest of the day is yours. I guess it makes up for Saturday!"

Surbiton, England

Toby Spencer-Drummond was sitting at the dining table of his 1930s semi-detached house in Surbiton, covering his toast generously with Aunt Mabel's home-made marmalade, when his pager vibrated on the white tablecloth. Checking the number, he proceeded to cut the toast diagonally, taking a large bite, savouring the zesty contents. Removing the tea cosy from the pot, he poured himself some tea, adding the milk last so he could achieve the colour he preferred most. Having placed the teaspoon in the saucer, he contemplated a sip, but, knowing it would be hot, rang the 'L' room first.

"Good morning, Toby!"

"It is, indeed, a fine morning today. News?"

"Yes, plenty of movement across all your warrants but, again, only one call of interest. Just after seven last evening. Muffled voice again, only words spoken were: 'Alpha 9'. Again, nobody spoke at the receiving end. SIM again remained active for a short period. We got your request for cell site; analysis placed it within a five mile radius of Iffley, with a small amount of movement between switch on, the call and off again. Do you know where that is?"

"Yes."

"Oh, you do? Well, in that case, it should provide you with some welcome news this Sunday. I had a quick peek into your operational taskings. I expect to see the results of them. It is becoming increasingly clear that your suspects have other means of communicating, ones that you are missing and know nothing about."

The line went dead immediately.

Toby was determined not to let the call ruin his Sunday morning or the newly-opened jar of his aunt's marmalade. He slowly finished the toast, the last morsel of which always seemed to be the best. He swallowed a mouthful of tea before calling Mr Pink.

"Good morning, Captain!"

"Greetings to you as well, Mr Pink. I trust you are with Mrs Pink today?"

"I am indeed. For that, I am in her good books. My phone has been active though. That, she is not happy about!"

"Good active?"

"Bad news first: ANPRs have been negative. I had a drive-by done, successfully captured the data from the logger on the first attempt, which seems to be rare these days. Hasn't been analysed yet. Cell site for the phone: the location tends to indicate a connection with TVP, don't you think?"

"You could be right. The good news anytime now would save my Sunday, Mr Pink!" Toby replied, taking a sip of his tea.

"Yes, of course. I took it upon myself to check which tactical researcher was on call this weekend and, would you believe our luck? It was Prisha!"

"This is, indeed, excellent news. What have you tasked her with?"

"Finding a connection between the ANPR, logger data and TVP?"

"Good thinking, Mr Pink. When might we learn something?"

"We just did; just before you rang. During the one hour before and one hour after the call was made there were eight vehicles of interest that passed one or more of the ANPR cars. These cars are all owned by people who work for Thames Valley Police in some capacity, or who belong to the International Police Association—many retired cops are and many of those have Masonic affiliations, so Prisha tells me. Two of these passed the same ANPR twice. Prisha then ran a full workup on those two. One of them lit up and could be the person who made the call."

"Prisha, Prisha. How many times has that girl saved my bacon. Go on, who?"

"Retired Chief Inspector James Martin King. Father of ADS Jane King, who works on COCET with DCI Tom Ross."

"Interesting. How long before the logger data is ready?"

"Prisha says she will get to it within the hour; all depends how much data is on there. I suspect there won't be a great deal, so probably by midday."

"The intelligence around the other cars?"

"All done today. Details will be in Prisha's final report."

"Do you have any availability tonight?"

"Yes."

"Do you have any more . . . loggers?"

"I do, but it would all depend where his car is, what it is, feasibility study. You know the drill."

"I sure do. Get it done asap please, Mr Pink."

"Yes, Captain."

Toby thought he would need to pass some of this information to Chief Constable James Galloway that day. It was going to be a difficult call and, as he didn't yet have the full intelligence picture, he decided to wait.

COCET, Aylesbury, England
At COCET Owen looked over his shoulder to Dale, "He has just come on, Sarge."

Dale used the wheels on his chair to slide across the room to the pod where Owen was working. Owen moved over slightly so the pair of them could see the central one of his three screens. A message from 'Alpha' user 'pureisbest' suddenly popped into the dialogue box. It read.

'The beef is ready; you must all be in Bangkok by Wednesday at the latest. Payment for the meal will be in advance. $25 US. There will be onward travel from Bangkok. Once I hear you are all here, I will make arrangements so we can meet up.'

"Shall I answer him?"

"Not yet. Let him wait, best speak to Nick first," Dale replied, picking up the phone and asking Nick to join them.

A couple of minutes later Nick entered the room, "How can I help?"

"Nick, is there anything on his hardware that indicates he may have divulged what his travel plans were to anybody?"

"Not that I can see or find. Of course, he may have had other means of communicating."

"That never came out in interview," Owen added.

Nick shrugged his shoulders and looked at Dale.

"Ok, confirm it, show proportional enthusiasm."

Owen typed out, 'Will be there, looking forward to trying Thai beef :-)' and sent it. He got a smiley face back in reply.

Dale slid his chair back so he could see both Owen and Nick.

"This is our opportunity to see if we can draw out one of the other users, get them out of the chat room and onto email. Nick, there has been very little chat between our target and the other two users, both of whom are behind proxies. Is there anything you have found that might shed light on this?"

"Short answer: no, although I haven't got through all his chat logs yet."

"That sort of corroborates his interview. Owen, wait until 'pureisbest' has left. Whichever one of the other two arrives first, once they have seen his message, get into them, suggest email, discuss concerns you have for being robbed. The price cannot be 2,500: that seems way too cheap. We know from the interview he was expecting somewhere between five to ten thousand. This would be a good point to challenge the price. It could be too steep for others."

"Will do, Sarge. Looks like he's gone already. From Nick's intel we shouldn't have to wait long. The other two seem to come on from 11am onwards."

"How're you doing over there, Anna?"

"It's going really well. They can't stop sending videos and images!"

"Great news. If you need help, just ask and I'll be there. Soon as you have enough for victim identification work, let me know."

"Yep, sure thing; won't be long at this rate. The first two will be urgent and they appear to be in the UK as well."

Nick looked at Dale with a smile. "God, I love this work!"

Dale smiled back. "We all do. This is why we do it, for days like this."

"You won't like looking at these," Anna interrupted. "Evil bastard. He needs locking up!"

Nick turned towards Anna. He could see the screen but didn't take in the image that was currently displayed. He had seen enough since working with COCET to know that he only viewed what he had to and nothing more. He had already catalogued 5000 images and videos since he began work on Harris's hardware. There were over 15,000 more to go.

"I'll leave you to it. I've got my own work to do."

Dale rang the extension for Jane King.

"Jane, Dale here. Heads up: there will be some urgent dissemination and victim identification work coming your way."

"How long?"

"About an hour."

"We'll be ready."

Anna Farley had received the results from the SPOC at headquarters, who had in turn received it from UK internet providers. They all related to undercover activity between Anna Wilson and the offenders she had been infiltrating. She set to work compiling a comprehensive intelligence dissemination document for forwarding to the home forces concerned. In these two cases, it would be Staffordshire and

Derbyshire. She was halfway through when Jane returned with her verdict, having completed the victim identification work.

"We can't get these checked through Childbase or Interpol in the short space of time we have. It doesn't matter though; they can do it themselves. I haven't seen these before. They look very new. There are English plug sockets on the wall, and in one video I can hear Sky News in the background. I'm sure they will trace the two children involved in this."

"How're we going to get the material to them? Are we using a biker again?"

"Yes, he will be here in about 25 minutes."

"Great. I will be ready by then. Have you rung ahead? What did they say?" Anna enquired, with more than just a hint of worry in her voice.

"Yes, I did. Both teams were alerted through the system the Chief set up. They will be acting today, as soon as we can get the packs to them."

"Awesome. I'll get back to work then," Anna replied. This time though she had hope in her voice.

"Sarge, one of the 'Alphas' has just come into the room. I'm going to send him the prepared text now," Owen said with excitement.

As he watched the text appear on his screen, he waited impatiently to see if he would get a reply. Dale joined him in the wait. After a few minutes of no activity, the 'Alpha' left the chat room without engaging the user known to him as 'youngsweetlips', who was actually a law enforcement officer working for COCET.

"Don't worry, he could just be busy. He now has your email though, so he might just reply later."

"One down, one to go. In the meantime, I've got another user here who's boasting about abusing his daughter tonight. I'm going to engage him now."

"OK. Need any help, let me know."

Surbiton, England
Toby's pager alerted him to call Mr Pink.

"That was quick work, or is there some other update?"

"Quick work. That's Prisha for you—seems like she wanted to get home early. She says it's all in the intel folder awaiting your perusal. I have a team briefed for tonight. Speak sometime Monday."

Toby opened his Government-issued laptop, placed an encryption box between it and the internet socket and made his way into the intranet, navigating his way quickly, until he found the folder he was looking for. Once there, he scanned the contents to see how much intelligence there was. Prisha had been busy! Although there was plenty of intelligence, not all of it could be divulged to James Galloway. He texted him and requested he prepare for an incoming call on his home Brent system. He prepared his own, waited a few minutes, then rang him.

"This had better be good. I've had enough of my weekend ruined."

"The intelligence may be good; what you are about to hear, though, might not be."

"Go ahead," the Chief replied, sighing.

"Another call. We are now at 'Alpha 9', same muffled voice. Cell site – yes we got there before you – put the caller around the Iffley area. That was before it was switched off. Our ANPR cars did not pick up your man, but it did pick up a number of cars that are owned by people who work for TVP. Two of those cars are of interest to us."

The Chief felt some anger rising in him.

"How the hell do you know who works for my Police Force?" the Chief demanded.

"First of all, James, it's not your Force, it's Her Majesty's Government. Secondly, I represent its Security Service. So, it's my job to know. Now, two of those cars passed the ANPR vehicles twice, both within the target period. One is owned by James Martin King, father of Jane King, currently working on COCET."

"James doesn't work for us now, he's retired!" The Chief almost shouted, the ramifications of what he was hearing still making its way through his thought processes. As was the verbal put down.

"How the hell did you pick that car out? You aren't telling me everything!"

"If you let me continue, I will tell you," Toby replied, in a calming tone.

The Chief took a huge intake of breath, to calm himself.

"Go on."

"James King is a member of the International Police Association, so we traced him through that. As for the second car, he is a serving officer: Terrence Miller."

The Chief had to sit down. He had not got to where he was without having a brilliant, quick- thinking mind. Right now, he needed to put it into action.

"From my knowledge, James lives near Iffley, if not actually there. I don't know where Terry Miller lives, but there is every chance that he could live in the same area. Just because they have passed those cars during that time is no more of a coincidence than the other six. Surely?"

"The first problem is, James, one of them has a daughter working on COCET with their team leader deployed in Cambodia, right in the middle of all of this. She is effectively COCET's de facto deputy and has full access to all the police intelligence relating to it. The second problem is Terrence Miller."

"What the hell has he got to do with this . . . ?" The Chief's words trailed off. His mind going back to Operation Hope. He suddenly had an awful, sinking feeling in his stomach.

"The problem, and that of both King and Troy, is that they all belong to the same Masonic Lodge, even though they have been ordered not to be members. Now, what I am about to tell you is part of your top-secret clearance, so it comes strictly under the 'strapping' you received.

"I appreciate you might not like being told things at your rank, but I am telling you now: this is being recorded. I am reminding you of your security clearance rating, one particularly bestowed upon you for this operation. I know that Miller fell under suspicion after Operation Hope. He was investigated and moved as a result of that suspicion, but ultimately cleared of any wrongdoing by none other than John Troy.

"I have had Troy under technical surveillance; he has been visiting Miller, so I know where he lives. I have video evidence that he has met King. You know, as well as I do, that Masonic influence throughout

Government, even in its most secret of organisations, can, and does, work against the state. It is one of the deep state actors.

"The combination of King, King's daughter and Miller wrapped around this, with the 'Alpha' scale now at nine, risen immediately after your disinformation, together with Ross locating the safe house, must be having some impact on your thinking. Surely?"

"There is no way Jane King is knowingly involved in this," the Chief said, as convincingly as he could.

"I agree. It's not me you will need to convince next week, though. And don't forget you have a man out there."

"If I take Jane King off the case, it could blow everything!" the Chief replied, plaintively.

"You can't. Tom Ross, for one, would object."

"So, what are we going to do?"

"Sit tight. Get as much feedback from COCET as you can, without alerting them. Keep tabs on Ross, all until next week. We get the meeting out of the way, get the strike done in Cambodia, then pick through the carnage it will ultimately create."

The Chief needed a drink. It was early, but he made himself a large gin and tonic, downing enough to feel its calming influence before he rang Maggie.

"Can you come and see me on Monday?"

"Of course, Sir. What time?"

"First thing. In the meantime, I'd like an update on COCET activity please."

"Just Cambodia, Sir?"

"No, everything, if you would. Just headlines for now, but I'll want a full written briefing on Monday, and by that, I mean a full one. Facts, evidence, intelligence, context, nuance, gossip—the lot."

"Headlines for Tom is: he has handed the intelligence log to Deena; she will hand that to Major Pich tomorrow at the earliest, as requested, which means they won't be hearing back on that until Tuesday. It is so sanitised that Major Pich will undoubtedly call a meeting to discuss what the log really means. Until then, they are both on weekend off.

"COCET, Operations Laverton and Blackwood have gone well, as you know. The offenders are both remanded in custody. Their identities have been assumed by the undercover officers. They are making good ground already with the infiltration phase, with one internal group having links to Thailand. As you know, it's that intelligence, in part, that is protecting Deena's on the ground assets."

"Are there any urgent cases I should be aware of?"

"I've just had an email, from Jane King. In it, she indicates they are currently disseminating urgent intelligence to Staffs and Derbyshire. Those forces are acting on it today. Apparently, local departments were made aware of possible work coming to them through the early alert system you set up with ACPO."

"Good, glad to hear something is working well today. Anything else?"

"The only other thing Jane mentioned was Interpol have sent Niall out to Thailand on a request from Tom. The internal group the UCs are infiltrating: one of the suspects has told the rest to be in Thailand next week."

"What more do we know about them since my last update?"

"Not a great deal, other than what I have just told you. There are four of them. We have assumed the offender Harris's identity. One of the remaining three has been traced to Thailand. That's why Tom has asked Niall to get over there. The other two are behind proxies, but the UCs are attempting to engage them outside of the chat room. Is everything alright, Sir?"

"Yes, and no, Maggie. There are some things I can't tell you. Some of the intelligence with Box has unsettled me. We are only getting part of the picture from the spooks, and it annoys me. They annoy me. On another matter, you've got bags of service. Have you ever heard of a police code system, similar to that of the ten-ten system, but used on an 'Alpha' scale?"

"No, I haven't, sorry. Why do you ask?"

"There's one being used that I can't tell you about. The suggestion is that police are using it. I've never heard of it."

"Nope, sorry. The only police connection I've had with that word, is with COCET."

"What on earth do you mean, Maggie?"

"The Thai group we're infiltrating! They call themselves the 'Alphas'."

CHAPTER FOURTEEN

Ban Mai Nong Sai, Thailand

It was early evening as Chenda approached Phnom Penh. At the same time, Chet and Umar were making their way across the border at Poipet; back into Thailand. Once through, they followed the instructions they had been given and turned down the track Chenda had been on earlier, driving to the end and parking in front of the warehouse. They left the engine running, whilst Chet rang a number. He let it ring three times, then hung up, then rang the same number straight back, let it ring once, then hung up again. They waited in the car as instructed, the air-con keeping them cool.

Umar looked behind him. Unable to see properly, he got out of the car, walking behind it, scanning the area, looking for signs of a trap. Returning to the passenger side he got back in, shutting the door.

"Not happy, brother?"

"Never happy where that Khn bā is concerned."

"Agree with you there. Let's hope we can strike up a deal, one where we can get rid of him!"

Umar began to look around a second time, when a silver Toyota ute pulled up alongside them. Chet switched off and got out to meet the driver, the sole occupant of the Toyota. Neither he nor Umar was carrying a weapon. If things got out of control, it was Umar's job to take the driver out. As he came into view, Chet could see he was a European in his fifties, slim and not in good physical shape. From his clothing and appearance, he was somebody who had been living in Thailand for some considerable time.

"Chet, Umar?" said the driver.

"That's us," Chet replied.

"I'm Brian. I hear you want some confirmation that your operation is safe once it all reaches me. Is that right?"

"Yes, and beyond. We don't want it tracking back to you and then us," Umar said, with enough abruptness, letting the European know they both needed to be satisfied.

"Follow me," Brian said, as he walked over to the glass doors of the warehouse.

Chet couldn't place the accent. He thought it was English, but there was another accent in the voice. One that he had never heard before. As Brian walked past them, Umar could see that, unless he had a gun attached to his ankle, he wasn't carrying.

Once at the door, Brian unlocked it. It was a single lock, one easily picked which didn't impress Chet or Umar. Inside though, and with the front glass door shut, things started to change. Umar noticed the discreet camera high up in the left corner of the foyer. He turned to find another one high up behind him, to his right. The placements meant there were no dead spots. There was a solid steel door off the foyer. This one had three locks. Brian unlocked it, then had to use both hands to pull it back, it was so heavy on its hinges. Chet looked through the doorway but could see only darkness until Brian pulled a major breaker switch on the wall just inside. They walked in, Brian closing the door behind them. As the lights inside began to burst into life, Chet and Umar couldn't believe their eyes. There was a whole second building constructed inside the warehouse shell. This shell had no windows, skylights or external doors, other than the one they had just walked through. There was a central passageway that stretched the whole length of the building with closed doors on either side. Brian went to the first door on the left, opened it and beckoned for Chet and Umar to look inside. As they walked in, the room lit up. It was a master bedroom with a large ensuite bathroom, incorporating a large bath: big enough for four people. The decoration and fitments were to a very high standard. It was, without doubt, five-star hotel grade.

"This way, please."

Brian led them to the next room along. Chet walked in and saw it was identical to the one they had just come from.

"Is everything the same?" he immediately asked.

"No. Follow me please," Brian calmly replied.

Umar, who hadn't entered that room, followed Brian to the next room. He walked in to find it was essentially a torture chamber: the sort of room the Khn bã probably had made for himself.

"Do you use this room?" Umar asked Brian, in a sinister voice.

"No, not personally. But I like watching."

Umar was about to launch a reply, but Brian got in first.

"You know exactly what these kids are for, you get paid well for it. Don't try and guilt trip me!"

Umar opened his mouth to reply, but Chet beat him to it.

"We'd like to see the rest, otherwise you won't be getting any more children, because without us, they won't reach here. So, just be careful when you speak to us in that tone."

Chet stared straight into Brian's face. He knew he could put fear into people with that stare, and it worked. Brian averted his gaze and walked to the final room on the left and opened the door.

Chet and Umar walked in to find a communication centre. Brian powered up six large screens, before turning to speak.

"Each room has a full set of hidden cameras that can be operated remotely, what they see can be recorded and then burned to disc from here. The buyers don't know they are there. We record everything from the moment they arrive outside, everything they do when they are here, until they leave. This is both insurance and profit making. It ensures their silence. Some are offered a copy as a living memory, the rest we blur out and sell on to selected customers. Follow me, please."

Chet and Umar took the few, short steps into the room opposite to find it was an iron-barred, caged cell block, identical to the one at their safe house in Cambodia. This one, though, was bigger and had more compartments.

"Do the cameras cover here?"

"Yes, it is good money maker."

"What's the sound transfer like between the rooms? You have a major road not far away and a store," Umar asked, knowing it had been a deciding factor in the selection of their safe house in Cambodia.

"The walls and ceiling are fully proofed to recording studio standard. Not a cry, scream or moan can be heard. You have my word on that."

"You're a sick fuck!" Umar shot back, unable to contain himself.

Chet knew the situation could get out of hand very quickly where Umar was concerned, so he needed to act quickly.

"Just show us the rest of the rooms, then we can talk about other aspects we have concerns over," Chet said in a demanding voice, flicking Umar a quick look, which he knew his brother would understand.

Chet and Umar looked into the other rooms as they made their way back up the passageway to the steel door. They were all accommodation suites.

"Have you seen enough?" Brian asked, back at the steel door.

"Yes," Chet replied.

"Good. What other concerns do you have?"

"Not here, not after seeing all that recording. It's our car or no kids, your choice?"

"Your car it is then."

Umar ushered Brian into the back of their car then he and Chet got into the front.

"What happens to the children from here?" Chet asked, as soon as the door was shut.

"Some are just staged here: nothing more. The buyers want them untouched, and they want video proof of their stay here. Some will travel by land, if they are going to Malaysia for instance. They are drugged and put into vehicle concealments. We've never lost one. Others that are going further afield are drugged, then shipped. Some are taken all the way, some are met just off the coast; it all depends."

"What about the ones that are used here?" Chet asked.

"We offer the same service; but they don't fetch as much. But we do guarantee they come in an almost new condition though, which helps."

"Have you had problems with customers going too far? What happens then?"

"Yes, we have. I'd rather not go into specifics. We just have to treat it as a loss and move on."

"What about interaction with this location and you?" Umar asked.

"Nobody comes here without a blindfold on. They have no idea where this place is. I have one trusted person who has been with me for years who collects them from Bangkok. An hour out, they get blindfolded until they get inside. Once here, they meet me. I have a mask on the whole time they are here. Same on the return journey to Bangkok."

"What about land or shipping transport: how exposed are you?"

"I'm not. I always use my single, trusted person. He would never say anything."

"What about him: how exposed is he?" Chet persisted.

"They don't know him. They know only a nickname. We change our SIMs constantly and, even if he was caught, he would never speak."

"How can you be sure of that?" Umar scoffed.

"One, he loves me. Two, he knows I'd have him killed."

Right at that moment, unknown to each other Chet and Umar, were thinking the same thing.

"We have one hot product. What are your plans for him?" Chet asked, wondering if they were just swapping one mad man, for another.

"Thought you might bring him up. He is a problem, one that has called for a one-off plan. He won't be going any further than here. But don't worry, he will still be worth it."

"Who's managing the disposal?" Umar asked, without any hint of emotion.

"Me."

"Done it before?"

"Yes."

"Any third party involved?"

"One, but you needn't worry about him. He's tied into it."

"But I do worry. I want to know," Umar replied in an insistent tone.

"The person harvesting the organs. He is well paid and hardly likely to be a weak link, considering what he's doing."

Chet looked at Umar, then looked out through the windscreen at the warehouse, pausing, before speaking again.

"Is that mobile number one that I can always get you on?"

"No. I change regularly. I have only a handful of people that need to know what number I'm ever operating on. I can include you on that list if you want."

"Yes, that would be a good idea. One more thing. How long have you known the Khn b̂ā?"

"I heard that's what you were calling him. I know him as Michael. We met a few years back, here in Thailand."

"Have you worked with him on business like this before?"

"Yes."

"Is this place a joint setup between you and him?"

"I understood you just wanted assurances. You're straying."

"I'm not, as you say, straying. I need to know your credibility. Simple as that."

Brian looked between Chet and Umar nervously. He didn't like the line of questioning but could see their point as well.

"Look. I've been in Thailand now nearly eight years. This place is mine. The refurbishment and recording capability are new; that's a joint venture between me and Michael. I don't need to be in business with him to make a living for myself. To be frank, if you stop the flow of kids, then that's fine by me. I will just go back to doing what I was doing before."

Chet felt the explanation had a ring of truth to it.

"You've been very helpful. Thanks for showing us around. We'd best be going."

"Are you satisfied now?"

"I am, but I need to speak with Umar here privately. We come together as a pair. If he isn't happy, then I'm with him. I'll text just a Y or a N, OK with you?"

"Fine, but make it quick. If things have changed, I need to know. I have people on flights on their way here right now. I need time to prepare alternatives."

"Ten minutes."

Brian returned to his car and drove away.

"Don't like either of them, Chet. They are both mad."

"I agree. Out of the two though, he might be a bit less insane!"

Umar laughed at Chet's comment.

"I think the operation is well planned at this end."

"I agree, Umar, it is. It does worry me, though, that he must live in the area somewhere and probably has for a while. I've never seen him before."

"Yeah, but we haven't been here that long really. In any case, we aren't into the boy or children scene, so our hang-outs won't be his."

"What's your thoughts on removing the Khn b̂ā and dealing with just him."

"Not sure on that, brother. Look, the setup here looks great. He appears to be professional, which is good. My now very hungry belly tells me we should do this run. Kill the Khn b̂ā, let a few weeks go by and then sit down with him and see what he has to say. But never again a European."

"Agreed. Now food!"

Thames Valley Police HQ, Kidlington, England

"Good morning, Maggie. Go straight in, he's ready for you."

Maggie shut the door behind her, handed the Chief her report and sat down. The Chief read through it, taking his time, before slowly placing it on his desk.

"Any update to that, since it was written."

"No. I expect to hear from Tom later this morning. Do you want updating once I've heard from him?"

"Yes. I need him not to be taking any action until after tomorrow."

"That won't be a problem, Sir."

"There are plenty of problems, Maggie. What plan is in place for Thailand, do you know?"

"Not yet, but I will know later today. When are we going to tell Tom?"

"That won't be just my decision. We will know more tomorrow. I will never leave a man behind, Maggie, but for now he's on his own.

We have a chance to settle the long-held rumour that we have a secret Police Service within our public one. We won't get another chance like this; we simply must take it."

"I understand. I know you can't tell me everything, but is the investigation getting somewhere? At home I mean."

"Yes, it is, Maggie. I don't want to admit that, but, yes, it is."

Jane entered the conference room at COCET to find the whole team already seated and awaiting her arrival.

"Intel cell first: Anna, bring us up to speed, please?"

"I think we all know that the urgent packages went out; they were acted on over the weekend. Two in custody. Full admissions. Victims in one case were the offender's own children. They are making enquiries to see if he has had access to others outside his family and, if so, if he has offended against them. He has a personal collection, across the offending scale, in excess of 5,000 images and movies. No evidence the wife knew, but the case officer says they aren't happy that she did not suspect it. Social Services are involved. Offender has been charged; due to appear for remand this morning.

"Second case identical to the first, but he's also admitted to offending against the babysitter who they have been unable to locate. His collection is expected to be around 20,000. He appears this morning on a remand hearing as well."

"Excellent job, everybody. Without your efforts this weekend, these children would have been sexually abused yet again by the one person that they should have been able to trust. Well done. Is that it, Anna?"

"Yes."

"Dale, where are we?"

"That summary has covered our urgent work from Blackwood. Anna has been supplied child abuse material from sixteen other targets, as of when she knocked off last night. Nothing there that looks new, and it's ready for victim-identification assessment. She starts again as soon as we have finished here.

"Laverton. We've been unsuccessful in luring the other two 'Alphas' out from behind their proxy, or even out of the room. One, however, has agreed to meet up with us in Bangkok, as they have worries about being robbed. Safety in numbers, I guess. Contact though, to arrange the meet up, must be through the room. This of course leaves us with two problems, one physical, one technical. Firstly, we won't be in Thailand. Secondly, it's possible any one of the other three might have the capability to recognise that we are logging into the room from outside Thailand, when we're claiming to be there."

"The physical solution is something that has to come from the Boss," Jane began. "I'll get onto him. You probably all know, and if you don't, getting a UC deployed into Thailand is just too difficult, especially within the time frame. Nick, what options do we have on the technical side?"

"You have three easy methods, as I see it. One, just stay as you are and, if challenged, front it out. Deny it. Two, get onto IT and get on a temporary proxy yourself. And three, the one I would recommend, is that you use Niall out there to act as a direct physical proxy, video it all at both ends and justify it through an SIO policy decision."

Jane looked at Dale, who raised his eyebrows.

"I'm liking option three. Dale, what say you?" Jane said, with her eyebrows raised.

"Yep, I'm loving it."

"Anything more from Laverton?"

"Yes. Owen and I have infiltrated 22 targets, using intelligence from Nick. They have all been successful. Nothing urgent. Victim ID work is on your desk."

Before Jane could speak, Anna interrupted.

"I haven't seen those in intel yet?"

"That's because they aren't there yet. But they will be, once we've finished here."

"In that case, back to your jobs, team. Well done everybody, keep it up. Dale, I'll get back to you once I've spoken with the Boss."

Phnom Penh, Cambodia

"Hi Niall, how was your trip?"

"It was good, how's things going with you?"

"Treading water. They have our intel. We're now waiting for them to come back to us on it."

"I've got an update from the RTP already, would you believe it?"

"No, I wouldn't. What's happened there since you left?"

"Seems like the techies really got their shit together. They're a different breed to the older guys. They're smart, switched on and learn quick. They aren't eejits, Tom."

"That's good to hear."

"Yeah, well. They've done a bit of digging on this warehouse. The person paying the bills on the internet connection is a Brian Kennedy. I've got his date of birth and passport details. The address they have for him is that warehouse. This is where it gets interesting: they did an immigration search and they found an exact match on his details on a single two-week tourist visa, both in and out again from eight years ago."

"How good are their systems?"

"Probably not great. But get this: he was Irish. So, I've done some checks. I've found what I believe to be the same Brian Kennedy, same date of birth, same passport number, who was born and lived in Dublin. He died six months after returning from his Thai holiday. He had cancer and the trip was on his bucket list."

"So, the person paying the bills on the warehouse has stolen his identity?"

"That's my guess. The RTP crew think the same as well!"

"Is there anything they can do without tracking him down and alerting him?"

"No, and they say the local cops up there will be on the take, which is why they are taking me there tomorrow, there and back in a day. Scope it out. They have an informant who is a male prostitute. They are going to take him up there with them. They will get him to go into a few bars, ask around to see if he can pick up some information on the local scene, who's running it, nothing too out of the ordinary."

"Great idea. Who's going to do the scope?"

"I'll get them to do it. Don't worry, I'll keep my white face well out of the way."

"Don't actually scope it until you hear from me. I know that Deena was getting some work done on the address. As it's in another country you'd better not tell them that though. It could be we already have what we need."

"What do I tell them?"

"You'll think of something, you've the luck of the Irish on your side!"

"Thanks for that. You got a plan yet?"

"Not really, but you will be the first to know when I do!"

"What about the identity you've assumed. I hear a UC is a no go?"

"Yeah it is. Maybe I might just pop over there and do it on the side?"

Niall didn't know if Tom was serious or joking.

"Tom, I think you know me well enough. Out here, there are no rules. I've got your back."

"It's more wishful thinking on my part. I've been thinking about it, just haven't worked it all out yet . . ."

Tom heard the incoming call vibration next to his head and checked to see who it was.

"Have to go, Jane is calling me. We'll speak tomorrow if not before."

"Sure, I must crack on and find the nearest bar that serves the black stuff."

"Hi, Jane. How are you?"

"Fine thanks, Boss. You able to speak?"

"Yes, I am."

"Two urgent disseminations to Staffs and Derbyshire went very well. Children rescued and two offenders for court this morning. Both remand files."

"Great work!"

"Yes, I think so too. We have a good number of, 'supplying cases' to the UCs on both jobs. Nothing urgent at the moment. Also, there are two issues with Laverton I need a decision on?"

"The Thai end?"

"Yes. Owen has tried but failed to lure the two 'Alphas' out from behind their proxies. One has arranged to meet us out there due to concerns about being robbed. Dale has concerns that they might be able to technically work out from the room IP that we aren't actually there. The elephant in the room is: how are we going to meet him?"

"It's been on my mind. Niall has just brought the matter up as well. On the IP side, has this been run past SDE?"

"Yes. Dr Nick thinks we have three options. One, front it out; two, we get behind a proxy; and three, which he personally recommends, and it has both mine and Dale's support, is to use Niall out there as a proxy for Owen. He gets guided through it all by Owen. Video it there and here. You make a policy decision, based on the circumstances— there being no other way."

"I like that. Consider it written up. I'll speak to Niall. On the UC front, this is between you and me only; are you comfortable with that?"

Jane knew the correct answer was that she needed to know the proposal first to know if she was comfortable with it or not.

"Fire away!"

"I have three options as well. One, I go across to do it and tell no one, see where it leads us. Two, we use Niall, although he doesn't know about this yet, to meet the non-Thai 'Alpha' and then through the RTP, identify him. Then use Niall via Owen, as you've described, to arrange the meet with the Thai end, but then just fail to show up. Maybe sow some seeds of doubt when he meets the first 'Alpha', so it gets fed in. Three, and this has only just come into the equation—we use an asset who belongs to the RTP."

"What sort of asset?"

"The human sort."

"Who?"

"A male prostitute."

Jane started to chuckle.

"It could work," Tom said, in a weak, defiant voice.

"Go on then, tell me?"

"Well, we get Niall to arrange the meet, then pass the details of that meet through intel dissemination to the RTP. I'll write a policy decision for it to go to them and the rationale behind that decision.

Once the RTP have it, it's theirs. They don't have their hands tied behind their backs like we do. It's their country and their rules."

"To what aim?"

"Backstop to action we want to take in Cambodia, which might never happen. Uncovering the criminality behind the existence of the warehouse. It's connected to what we're doing with Laverton, and all the intelligence points to it being connected with Veritas."

"I agree we have IP data linking the warehouse, but we've been down that route before with the RTP when we missed Michael. Everybody was hooking into everybody else's internet. This could be the same."

"It could, but I just heard from Niall that the subscriber for the connection was an Irish man who died years ago. The person currently paying the bill on that address has stolen his identity."

"Well, now you tell me that, it sounds like a plan. What about a Thai male prostitute turning up there, purporting to be Harris, who purported to be 'youngsweetlips' who is actually us?"

"Fair comment. But they are all purporting to be somebody they're not. That's our advantage. They have no idea who 'youngsweetlips' really is. If he is challenged on IP data, he just says he spoofed it. Don't forget what this is really all about from their end: money."

"About that then. We think the price must be 25,000 US. Where's that going to come from?"

"Not sure yet, but I'll get it. You still comfortable?"

"Of course I am. Sounds bloody awesome."

Tom first checked his watch, then texted Maggie. He got an immediate reply. He opened his laptop and connected to her on Skype.

"How's it going there, Tom?"

"Good, I have an update!"

"Fire away."

Tom waited, seeing that Maggie was opening a notepad. As she dropped her head, he began.

"We've done a scope of the warehouse address in Thailand. That was achieved by Chenda, Deena's driver. We won't have the update from that until she gets back."

"Any problems?"

"No."

"Continue."

"Niall is here. He has met his RTP contacts. They provided him with intelligence on the subscriber for the warehouse. An Irish national. Niall did the checks on that person and has found out he died many years ago, having visited Thailand as part of his bucket list."

"Stolen identity?"

"Yes."

"What's your plan with Thailand?"

"Shall we discuss Cambodia first?"

"No, Thailand, please."

Tom really didn't want to discuss it further, but he had no option.

"Our UCs have managed to get an agreement with one of the 'Alphas' to meet him in Bangkok, on the pretext of discussing personal security. My plan is for the RTP to identify that person and take it from there to the warehouse, taking action either from what they see, or working from intelligence dissemination from us and our activity in Cambodia."

"Sounds good. Who's meeting the 'Alpha'?"

"We can either just not turn up, or the RTP can use one of their people."

Maggie looked up sharply.

"You really think either of those will work?"

"Yes, for sure."

"Even when it comes to the Thai contact?"

"Yes."

"Are you telling me everything, Tom!" Maggie said, in a stern but frustrated voice.

"What are you saying?"

"Don't turn the line of questioning. Is there anything else?"

"Yes, Niall is going to the warehouse location with the RTP tomorrow, just to check the location. They won't need to scope it again. Just check the area out sort of thing. Cambodia now?"

Tom saw Maggie's head drop before he heard her speak.

"Continue."

"The Major has the intelligence. We're still waiting to hear back."

"Anything more?"

"Nope."

"Text me when there is."

No sooner had Tom finished the call than there was a knock at the room door. He opened it to find Deena, Sarah, Chenda and a concierge holding a tray of drinks.

"There's no such thing as a free day when you are working away from home," Deena said, striding confidently into the room, followed by Sarah, not for the first time her perfume penetrating his senses. Tom, who was about to tip but realising somebody had already done it, closed the door and picked up his Tiger beer.

"Nice call. Whose idea was this?"

"Mine," replied Deena. "We have some news—Chenda?"

"Yes, absolutely for sure, Deena. I went to the address just over the border in Thailand. It's well hidden, off the road at the back of two other commercial buildings. I have pictures and a plan of the area."

Deena produced a laptop from her large handbag, placing it on the coffee table.

"I've downloaded the pictures, take a look."

They crowded around to watch, as the screen slowly cycled through the still images. The one thing that struck Tom was that it was totally nondescript. His gut told him it was dirty. As the slide show ended he took the plan from Chenda and examined it. She had done a good job. It was tucked away for sure.

"This is good work, Chenda. Well done. Were you seen?"

"No, absolutely not."

"And you came straight back!"

"Of course. This is important information."

Tom turned to Deena and Sarah.

"I have some news as well. Niall is going to this location tomorrow; the RTP are taking him. I will tell him not to go to the warehouse. This scope is enough for what we need. The RTP are taking an informant with them: he's a male prostitute. They will deploy him into a few bars to see if he can gather information as to who is running the male sex scene in that town.

"The officers that are dealing with Niall are the same ones we dealt with before. They did some research on the subscriber, Brian Kennedy. Turns out Brian Kennedy was an Irish citizen who died many years ago; one of the last things he did was visit Thailand for a holiday. Whoever is paying for the internet connection at this warehouse is not who he says he is," Tom said, whilst pointing his finger at the plan of the warehouse.

"That's significant, Tom!" Deena replied, taking a sip of her gin and tonic.

"It is, and there's more from COCET. The UC who's purporting to be one of the 'Alphas', has agreed to meet one of the others in Bangkok, prior to onward travel. So, we have a chance to identify him . . ."

"How are we going to do that, meet him that is?" Sarah interrupted.

"I was thinking we either use Niall, or the RTP informant."

"Is Niall a UC?"

"No, he's not, which is why I favour the RTP to run that side of things. The only problem is, if the offender Harris was really here, he would have to access the room to make arrangements to meet up with the other 'Alpha' and then the Thai contact for onward travel. Dale is worried that they may see the incoming IP, and, if they do, that it's a UK one."

"Is there a technical solution?" Sarah asked quickly.

"Yes, we get Niall to do it in Bangkok but under instruction from Owen back home. Video it all. I'll authorise it and write up the rationale for it. Look at it as a proxy server, just a human one."

"Will this work, using a Thai to meet what will probably be a white middle-aged Western man?" Deena asked, with surprise in her voice.

"With the 'Alpha', yes. The meet can be short, in the open, strict instructions to stick to the script. I know it's not ideal. But what you have to remember is: nobody knows who's coming, where they're from or who they are. The 'Alpha' will have travelled, he's in a foreign country, makes contact through what he thinks is a secret, online group, behind a proxy. The last thing he will be thinking about will be UK cops."

"When you put it that way . . . sounds solid," Deena laughed, taking another sip.

"What will be your objective, or should I say, what will the RTP's objective be?" Sarah asked, giving Tom a sly wink that only he could see.

"I guess their objective will be to follow him off and identify him."

"Your explanation for using a Thai against the 'Alpha' stacks up. But what about the Thai end. You may have Thai against Thai: there must be some danger?"

"There's always danger in this type of work. I accept it will be a surprise, but I think we have an edge to help them over it."

"And what would that be?"

"The payment, they want 25,000 dollars US. That will help them see past any concern they have. And don't forget, they will not be suspecting UK cops and RTP even less."

"One problem with that plan, Tom, where the hell are you going to get the money from?" Sarah asked in an incredulous tone.

Tom paused, shuffled his feet, downed some beer, then sat down, not taking his eyes off Sarah.

Meanwhile Deena, who had got her phone out, took a large swallow of her drink, stood up and walked to the doorway of the adjoining second bedroom before turning back.

"Small or large denominations?"

"Twenty in large, as that's what you can bring in. The other five in twenties and fifties."

CHAPTER FIFTEEN

Phnom Penh Cambodia

As Major Pich sat down, his body language and stern demeanour provided the advance warning that all was not well.

"This report poses more questions than it answers. How've you come by this?" The Major demanded, addressing Tom.

Sarah glanced at Deena, who was showing no signs that etiquette had been broken by Pich addressing Tom first and ignoring her.

"Through online chat," Tom replied, as friendly and openly as he could.

"With who?"

"If we knew that, you would know. It's commonplace to use proxy servers to protect identities: especially when someone is committing this level of crime. They don't want police to trace them."

"We don't have this type of crime here. It must be other nationalities who are behind it, maybe Russians. We have intelligence of a Russian operating out of Sihanoukville. The story, though, has authenticity. I need to know more about this gang. What are their names?"

"We don't have that, and we won't be able to get it either."

Major Pich stared at Tom, who saw the suspicion in his eyes.

"I've tasked my undercover officers with trying to engage one of the suspects to lure him out from behind the proxy. Hopefully we will identify that person soon."

"Is he the one that's told you this story?"

"No, it's one of the others involved."

"Is he traceable?"

"Not at the moment."

"Yet he can tell you this story of a safe house being used by a child trafficking gang; local police involved; children taken off the streets of Phnom Penh and smuggled out of the country. You can see how that sounds and looks?" Major Pich said, slowly and deliberately, his command of English now very evident. Tom, though, had planned for it.

"This is how online undercover policing works. It's a game of cat and mouse. We don't know who they are. They don't know who we are. Sometimes to the very last minute."

"Without the address we can't do anything, so you must get it."

"I expect to. When we do, will you search the address?"

"I haven't got clearance yet. But I expect to by tomorrow. If you get the address, you will come with my team, the two you have already met, plus the interpreter. We will all go together."

"The gang have guns. Will you be taking any soldiers?"

"I don't believe that talk. Yes, there are some who have guns. But nobody is stupid enough to use them against the Immigration Police. I have a gun. We can take that. You, though, must get the address. Without that, we cannot do anything."

The Major stood up, nodded at Deena and Sarah, and left.

"All things considered, good outcome," Deena said, cheerfully.

"Do you believe him?" Sarah asked.

"Yes, I do. I have to leave for a meeting on the other side of town. I'll be back later this afternoon. We can discuss this further then. Will you be able to get an update from Niall on my return?"

"Yes," replied Tom.

It was 4pm by the time Deena and Chenda arrived back. Tom rang Sarah's room, to let her know they were back, and she let herself in with a second door pass.

"Who would like to go first?" Deena asked.

"I will," replied Tom. "Sarah and I have been doing a lot of talking whilst you've been gone. Sarah rightly has concerns about the level of risk around our knowledge of the fire power which the gang has access to. What do you think?"

"Guns are out there. The criminals have them. There are people who will use them. It was only a few weeks ago when one of the US mothers was dropping her kids off at school, and she was robbed at gunpoint. I've never heard of the Police being attacked or ambushed though."

"Is that just because they don't do proactive work here?"

"Yes, that will come into it. Some of it will be because they, the police, have been bribed. Some of it will be because of fear. So, I do get where the Major is coming from. At the same time, they don't know what we know. Do you have a plan?"

"Yes, I have two, although one of them relies on gaining intelligence at the right time."

"Go on."

Tom looked at Sarah before speaking.

"Plan one, is to stay the current course and just go there with the Major and his team and let it all unfold. Plan two, is to do the same but use intelligence from Sopheap's sister to tell us when most of Chakra's men are at her location, then go and search the address. It will mean coming up with a believable reason why we may have to suddenly hold off the search."

"Which do you favour?"

"I favour just going as the Major suggests. Sarah prefers waiting until Sopheap can provide intelligence to suggest there are fewer gang members present."

"The operational side is a matter for you, Tom. But I'm with Sarah: lessen the odds."

"OK, we'll go with plan two then. Shall I call Niall?"

"Yes, but before you do, I have the money. It will be available in Bangkok from 9am tomorrow. There are, however, some caveats. The money cannot be stolen, lost or go across. Otherwise, there will be hell to pay."

As the call was answered, they could immediately tell Niall was travelling in a car.

"Wait there a minute, Tom, we'll pull over."

As the background noise lessened, call clarity increased.

"Top of the afternoon to you, Tom," Niall said, his strong Irish accent evident.

"Hi Niall, I have Deena, Sarah and Chenda with me. Are you able to give us an update?"

"Sure am. This trip was really worth it. We stayed away from the address as you suggested, spending all our time deploying Coco, the RTP source, into the bars that were open. The male prostitute scene is run mainly by a white guy they all know as Brian. I think we can take it, that's Brian Kennedy. He has a male partner and lover who is a Thai, called Somsak. They have been working the scene here for a few years. Somsak is the enforcer. They're both ruthless and brutal. Brian now only wants very young boys or older boys who look very young. There is a rumour that Brian has been supplying very young children to foreigners who use his warehouse. That's it, nothing more."

"You did well. Is this to your ear?"

"Yes, I'm out of the car on my own."

"Can you call Dale when you get back to the hotel. I want you to be a human proxy for Owen. Are you alright with that?"

"Of course I am. He'll have to walk me through it, though, step by step. What's it for?"

"Phase one, we want you to arrange a meet with one of the other 'Alphas'; he's in Bangkok as well. He has concerns about being robbed and has already agreed to meet up to discuss mitigating that risk."

"You want me to meet him?"

"No, I'd love you to, but you know what our laws are. Can you broker a deal with the RTP? I'd like them to deploy their asset to meet him, then tail him off, house and identify him for us. That operational decision must be theirs though."

"I'm sure they would love to do it. I'll get it sorted. So, if that's phase one, what's phase two?"

"Two is a bit more complicated and requires more involvement from the RTP and their asset. First thing, though, is to be a proxy again, this time for the 'Alpha' that's arranging all this at your end.

Depending on what he says, will depend on what we ask of the RTP."

"Done. I'll call you back later tonight, hopefully with some good news."

"Before you go, can you find out if the RTP can use their SWAT team and, if they can, will they use them at Ban Mai Nong Sai."

"Will do."

"SWAT team?" Deena enquired, with a sly grin on her face.

"Just thinking ahead," Tom replied, innocently.

"Are you thinking about letting the children run into Thailand?" Sarah asked, surprised.

"If we can confirm that's their destination, then it's an option. In any case, we want Kennedy taken out. Mainly though, it's a backstop."

"I'll leave you two to thrash things out. I have somewhere I need to be. Chenda, contact Sopheap, we need him to be visiting his sister as much as possible over the next two to three days. We want his sister to keep a sharp eye on who is, and who isn't, there at all times please. In relation to Niall, it doesn't matter what time he calls, ring me."

MI5, Thames House, London, England

The Chief finished one last read of the update report from Maggie. Looking up, he could see they were stuck in traffic on Vauxhall Bridge.

"Is it an accident, Gerry?" The Chief asked his driver.

"No, Sir. Just weight of traffic. We'll get through this junction in another three or four sequences. You'll still be there on time."

The Chief checked his watch, got his phone out and rang Tom.

"Hi Tom, it's the Chief here. How're you and Sarah?"

"We're fine thanks, Sir. Sarah's here with me now."

"Send her my regards, please. I'm about to go into a meeting about Veritas. I have an update report from Maggie, but it's now 24 hours old. I guess you've been busy in the meantime. Can you bring me up to speed?"

"Yes, of course."

Tom outlined the meeting with Major Pich – not mentioning the request for him to be on the search – the action surrounding the warehouse, the plan for identifying the 'Alphas' and the proposed involvement of the RTP but minus the second stage of undercover activity, as they had not yet agreed to it.

"You have been busy. Thank you for that update. Is Deena happy with the way things are going?"

"Yes, I think she is. Her informant is protected, so she's happy."

"And the search?"

"Yes."

"Do you have everything you need there?"

Tom suddenly felt uneasy with the line of questions.

"Yes, Sir."

"Do you have PPE and first aid?"

"Some PPE. First aid is a brand-new set put together just for this trip. Has everything in it."

"Good to hear. I will await more reports as and when. Good evening to you both."

Gerry pulled up outside Thames House, where the Chief quickly got out, made his way through all the entry protocols for the UK's Secret Service, then waited for Toby to arrive.

"Good morning, James. We're all here. Follow me please."

Toby led the Chief upstairs, along a corridor to a large wooden door, which had a sign hanging on its handle which said, 'Do Not Disturb'. The Chief entered, to find a medium- sized conference room.

"May I present James Galloway, Chief Constable of Thames Valley Police."

The two occupants of the room stood up.

"Howdy, James. I'm Larry, pleased to meet you," Larry said, in what the Chief thought was a Texan accent.

"I'm Arthur, pleased to meet you too," said the other.

Both men sat down, whilst Toby positioned himself at the head of the table, leaving the Chief, with a choice of three seats opposite Larry and Arthur. He took the middle one.

"James, can we see the report from Superintendent Burrows?"

The Chief produced three copies, sliding them across the table. All three read the contents quickly.

"I've an update," Toby began. "One of my subjects hit a flag as he exited the country. Destination Thailand. He's currently in Bangkok. We were also unexpectedly presented with an opportunity yesterday and installed a keystroke logger on another subject's device. That proved positive, in that we have secured a password for a Hotmail account I think all my subjects have access to. They then use the draft folder to leave messages, ask questions, receive instructions, deleting them as necessary."

"I've had that before," Larry said, in a matter of fact tone of voice.

"James, do you have intelligence you can share that isn't in this report?" Toby enquired.

Yes, yes, I do," the Chief replied, who then read the notes from his earlier conversation with Tom.

"Wow, James. Thought you Brits had your hands tied behind your backs. This one's expendable, is he?"

The Chief did not blink, move or bristle at the comment. In his head, though, he really wanted to tell the American where to stick his words.

Toby interrupted quickly, sensing the building tension.

"Arthur, I believe you might have something for us?"

"Yes. We have a regional asset that has produced intelligence indicating a purchase of Russian mines destined for Cambodia—to protect a stronghold. As a result, we made a number of taskings, one to Larry and the US Embassy in Phnom Penh. They have supplied us with satellite intelligence which we have analysed. Your report now confirms that these mines are deployed at the safe house you intend on getting the Cambodian Police to search."

"You need to send in the SAS, James," Larry quipped.

"That's one plan, however, there is another."

"What's that, Arthur?" The Chief asked, ignoring Larry.

"We assess that the mines have been laid in two areas. Those two areas can be avoided quite easily. But it does mean you will need to stick to the driveway and courtyard. Don't venture further out. We are prepared to provide you with a short window of intelligence that could tell you when the best time to undertake the search . . ."

"That comes courtesy of us, James. Just so you know," Larry

interrupted.

This time it was Arthur's turn to ignore Larry.

"You will be able to use it to corroborate what you are getting from sources on the ground."

"Thank you. That will be most helpful."

"There is one stipulation, though, as there always is with these things. I understand you are working with the Canadian Ambassador. Is that right?"

"Yes, we are. She will not be anywhere near the search though. I can assure you of that."

"That doesn't matter. She has to be sighted on this and straight away."

The Chief was thinking about the ramifications of briefing Deena in, but not his own man, when Larry spoke his thoughts for him and the room.

"Tough job, leaving a man out there in the cold."

"If you knew the officer, you would know he can look out for himself. We have the one and only opportunity to bust open a rumour that has dogged me and previous chiefs for at least 25 years. I simply have to take it. And, contrary to what you might think, Larry, I won't be leaving a man behind.

Toby, who had let the exchange go too far already, decided it was time to intervene.

"I think we can move forward and formalise some actions for the next 24 to 36 hours at least. Arthur, you will provide me with intelligence that I will pass to James: is that agreed?"

"Yes."

"James, you will brief the Ambassador today and let me know how the undercover operation develops. Also, I will need to know who you intend to arrest and when."

"Agreed."

"I'll be liaising with the Met's Special Branch to arrange for my subjects to be arrested and interviewed. I'll need to wait for the Thailand side of things to develop, before being able to make plans there. I'll brief your Professional Standards, James. Are we all in agreement?"

Phnom Penh, Cambodia

Tom had just finished dressing for dinner, when he received a text from Maggie. He opened his laptop and dialled her.

"Hi, Tom. The Chief wants a report on where you are at the moment."

Tom looked over the screen to Sarah, who gave him a perplexed look. He was about to speak when his gut told him not to.

"I'm just about to go for dinner. Will a written one be OK, when I get back in?"

"Yes, fine. Just don't forget."

"I won't."

Tom shut the laptop, feeling his stomach begin to churn as he did so.

"That's odd, that's very odd. Are you alright?"

"That's unsettled me."

"What are you going to do about it?"

"Not sure."

"You have to speak to the Chief."

"I don't think I've even got his number. Maybe I should just ring Stuart."

"He will only have to ring the Chief."

"I have his number," Sarah replied, studying Tom's demeanour before dialling the number herself, handing the phone over when she heard the Chief's voice.

"Sir, it's Tom again."

"Hello, Tom, what can I do for you?"

"Sir, I need to be up front here: I've just had a call from Maggie saying you want an update report from me. Is that correct?"

"No, it's not. What did you say?"

"I said I'd provide a written one later."

"Provide nothing more than you told her last time. Understood?"

"Yes, Sir."

"And don't breathe a word to anybody about this. Nobody. Got that?"

"Yes, Sir."

"Until you hear from me again, don't call or take a call from Maggie.

If you get any updates tonight or tomorrow, I want them immediately. You report to me until I tell you otherwise. I want it all by email. Text me when you send it."

"Sir, you have me worried."

"Don't be. Just do your job and do what I tell you."

Tom looked at Sarah, who had a look of bewilderment on her face.

"Did you hear all that?"

"Yes, I did. I guess that gets you off the hook. I think I need a cocktail before we go out, just to get my appetite back. Are you buying?"

Oxfordshire, England

The Chief sat stony-faced in the back of his car as it sped along the M4 motorway. Maggie could just be thinking ahead. That must be the case he told himself. Time would tell. Just the thought of it made him feel sick. This was exactly why he was doing what he was doing. This had to stop. The buck had to stop with him. He would ring Stuart. Now, though, he had to get hold of Deena.

"You're speaking to Deena Potts, Canadian Ambassador to the Kingdom of Cambodia."

"Deena, it's James Galloway are you able to speak?"

"Yes, I am."

"Can you take intelligence over your mobile that's classified as secret?"

"No, for that I'll have to call you back. Shall I do that?"

"Yes, please."

Moments later his phone rang.

"Nice to hear from you. How can I help?"

"I need to brief you in on a parallel operation to the one you're working on. In short, there's a Security Service operation running in tandem to what you are doing with Tom. It has long been suspected that ministers, senior level civil servants and police have been operating clandestinely for a great many years, working together for promotion, monetary favours, sexual favours and in some cases even children.

"Their reach is believed to be huge and run deep into many state departments and functions. Freemasonry has played a role, though to what extent nobody really knows. Every police force in the country is possibly involved to some degree, mine included. I was approached by our Home Secretary to be the one to work with the Security Service on it.

"Veritas is part of that. We believe that one of the 'Alphas', the one in Bangkok, is possibly a senior civil servant. I guess we will find out tonight. When you search the address and make arrests, it will trigger a large number of arrests throughout the UK. Some will be from Thames Valley Police.

"I have received good intelligence to suggest that the safe house has been booby-trapped with trip mines. The same intelligence, though, says the safe areas are the driveway and courtyard. The mines are all outside that area. The security agencies involved have cleared you to be sighted on it."

Deena decided not to let on that she had suspected Security Service involvement.

"Well, well. Does Tom know?"

"No, and he mustn't. There are good reasons for it."

"What about Sarah?"

"She doesn't know either. That is why she is there. This will make the front page for a number of days."

"I did wonder about the mix. Makes sense now though. OK, well thanks for briefing me in. Now that you have, if anything changes, I will need to know about it."

"Agreed."

"As for Tom, you do know there is no way he cannot go on the search? They simply won't do it without him."

"Yes, I do know that. That is why he was picked. I knew all along he would go."

"How do you want me to play the presence of the mines?"

"I haven't got a clue. I was hoping you would think of something."

Phnom Penh, Cambodia

Tom and Sarah were back at the hotel, full, yet exhausted from discussing the call from Maggie and the Chief. Neither of them was ready for bed. They ordered drinks and sat outside, staring out at the mighty Mekong.

Tom was enjoying the heat, sights, sounds and the occasional scent of Sarah's perfume. Whatever it was that she wore, he found it intoxicating. His enjoyment was abruptly broken—by his phone.

"Tom, it's Niall."

"How did it go?"

"Like a charm. Coco the informant had to fight him off, he was that keen. I'm sending you his details now. He's a Brit."

"How about the second part?"

"Did that. The meet is Thursday afternoon. All three, plus the fixer, are travelling in one vehicle. The RTP are prepared to use Coco again, but we have a problem. Money has to change hands at the meet. Coco will then be taken for the meal. The restaurant is an overnight stay, back the next day. The 25-dollar meal is 25 thousand. The RTP want to know how you propose they get around that?"

"I have the money. It can be collected from 9am tomorrow. I'm going to need to sleep on it though."

"Second thoughts?"

"Sort of. How will the RTP follow them?"

"They won't. They are looking for Coco to text them where they are. They're thinking it will be the warehouse, so they will have a team, ahead and waiting."

"I'm just a little uneasy. Worried, I guess. I think if we know where the meet is, they can cover that, pick up the car, get the details, pass it to the team who is ahead and just go from there."

"That does lessen the risk on Coco. The problem is not turning up may spook them. They may then change plans, go elsewhere, change vehicles, even call it off."

"The other issue is, the money cannot go across."

"We'll get it back."

"Famous last words. Money may go straight to another and off the plot."

"Fair point. How about a flash of the cash? Let them count it. Then refuse to hand it over: payment on delivery."

"The deal has always been money up front. I get what you're saying; it would be done like that back home. At home, though, we would have an operational team as back up, full surveillance, tracker, phones hooked up. Give me the night to sleep on it. SWAT team: what's the go there?"

"Yes, they're available. Plans are being made on that front."

"Speak in the morning, Niall. Well done."

"You get that?"

"Yes. You normally push the envelope on the UC front, why not this one?"

"Today's call from Maggie, and then the Chief, it's unnerved me. I guess it's a bit like your call with the search. Lesson the odds."

"Best you call Deena. Are you going to tell her about your concerns over the call?"

"No, she'll think I'm going all soft and anxious. It'll probably just turn out to be nothing, just as we discussed."

Tom rang Deena, outlining what Niall had told him.

"The money can't go across, Tom, that's the deal."

"I know. I just need to work it out in my head. Make sure I'm not missing something."

"That's good practice. For us, though, it seems like we should be undertaking that search on Thursday morning. Which means we should be in Battambang tomorrow night for an early start the next day."

"Agreed. So, I provide another intel log tomorrow morning with the address on it; you call a meet with the Major; we ascertain if he has permission; if he has, we hand over the address and travel to Battambang."

"Yes. Sarah and I will travel to Battambang with you. You can then go on the search with the Major and his team."

"Sounds like a plan."

"It does. Speak in the morning. Goodnight, Tom."

Sarah swallowed the last of her drink.

"I guess you have some emails to write before bed. Two big days ahead. You go up and get started. I'll get us two refills, meet you up there."

Oxfordshire, England

"Stuart, it's the Chief. Can you speak?"

"Yes, Sir."

"What's in our Crown Jewels for Maggie Burrows?"

"Nothing. She's even had a stint on here."

"Would she have seen everything whilst there?"

"Yes, and she was on here when there were strong rumours about the cabal. Why do you ask?"

"She has asked Tom Ross for a report in my name, when I hadn't asked for it."

"About Veritas?"

"Yes."

"Has there been opportunity for her to provide you with his report?"

"Not yet, it was a short while ago, Tom won't have sent it yet."

"We'd better wait a few hours. If she hasn't done anything with it by the end of the day, then . . ."

"I know Stuart. It's unthinkable. Are you sure there's nothing there?"

"The only thing I can recall is, in her early years, there were a few sex scandals around her. Nothing on our database about it though. I personally always thought she had something going with James King. That's not written down anywhere either. But, since I read the intelligence from Box, I guess I should have thought about it. Sorry I didn't mention that earlier."

"What made you think that at the time?"

"Just the way they were around each other. There was just something there."

"Did it last long?"

"Yes, right up until James retired."

"Alright. Let us hope it's just something and nothing."

"It's not nothing, Sir. She asked for a report in your name, when you hadn't asked for one."

Phnom Penh, Cambodia

Back in his room, Tom opened his laptop, wrote an update report containing nothing new, attached it to an email and sent it to Maggie Burrows. He then checked his inbox. Seeing the message from Niall, he read it, copied the details of the 'Alpha' into a fresh email and sent it to the Chief along with Maggie's update report. He was texting him, when Sarah arrived with the second round of nightcaps.

Moments later the Chief received Tom's text. He opened his Blackberry, found the email and read the contents. He dialled Toby immediately.

"This can't wait. I won't be discussing product. You OK with that?"

"Yes. If this is about Larry, he's like that with everyone."

"No, it's not, although the man's a dick. This is far more serious. I have just found out the identity of one of the 'Alphas.' I'm forwarding the details to you now. Tell me when it arrives."

The Chief looked out of his car window, watching the traffic speed past him as it headed into London. The clock was now ticking. Whatever happened from here on in would probably define his tenure as Chief.

"It's here. I'm opening it now. Well, well! That 'Alpha' is my senior civil servant suspect. This is indeed excellent news, James. What a start! Thank your staff for me. When the time is right, of course. I know Arthur and Larry are still in the building, I'll pass it on to them. Bye for now . . ."

"Hang on. I'm not finished. You may wish to temper your enthusiasm with a possibility of compromise."

"What on earth do you mean?" Toby replied, his tone changing in an instant from one of elation to one of anger and fear."

"Maggie Burrows. She may be working for the opposing team!"

CHAPTER SIXTEEN

Professional Standards units are relative in size to the constabulary. They are small, reflecting the fact that the vast majority of police are honest, trustworthy and above reproach. This, however, is their Achilles heel. When police officers are truly corrupt, the same departments do not have the capability to investigate. Instead, they employ omnicompetent detectives who normally police organised crime. This has one critical advantage: corrupt cops are normally involved with other serious crime groups. Catch one of them, and they will hand the cop over in exchange for a deal.

—I. R. Tyler

Phnom Penh, Cambodia

Tom and Sarah were in the hotel lobby, waiting for Deena to arrive.

"How do I look?"

"How'd you mean?"

"Do I look worried?"

"No. You do look tired though. As if you have been up half the night. Here's Deena coming now, and the Major's right behind her. You'd better snap out of it."

It was all he could do to muster a smile.

The Major, ignoring formalities again, sat down, whilst casting a brief look towards Deena, before resting his gaze on Tom.

"Good morning, Major. Are you allowed to search the address?"

"If you have the address, yes."

Tom produced the additional intelligence document, handing it over.

"This is the address we have. This is how it was relayed to us," Tom replied.

The Major took the document and quickly read it.

"The address means nothing to me. It looks real. I can check it exists when we get there. OK, this is what we're going to do. We will all travel to Battambang this afternoon. You can stay in your hotel; my team and I will stay in ours. We can meet up for dinner and talk over plans for the next day. In the morning Tom, my team, and I, will go to the address. Then we will see what is going on there."

"Is this an early morning visit to catch them off guard?" Tom asked, trying to hide his real reason for asking.

"No, we can't do those things here. We will eat breakfast at eight, and then all meet up after that. That's early enough."

"What about the suggestion of firearms?" Deena enquired politely. "Do you still feel the same way on that?"

"Yes. This is just talk. We won't have a problem. Now, I must go. I have other things to do before I get my team together. It's a long drive to Battambang. Ambassador, please call me when you arrive."

With the Major gone, they reassembled in Tom's room, Chenda joining them.

"Can I suggest, Tom, that you deal with all things operational, both here and Thailand, and I'll manage the informant."

"Agreed. Tonight's dinner then. We should keep that as short as possible. Any side talk or questions involving this operation, we just stick to our story. We need updates over the course of today from Sopheap. I don't know how he's going to manage it, but we really need one, last thing at night, and again first thing in the morning. No later than eight."

"Chenda, ring Sopheap now, please. Tell him what we need from him and Nuon. Make sure he has enough credit and charge on his phone and that he remains in signal range at all times. Use the other room."

"Yes, Deena."

"Go on, Tom," Deena said, as Chenda disappeared into the other bedroom to make the call.

"Plan A is most of Chakra and his gang are at home. I'll go with the Major and his team, enter the safe house and see who and what's there. At that point it will just unfold, and we'll deal with it as it does. Plan B is we have to stall because intelligence suggests too many gang members are not at Nuon's and therefore could be at the safe house."

"How are you going to stall?" Sarah asked.

"During the dinner I'll sow a seed that I've asked the undercover officers to be online over the period of the search. Bit before and a bit after. If the intel in the morning is that the gang are all out, I'll say that intelligence suggests we do not undertake the search because we believe there's nobody there."

"What happens if the intel changes en route?" Deena asked with concern.

"We just have to hope that doesn't happen. If it does, we just roll with it."

There was silence between them as Tom's words sank in. The silence was broken by the arrival of Chenda.

"He's going over there after lunch and will stay as long as he can. He says he can't go back tomorrow morning before 8am. Any earlier, and Chakra will start asking questions."

"That's probably good enough, Tom. By the time they have eaten breakfast and we all meet up, it will be after nine by the time you get there."

"Once there then," Tom sighed, "hopefully we find the kidnapped children and Michael. At that point the Major will have to make arrests. We stick with him, provide as much assistance as we can. Just deal with it as happens. Could be a long few days."

"Where will we base ourselves? I'm going to need access to phone and internet," Sarah asked.

"I'd imagine the Major and his team will check out after breakfast. We won't. I'll arrange for a late checkout. If necessary, I'll pay for another night so we can leave when we want. I think the Major will want to take any prisoners back to Phnom Penh, because that's where the offences occurred. Where we're staying in Battambang you will get good coverage. We should also keep our rooms here though. If necessary, Chenda can bring you back if the connection breaks down there," Deena replied.

"That's it for here. Any questions?"

"Yes. What are you going to do if firearms are produced?" Sarah asked. Her tone carrying a sense of urgency.

"I won't be leading from the front. This is the Major's show. It's his turf. He will also have a gun, and don't forget who they actually are and that this is Cambodia. It's the Major's finding that having a gun and using it against them are two entirely different things. We have to believe that."

Sarah didn't respond, instead letting her look make it clear what she was really thinking.

The situation wasn't lost on Deena, and she seized the opportunity she had been seeking.

"There is one other thing you should bear in mind, Tom. The area between Battambang and Poipet was heavily mined during the war. Extensive demining work has been undertaken and still is, on an almost daily basis, by many organisations including HALO who have been doing it since the early 1990s. The area around the safe house could easily have mines in the ground. You must stick to the driveway, any courtyard, or hard-surfaced areas. Do not venture from that under any circumstances. Do you understand?"

"Hadn't thought of that. Good thinking."

"Also, do you have a first aid kit?"

"Yes."

"Good. I take it you know how to use it?"

"I had my annual refresher before I left to come here!"

"Thailand then."

Tom dialled Niall, placing the phone on the coffee table with the speaker switched on.

"Top of the morning to yer, Tom. Have you come to a decision, because I could do with knowing what that is!"

"Yes, I have. Can you suggest to the RTP that they don't deploy Coco? Ask them to deploy one team to cover the meet; get as much evidence of that, car numbers, photos, video that sort of thing. If they can perform a small follow, just enough that would place the vehicle en route to Ban Mai Nong Sai, that would be great. Then get a second team to pick the car up as it approaches the town. From there we need to know where it goes, what it does. Then remain on standby to either make arrests or use the SWAT team at the warehouse."

"Done. The meet is this afternoon. If I'm in a position to watch it, which I'm told I should be, I'll call you. Speak soon."

Tom clarified the plan for Thailand.

"First of all, I'm assuming that Thailand is linked to Veritas. The warehouse gets hit by the SWAT team no matter what we find at the safe house here. That way, if we've missed any children, we get another chance to rescue them further down the pipeline. If it's not linked, then the warehouse gets raided anyway, due to the infiltration that we are currently undertaking at COCET. Plus, the RTP should know where the 'Alphas' are so they can make an arrest."

"Sounds good. In that case, get yourself packed. Enough for a couple of nights at least. Chenda will collect you at 2pm."

Tom, Deena, Sarah and Chenda had been travelling for about 35 minutes when Tom received a call from Niall. He switched on the speaker, turned the volume up to maximum and leaned forward, holding the phone flat on the central console. They overheard Thai voices in the background before Niall spoke.

"Two white males, both carrying holdalls have just arrived at the location. One of them is the UK civil servant we know about. The other is about 50 years old. I would say, by the looks of it, they know each other or have met before. They are deep in conversation. A white Toyota, what looks like an Estima, has pulled up. It has blacked out windows. A dark-skinned male has just got out and walked over to the pair . . ."

Tom heard a male voice in the background say something.

"That person is a Thai, I've just been told," Niall said, continuing with his observations. "All three are in conversation. The driver of the Estima is looking all around. He has checked his watch, now beckoning the white males towards the car. They are all getting into the rear through the sliding side door; the door has closed behind them. Are you getting all this?"

"Yes, loud and clear, Niall. Have the RTP got anybody on the ground, to see what's going on inside the car?"

"They do have some, but it's only to ensure they get the registration plate and good video footage of them. Where are you?"

"On our way to Battambang."

"The side door is opening. The Thai has come out and is looking all around again. He's clearly looking for Coco. He's going back to the side door and looking into the car. He is having a conversation with whoever is in there. Looks like the conversation is getting a bit heated. The Thai is gesticulating with his arms towards the inside of the car and now behind him where the two white males first met up. You still getting all this?"

"Yes," replied Tom.

"The Thai is using his mobile phone, walking away from the car a bit as he does so. Looks like he is having a conversation. He's gesticulating with his arms again. It appears he's not happy. Moment of truth fast approaching Tom!"

"I know. He's reacting as he should."

"Call's finished. Back to the car. He's closed the side door and making his way around to the driver's door. He's in. Car moving off. It's away and out of my sight."

"What happens now?" Tom asked, excitement clear in his voice.

"We're bugging out of here quickly. I'll call you once we know what route he's on."

Forty minutes later Tom's phone rang again.

"Go ahead, Niall, you're on speaker."

"He's en route for Ban Mai Nong Sai. We are following some distance behind now, can't see the car anymore. Our plan is to close the gap occasionally, just enough to make contact before slipping back out of sight again. The team ahead have been alerted. We will close right up as we approach them.

"The RTP tell me that the car has registration plates that were issued from the district covering Ban Mai Nong Sai. They are currently doing some checks on the car, but they are already saying they believe the details held will be false. They believe that the car was previously written off two years ago."

"How long will it take you to get there?"

"It was over four hours last time."

"We should be at Battambang by then or near it. When you call, make sure I can speak."

Thames Valley Police HQ, Kidlington, England

"Come in, Stuart. Shut the door please," the distress in his tone immediately apparent.

"How the bloody hell did we get ourselves into this mess?"

"This mess began long before us, Sir. I am assuming you haven't seen anything from Maggie?"

"No, I haven't. But then that's hardly surprising. She doesn't know anything more than I currently know. I told Tom not to let her have anything new."

"What's happening on that front. Are you able to tell me?"

"Yes, I got you clearance. Toby rang me last night, wants you read into everything. He wants Maggie arrested and kept incommunicado until after the search and arrests in Cambodia and Thailand. He's got one of his targets out there, wants him caught red-handed to turn the screws; get him to spill the beans on the rest."

"What have you told him?"

"I told him I'd get back to him, once I'd had a chance to speak to you."

"Delaying a phone call is one thing. Incommunicado is another. However, this doesn't get much more serious than this, so I guess we can do it."

"How about arresting her?" The Chief enquired, lifting his eyebrows.

"As you know, we've been building our arrest plans as we've gone along. I wasn't expecting to add Maggie to the list though. I would prefer that we waited at least 24 hours to see if she steps forward with some sort of report for you. Something that might explain all this."

"I would as well. The fact is, we simply don't have that time. The very most I can give you is four hours."

"What about putting it to her, to see what her response is?"

"Thought through that with Toby. Too risky. We either arrest her, or we don't."

"And if we don't?"

"I'm due to see the Minister and probably the Home Sec this afternoon. No prizes for guessing how that will turn out!"

"What about the rest of them?"

"Not until the coordinated strike. Maggie is the one that can compromise all of this. She's the one that has to be neutralised. That way, the rest of the operation can proceed as planned."

"In that case, there's really only one option available to us. Maggie Burrows will be arrested at midday today."

"Correct."

CHAPTER SEVENTEEN

Battambang, Cambodia

Tom had just settled into his hotel room at Battambang, when Niall rang. He could tell by the sound of the call that Niall was in a car and travelling at speed.

"Can you speak?"

"Yes."

"We're about 20 minutes from the outskirts of Ban Mai. We just caught up with them. The team ahead have been alerted. There's a major junction in about ten minutes. They're going to take over the follow there."

Tom heard a knock at his door.

"Hang on a sec."

Tom went to the door and let Sarah in.

"I'm back. OK, once the other team have taken up the follow, follow their car, and then call me. I'll get the team together."

"Going well?" Sarah enquired.

"Yes. So far anyway."

"Have you heard back from Maggie or the Chief?"

"No. I have to update the Chief though, but I won't be doing that until what's going on in Thailand becomes clear."

"Do you want me to get the others?"

"Yes please. Tell them to shower and change before coming here though. We're going to be tight on time."

"Will do. I'll shower and change here if that's OK?"

"Sure. I'll jump in now, so it's free for you."

Showered and dressed for dinner, Tom answered the door to Deena and Chenda. As Chenda walked by the closed bathroom door she could hear the shower running. She looked at Tom, noticing he was wearing fresh clothes, looking refreshed.

"Where's Sarah?" Chenda asked, with a smirk on her face, her eyes widening as the sound of the running shower suddenly went silent.

"We're stuck for time, Chenda." replied Tom.

"I believe you, Tom. Absolutely, for sure."

"Don't be so cheeky, Chenda," Deena said, with all seriousness, then burst out laughing.

The bathroom door suddenly opened. Sarah walked out in a three-quarter length pastel blue linen dress. She passed by Tom – who caught her perfume again – sitting next to Chenda on one of the sofas.

"You look beautiful, Sarah!" Chenda said in admiration.

Tom looked at Sarah and started to feel a bit awkward.

"Let's ring Niall shall we . . ." Tom began, just as his phone rang.

"Tom, can you speak?"

"Yes, go ahead."

"We've handed over. Went smooth as Thai silk. We're heading into Ban Mai now."

"Did the vehicle have any stops en route?"

"No. Just giving you the heads up: RTP have said that once this car goes to ground they will be knocking off for the night. We're paying for their lodgings, food, fuel and that of the SWAT team."

Tom looked at Deena who just shrugged her shoulders.

"There's very little difference between here and there, Tom. If you want them to do anything, you'll have to pay for it. You can't go all British high and mighty when you work out here. You won't get things done."

"Well, considering I'm personally breaking enough rules to get me sacked or demoted back to constable, a bit of local graft is just a drop in the ocean, I guess."

Sarah gave Tom a small wink as she continued to towel dry her hair.

"You got the company card?"

"I sure do, I know how to use it as well. I'm going to have to hand over some cash though. Luckily, I've brought plenty, having learnt from my last trip. At some point in the future, Interpol will ask TVP to pay them back. I'll have to tell them you authorised it."

"Authorised. You have three witnesses here. What's going on?"

"We're on the outskirts of Ban Mai now. Wait a minute, something's up. I'll call you back."

A few minutes later Niall rang back.

"He pulled over and got in the back. We don't know what for, but he's back in the driver's seat and off again. It's dark, Tom, we're all bunched up, too tight really. Hopefully the driver won't be looking for cars following him."

Deena's phone beeped as a text came through.

"That's the Major. They're all at the restaurant. Wants to know how long we'll be."

"Hang on a sec, Niall. How far is it?"

"Five minutes."

"Tell him 15," Tom replied, giving Chenda a small nod.

"Only works in Phnom Penh, Tom."

"Of course it does!"

"OK. Go ahead Niall."

"We're headed in the general direction of the border. Just thinking, what are we going to do if it heads over the border. Are we going after it?"

"Can't ask the RTP to do that, even if they wanted to. You'll just have to let it run."

"We're almost at a junction for the road that leads to another road for the warehouse. Nearside indicator on the RTP car that we're following. They're turning left onto that road. We're now on it as well. This will lead us to the road that the warehouse is off. We will be at that junction soon. I think I can see it ahead now. It's dark. but I'm sure that's it. Yes, were at it. I can see the Estima one car in front of us. It's turned left towards the warehouse. First RTP car has done the same. We're holding back for a moment, give them a bit of room. OK, we've turned left. I know the turn off for the warehouse, they will be at it any moment—yes, the Estima has turned right. The following car has gone straight past. We're about to drive by. I can see brake lights on the vehicle right at the end of the track!"

A simultaneous cheer went up in the hotel room at Battambang.

"Great work, Niall. Tell the team 'well done' from all of us here. What I'd like is the SWAT team and you guys to be ready from about 8.30 and not to do anything until we have gone in here."

"No problems, we'll be ready by 7.30 anyway because of the SWAT team. We've had to stay well away from here, just so we don't start the jungle drums. Best of luck in the morning. I'll await your call."

"That's fantastic, Tom!" Deena said, as the call ended.

"Yeah, absolutely for sure. I was right there with them in the car!" said Chenda.

"Love it, when things go right!" Sarah said, nudging Chenda next to her.

"Right. I need to quickly update the Chief with a short email, then a text, then dinner!"

Ban Mai Nong Sai, Thailand

Umar checked the false compartment in the rear of the Landcruiser. Satisfied that everything was as it should be, he collected his overnight bag, placing it in the front passenger seat footwell.

"You ready to go?" Chet asked.

"Yep, I'm off."

"Try not to kill him on the way back!" Chet said, mischievously.

"Can't promise anything on that front. I'll be glad when this run is over. With his operation so close to where we live, I want some space between us."

"I'll have breakfast ready when you get here. This time tomorrow, it will all be over!"

Umar started the engine, gave Chet a thumbs up before driving off for Anlong Run and the safe house.

Battambang, Cambodia

They arrived back from dinner, assembling in Deena's room, as it was the largest. Chenda made tea for them all.

"We should debrief tonight," Deena began, "just to make sure we all know what was said and how they reacted. I'll start. It was clear right from the start that they were each given someone to concentrate on. I was the Major's. He was perfectly polite and very capable of interacting at my level over dinner. He never once dried up or went anywhere that made me feel uncomfortable. My view is that he is destined for one of the top jobs. Narith Pich is the real deal. How he will react tomorrow if it all goes sideways, who knows? Tom?"

"I got Captain Chey Leap. His English is about as good as my Khmer; which is non-existent. Their interpreter was sandwiched between the Captain and the Lieutenant who had to cover the conversations between me and Sarah. Chey spent most of the evening trying to convince me to go to a karaoke tonight. That was pretty much it. He appeared disappointed that I wouldn't go."

"If you had gone, all of them would have gone. It would have been Black Label, beer and prostitutes. That's Leap's job, try to compromise you should they ever need it. Sarah?"

"Samlain wasn't very communicative. He giggled a lot. Kept touching me. Asked a few personal questions. Did I have a boyfriend? What car I drove? Briefly touched on my communications role. When I described it, I got the impression he didn't really understand. That's it."

"Chenda?"

"Nothing. Nobody said a word to me. Beef steak was good though."

"In that case, I think we handled that well. Early night for us all. Before we do though, Chenda?"

"For sure, Deena."

Chenda rang Sopheap, placing the phone in the centre so everybody could hear. Chenda spoke first, in case Sopheap was near Chakra or one of his men. She ended the call after a single exchange in Khmer.

"He will leave and call us when he gets away."

After a few minutes the phone rang.

Chenda again spoke first, then nodded at Deena.

"Sopheap, how are you?"

"I'm working very hard putting my life at very great risk, Bong Srei.

I trust you will remember this, when the time comes."

Chenda shook her head, tutting.

"I will remember, Sopheap. What do you have for us?"

"Everybody is here, but two are missing?"

"Do you know who, or why?"

"I know who, but not why, Bong Srei."

"Would you like to tell me who then?"

"Yes, of course. It's his two most trusted men. Keo and Utey."

"So, except these two, were they all there throughout the day?"

"No, they were all away most of the afternoon. When they came back, Keo and Utey were not with them. They have all eaten and most are asleep already. Nuon overheard Chakra telling them there was to be no drinking tonight. This is all we know. I will be back there in the morning at 8am."

Deena looked at Tom questioningly.

"Sopheap, Tom here. Do they have their weapons with them?"

"Yes."

Tom looked at Deena, shaking his head slightly from side to side.

"Thank you, Sopheap. We must have that update from you at 8am. You must ring Chenda. We will not be ringing you. You cannot be late. Do you understand?"

"Yes, Bong Srei. I will speak to Chenda, my favourite woman at 8am."

Once the call had ended, Chenda muttered something in Khmer under her breath.

Deena stood up, flattening her dress.

"Everybody to bed. Breakfast in the restaurant at 7.00am."

Home Office, London, England

The Chief was on his way to London, when Stuart Simmons rang him.

"Go ahead, Stuart."

"Have you heard from Maggie, Sir?"

"No."

"Right, well, she's gone sick today. I'm sending a team to her address now. I've secured an unused custody block just inside the Met.

They're providing vetted staff for the duration. I've briefed the area commander."

"I know the Commissioner personally; I will call and thank him."

"Thank you, that will oil things. I'll update you once she's been booked in."

"I have an update for you. The Thai end has gone well. Toby's man has been taken to a warehouse we identified through COCET. Tom is ready to search the safe house tomorrow morning their time. There's no going back now. God help us."

As the Chief's car entered Marsham Street, Stuart rang.

"We found her at home. She didn't appear sick. She's been booked in. She was very calm, never questioned a thing. Requested her phone call, which was denied, then requested a solicitor, which was also denied. I've heard at that point, she became distressed. The search team are still at the address and will be there for a while."

"Anybody with her?"

"Yes."

"Who?"

"James King."

"Oh, fuck!"

"I said something similar."

"What've you done?"

"We had no option. We arrested him as well. It's a day or two early, but it presents us with a ticking time bomb . . ."

"You're not wrong there," the Chief said, interrupting. "Have you got a plan?"

"Yes."

"What is it?"

"With Maggie, it's pretty straightforward. She went sick, so that gives us 24 to 48 hours, which will be enough. Any calls about her through our normal channels, we'll get them and act accordingly to protect the operation. James King is where the real problem lies. We had a plan for Jane, but that was for when everybody was arrested and there was no need for secrecy. Now, we have two options. Neither is great, for differing reasons."

"Give me number one."

"James King's wife will sound the alert once he doesn't come home. She will ring Jane, then report him missing. As an adult, not at risk, we can manage that for 48 hours. The problem is we're misleading them."

"Don't like that one. Number two?"

"We inform Jane. Get her to attend the search to help the mother. Brief her, swear her to secrecy. Stand her down, manage her until we get past the next 24 to 36 hours. She will have to be formally instructed not to contact Tom until after the searches."

"Go with that one, but don't stand her down. Call me if you need me to speak to her."

"Yes, Sir."

The Chief got out and made his way to the Minister's office.

"Hello, Ayesha. Is he on time?"

"Hello, James, lovely to see you. Yes, he is. They're waiting for you. Go straight in."

"They?"

"The Home Secretary and Toby."

As the Chief walked in, he thought to himself, 'At the end of this, I'm never working with the spooks ever again.'

"James, thank you for coming!" Patrick Hall, the Minister for Security announced. "Please, take a seat."

The Chief nodded. "Good afternoon Minister, Madam Secretary, Toby!" The Chief let his stare linger on Toby just long enough to let him know how he felt. It was a slight, deft movement, but one not lost on the Minister.

"I was having my own meeting with Toby and asked him to stay on for this one. Hope you don't mind, James."

"Not at all," The Chief replied, through gritted teeth, taking a seat.

"I'm here, James, because I understand Operation Phobos is about to come to a head. I've been kept up to speed over the duration by Patrick and Toby. I thought it best we all got together before the storm. I'll be getting questions on it in Parliament, no doubt. So, Patrick, take it away," Rachel Abrams, the Home Secretary said.

"Toby, you first please."

"Home Secretary, Minister, James, you all have my report. Phobos, as you know, is the forerunner for other such operations in the future. Their success, or indeed even existence, will probably rest on the success or perceived success of Phobos. From my side, Special Branch will be making eleven arrests following action in both Cambodia and Thailand. As you know, this will entail the arrest of some senior civil servants and politicians. There's currently an undersecretary in Thailand. I'll release a joint statement with James. James will represent us when he fronts the media."

"James?"

"You have my briefing report. The head of COCET will be searching a safe house in Cambodia tomorrow. He'll be overseeing a raid on a warehouse in Thailand where we believe the undersecretary to be. I have a corporate communications officer out there who'll work jointly with Toby's staff. We've had to make an early arrest. Are you aware of that?"

The Home Secretary and Patrick nodded, in confirmation.

"That arrest was made just before I got here. What you won't know is: the officer arrested was with James King who was due to be arrested on Phobos. As you know, he's a retired officer and the father of Jane King who works on COCET."

The Chief glanced at Toby, who gave no reaction to the news.

"We have a plan to ensure there's no compromise to the ongoing operation. We will undertake joint action with the Security Service and will make a further three arrests. I will put out our joint statement and then do a press interview once we're ready."

"And you are 100 percent certain you can contain those two arrests?" the Minister asked slowly, with a hint of warning.

"Yes," replied the Chief, meeting the Minister's gaze.

"I understand you're working with a Canadian ambassador. Is that right, James?" Rachel Abrams asked.

"Yes, we are."

"I'd like to confirm she's been fully briefed on the level of danger in this search. By that I mean, she is fully aware of the extent of firearms and mines at the Cambodian safe house?"

"Yes, she has. It was her informant that provided the intelligence for the firearms and I personally briefed her on the mines. She will not be at the safe house, nor anywhere near it. Nor will the communications officer."

"Good. I don't fancy an awkward call with the Secretary of State for Canada—one where I have to tell him his Ambassador is dead due to a botched UK Police operation. Will we be including them in our press statements?"

"Yes, our communication officer will ensure that."

"Good—that leads me to your staff. Just so we are all clear here, it's been your decision to keep Ross out of the intelligence loop, and it will be Ross going into this fortress tomorrow with not so much as a set of body armour with him?"

"Yes, that was my decision. My policy log contains the rationale for it."

"I'm sure it does, James. And the mines?"

"That as well."

"Really? Assuming he survives this – I've had a dossier compiled on him – what are you going to do with him afterwards. This won't be sorted with a pat on the back and a gong. Now will it?"

"The Police family will wrap our arms around him. We will provide him all the support he needs. Had he known, he would have done it anyway, but the knowledge would have been a greater danger to him."

"What about this communications officer? I see she's on loan to you via the NCS, and they, via Yorkshire. I've had a dossier compiled on her as well. Do the NCS and Yorkshire know she's in the middle of enough weaponry to start a small war?"

"No, they don't. They're not cleared for this operation. Sarah is with Deena—the Canadian Ambassador, far away from danger."

"Your officer Jane King, daughter of James King, one of your arrests. I have a file on her as well. I understand she's very highly regarded within Thames Valley Police, and indeed by you. What are you going to do with her once this all becomes open knowledge?"

"Jane's an outstanding officer. I will not allow the sins of her father to ruin her career. She has a bright future ahead."

"I applaud your comments, James, although it may not be in your gift to achieve them. I have some thoughts on Ross and Dorsey, but that is something we can talk about once this phase has passed. For now, are we all ready?"

CHAPTER EIGHTEEN

Anlong Run, Cambodia

Umar's phone alarm activated. He fumbled for it in the dark, finally locating it. Keeping his eyes shut, he pressed a number of buttons, guessing their position, until he got the right one; blissful silence. He got up, grabbed his torch and went out to the generator. With power restored, he washed his face then cooked rice porridge for breakfast. He was finishing his porridge when the Khn b̂ā walked in.

"Are they ready?" Umar asked gruffly.

"Yes, they are. Is there any porridge for me?"

"I left you some! Be quick. I want to be on the road by four at the latest."

Umar left to clean his teeth and pack his belongings. By the time he had loaded the car Keo and Utey were awake.

"Do you need our help, or can we go back to bed?"

"Go back to bed. I've got this. If there's a problem, I'll fetch you."

"We have to ring Chakra to let him know you got away safely."

"I'll do that. Get some sleep."

Umar left and found the Khn b̂ā in the caged room.

"Can you pick the small one up and put him in, then come back to help me with the other one?"

Umar didn't answer. He picked up the unconscious child, took him outside, gently placing him into the false bottom compartment. He returned, took hold of the European boy's legs, and together they took him out, placing him alongside the first one. Umar put both boys in the recovery position, wedging them into place with cushions so they would not move during the journey. He then closed the lid on top, placed rolls of cloth on top of it and closed the rear door.

"Are you ready?"

"I'll just get my bag"

As Umar waited, he rang Chakra.

"Chakra, it's Umar. You're not needed. We're about to leave."

"Thank you, Umar. Did Keo and Utey get up?"

"Yes, they did. They weren't needed though. See you on the next trip maybe?"

"Yes, see you then."

As Umar finished his call, the Khn b̂ā arrived back. He put his bag in the back on top of the rolls of cloth, got into the front seat, and Umar drove off for the border crossing at Poipet.

Arriving nearly three hours later, Umar drove to a lock-up garage near the crossing. He reversed the car up to its roller door and manoeuvred in, once the door had been opened by the waiting street trader. Inside was the trader's large, hand-pulled cart. The trader pulled down the roller doors from the outside, leaving Umar and the Khn b̂ā inside, alone and out of sight. They quickly removed the still unconscious children, loading them into the centre of a large container, which had three sections. The boys were inserted into the centre section on small seats. They were then secured in place by rope. The centre section was then closed off from both sides with wooden inserts, which fitted tightly into position. The two remaining sections were filled with an assortment of light cooking utensils and rice bowls. Finally, the container was covered in an old tarpaulin.

Umar went to the roller doors and knocked gently three times whilst the Khn b̂ā got back into the car. By the time Umar had joined him, the doors were up, and they drove out and joined the queue to cross into Thailand. Once through, they drove to another identical garage on the other side and waited for the trader to arrive. It wasn't long before he did. They then performed the reverse routine as before, loaded the children back into their car, paid the trader, and drove off to the warehouse where Brian Kennedy was waiting for them. When Kennedy saw the Landcruiser appear on the track, he opened the garage doors, and Umar drove in. Ten minutes later, Umar was back at his own base eating a second breakfast.

"How did that go?" Chet asked.

"Easy. I hate being in his company, but it all went smoothly."

Outside, a car containing two RTP cybercrime officers, who had previously been undertaking observations on the warehouse, slowly drove past Chet and Umar's base, videoing the house and its surroundings. One of the officers reported what they had seen to the officer in charge of the SWAT team, who was still eating breakfast many kilometres away.

Chenda's phone rang at exactly 8am. She answered it, immediately activating the speakerphone. They were all listening.

"Sopheap, this is Deena. What news?"

"They are all here except the same two, Bong Srei."

"Anything else?"

"Only that Chakra took a call a bit before 4am. Nuon couldn't hear the conversation, but it was a very short call. Afterwards Chakra went straight back to sleep, and he's still asleep now. So are his men."

"Thank you, Sopheap. If anything changes suddenly, especially if the gang leaves, please call me when it is safe for you to do so."

"I will, Bong Srei."

"Over to you and Narith, Tom, Chenda will drop you off."

Tom got into the rear offside seat of Narith's own personal, twin cab Hilux. Samlain sat beside him in the middle with Thy, the interpreter, next to him. Leap got into the front with Narith, who immediately drove off.

"Tom, Leap has researched the way. He will guide us there. When we get to the address, you must stay in the car with Samlain and Thy. Once I have control, and it is safe for you to come out, then you can leave the car. You must stay with Samlain at all times. Thy will be with you, so if I'm not there, he can interpret for you."

"Understood," Tom replied, his head bending forward so he could hear Narith. As he withdrew into his seat, he saw a leather gun holster with a black handgun wedged between the central consul and the front passenger seat.

Samlain said something to Thy in Khmer. Thy then bent forward towards Tom.

"Samlain says, 'What's in the black bag by your feet?'"

"It's a first aid kit. Just a policy thing. Wherever we go at home, we must have access to one of these."

Thy interpreted Tom's reply to Samlain, who nodded slowly before replying back in Khmer.

"'He says, when we get back, can he have some headache tablets. He has one from staying too long at the karaoke.'"

Tom looked at Samlain who smiled back him. Remembering what Deena had told him, he kept a straight face before answering.

"Of course."

It was just after 9.00am when Narith turned up the dirt track to the safe house at Anlong Run. Tom immediately recalled Sopheap's description as it came into view. They travelled around a small bend past the thick jungle growth, allowing Tom to see the house for the first time. The track to the house was over a small bridge with a hump in it, spanning a moat full of dirty water. Narith drove over the bridge, coming to a halt abruptly, just the other side.

Tom could see they were in a courtyard with only one way out: the way they had just come in. They were surrounded on three sides; the main house on the right stopped just short of the moat. On the left, there was a flat deck ute. On it, was something covered in a tarpaulin.

Another car was parked at 45 degrees in the top right-hand corner of the courtyard. Behind it, the buildings were completely open to the front. He could see beds, sofas and what looked like a small kitchen.

Narith and Leap got out of the car. Narith shut his door noisily, Leap left his open. They were both dressed in uniform. Without warning, two men appeared from behind the car at the top of the courtyard. Both of them had rifles which they immediately pointed towards Narith and Leap. They began shouting in Khmer.

Narith shouted back at them commandingly at the top of his voice. He began pointing at his uniform, then at Leap and then at the car.

Leap then began to angrily shout back at the two men. Samlain began to shout out from the car. Tom couldn't understand what was being said, but he felt Narith was telling them to put down the guns, as they were the police and their uniforms proved it.

The two men both fired one shot each. Neither appeared to hit anybody, and Tom thought the shots went above the car as a warning. Samlain started to almost scream from the back of the car. Thy began shouting something to Leap. Narith backed up towards the car still shouting angrily at the men, gesticulating with his arms at the men and then at his uniform. Leap, whose door was open, made his way to it but hesitated, not wanting to get in until he knew what Narith was doing. Narith shouted something one more time, before opening his door and getting in. Leap then jumped in.

Narith started the car, swung left before being forced to turn hard right because of the car parked halfway up. The attempted single U-turn in the courtyard failed at its three-quarter point: Narith being forced to reverse backwards to gain enough clearance. Bullets then began to hit the vehicle all across the rear, with some passing through the rear compartment bulkhead. Some travelled through to the front, exiting the windscreen causing it to splinter. Tom felt thuds all around him, matching the sounds of the bullets being fired. Panic set in. Samlain suddenly began to scream in pain. Everybody tried to hunch down to avoid being hit. The car lurched forward, then suddenly slowed before hitting the low, nearside stone wall of the bridge. As the car came to a halt, Tom heard the shooting intensify.

They were trapped.

The screams mixed with flying glass, metal, fabric, clothing, and dust. Tom's heart rate slowed down, his senses shutting out the noise and danger. Whether it was his Royal Marine training at Lympstone when he was young or his many years of service as a police officer, he couldn't tell. But, right at that moment, he was totally calm. It was like he was acting in slow motion, whilst everything around him was at full speed, flying through the air.

He reached through, grabbing the handgun that was wedged next to Narith's seat. He removed it from the holster, noticing the extra rounds attached to the outside of it, one of which looked much older than the rest. The gun was a CZ 75, with a magazine already inserted. The safety was on, the hammer closed. It was a semi-automatic. He had no idea if there was a round in the chamber or not. Now was not the time to find out or ask. They were about to die. He pressed the magazine release button, pulled it out, saw there were rounds in it. How many, he couldn't tell. He slammed it home, racked the slide, ejecting a round. "'Damn,'" he said to himself.

He let the slide go and thumbed the safety catch off. The rounds hitting the car increased in number. They were going in for the kill. It was now or never, he had to get some rounds going back in the other direction if they were to stand any chance. Feeling he was about to be killed, he suddenly thought of his son Struan, who would be asleep on the other side of the world.

He opened the car door and stepped out, keeping low until his legs were behind the rear axle. He brought the gun up in front of him but off aim, seeking the position of the two gunmen. Seeing they were both exposed in the open, he took aim for the one on the left, firing off three quick rounds. The third bullet hit the target, causing the gunman to go down. He took aim again, firing once more into the lying man, before looking up to locate the other gunman, who had disappeared.

Without warning, the other gunman reappeared from behind the car, holding an RPG-7 on his shoulder. He began to swing right to bring the rocket launcher in line with their car when Tom fired four rounds in quick succession. The impact of at least one of the rounds that hit him, caused the rocket launcher to fire before it could be fully aimed at their car. The rocket hit the main house and exploded. Tom dropped below the deck of the car to protect himself from flying shrapnel until the explosion subsided. He then crept around the back of the car and could see the second gunman lying on the floor motionless. It was then his focus snapped. Fear and uncertainty began to engulf him. How many more were there? Could he be seen?

He knew he was outgunned. He needed more firepower. He ran towards the enemy car and the nearer gunman. Seeing he was clearly dead, he picked up his rifle. Using the car as cover, he went around the rear to find the second gunman motionless and kicked his rifle out of reach.

Hearing screams of pain coming from their car, he backed towards it. When he got there, he found they were all in shock. Narith was trying to get the car started, but the engine would not fire into life. Leap was in the back seat with Thy trying to comfort Samlain. Tom could see that Samlain's shirt was soaked in blood.

Narith joined Tom and retrieved his handgun.

"There may be others in the buildings or the house. We must clear it Narith. To protect ourselves."

"Samlain is shot. We must help him first!" Narith replied defiantly.

"If we don't protect ourselves, we won't be able to help him. A quick clear of the buildings. Both of us."

Tom could see that Narith was breathing heavily, visibly angry and upset. But he was experienced and considered the proposal.

"OK, quickly."

Narith said something to Leap, who turned and nodded.

Tom and Narith checked the buildings on the left to find them empty. The buildings at the top of the courtyard were rough living quarters, but empty. They made their way past the gunmen, Tom noticing the one with the rocket launcher was also dead. They entered the main house, the front door opening straight into a large kitchen. Nobody was present, but there were clear signs that people did live there. Off the kitchen was a corridor, which ran the whole length of the building with doors only to the left.

The Major shouted something in Khmer. With no reply, Narith entered the first room whilst Tom stayed at the door. Tom glanced inside. There was a caged area with a small bed and a chair. Nothing else.

Tom moved further along the corridor, entering the second room. Inside, it was the same as the room before. Narith then moved further along the corridor and entered the next room. Inside it was a bedroom full of personal items, but again nobody was there. With that room clear, Tom moved to the last room off the corridor. The way forward was partially blocked from where the rocket had hit the building. They both climbed over the broken stone bricks that had previously been an exterior wall, to find a final room full of TV screens, recording equipment, cameras, camcorders, tripods, chairs and a rifle propped up in the corner with a safe next to it.

Narith checked the safe. It was locked.

"Clear. Let's go and help Samlain," Tom said, relieved, wondering to himself where Michael and the children were.

They both raced back to find that Leap and Thy had pulled Samlain out onto the floor. Tom collected the first aid kit.

"Is he shot?"

"We think so," replied Thy.

"Get his shirt off him," Tom replied.

Thy said something to Leap in Khmer, who was on the other side of Samlain, and they quickly removed his shirt.

Tom could see that Samlain was ashen, in severe pain and struggling to breathe.

"Keep his arms to his side and his legs together. Roll him onto his side!"

Thy interpreted, then they both rolled him over. With his back exposed, it was clear he had been shot or something else had entered him. With no evidence of blood elsewhere, it appeared there was no exit wound.

"We must get him to Battambang!" Narith said urgently.

"Call an ambulance!" Tom replied.

"We don't have them," Thy replied, before Narith could.

"Thy, find the keys to that car. It might be in one of their pockets. Narith you hold him. I'll get a dressing on," Tom said, opening the first aid kit.

Part of his training was to know what your kit held, where it was located, what it was for and how to use it. He knew what he wanted before he unzipped the black bag.

He unpacked the largest field dressing he had, placed the dressing on the entry wound and began to hold it in place with a roll of cling film when Samlain's condition suddenly deteriorated. His breathing became severely restricted, and his face began to go blue. Tom stopped rolling the cling film around him.

"Lay him back down."

Flat again, Tom could see the right side of Samlain's chest was sunken. The left was risen, and his lower throat appeared to be pushed to the left. His training made him recognise the condition, but it also taught him that it needed a proper medic to relieve the pressure building in Samlain's chest. He knew what had to be done to relieve the pressure, but it wasn't his job to do it. Samlain's breathing began to worsen.

"We must get him to Battambang!" Narith shouted.

Tom looked over to Thy who had just found the keys to the car.

"He won't make it. He has pressure in his chest. We must let the pressure out if he is to stand a chance of making it to Battambang alive."

"Can you do it?" Narith asked urgently

"I know what to do, but I've never done it."

"You must do it."

Tom thought about the request.

"If I can find the right spot. I'll try."

Tom felt for the right clavicle bone. Finding it, he moved his fingers both ways until he was sure he knew its length, before selecting the halfway point. He then placed two fingers, side by side underneath the clavicle, and searched for the second intercostal gap. Having found it, he felt further down for the next one until he got to the fifth. Concerned he was not in the right spot, he did it a second time. Once he had it a second time, he felt along the side of the rib until it reached its side. He kept a finger on the spot.

"Leap, tear open some of those alcohol wipes. Then take the top off that scalpel for me."

Narith interpreted for Tom.

Tom wiped the area and took hold of the scalpel. He felt again for a spot closest to the lower rib. He looked at Samlain. He had to do it. Samlain was dying in front of them. Taking the scalpel, he inserted it about half the blade length and then cut down about 10mm, following the line of rib. Air suddenly burst out; the wound was bleeding, which he wiped away, but air continued to bubble out and Samlain's breathing eased. His face started to lose its blue colour and he became calm.

Thy arrived alongside them, driving the gunmen's car.

"Let's get this dressing on his back as lightly as we can with the cling film, then use his body weight to keep it in place by keeping him on his back." With Thy interpreting, they got the dressing attached and Samlain into the back of the car. As Narith was talking in Khmer to both Leap and Thy, Tom stepped back and got his phone out, wondering if he would get a signal. Amazed he had, he rang Niall. Turning his back, he prepared to drop his voice.

"Niall don't talk, just listen. Michael and the children aren't here. There were two gunmen. Both of them have been shot dead. They shot our car up with us in it, one of the Cambodians has been shot. I need you to go in there straight away. Tell the SWAT team to expect firearms and take any other action you think necessary. I've got phone coverage here, but if I move, I probably won't get it again until I'm back at Battambang. This is a fluid situation here."

"Holy Mary Mother of God! Are you injured?"

"No, I'm fine."

"Thank God. It was a good thing you stayed out of it, that could have got really messy on a number of fronts."

"I shot the gunmen, Niall."

"Fuck, Tom. How?"

"Doesn't matter now. Just get in there. Hopefully, we can salvage this, because at my end, the only two we had to help us out are dead. I have to go. Good luck!"

As Tom finished the call. He was joined by Narith.

"Leap will drive into Battambang. He will get Samlain to the hospital there. He will then get reinforcements and a mechanic for my car and come back here. We will stay here until they arrive."

"OK, I need to let Deena know what's happened. Am I going to be OK with the authorities over what I did here?"

"I'm in charge. I told you what to do and you did what I requested. There's no problem. What I say, is what will be recorded. Don't worry

237

about it. Thank you for what you did. When the local police get here, they better start talking, because there's clearly more behind this than those two!"

Tom rang Deena, as Narith used his phone to call someone else.

"Hi Tom, it's a small wonder you've got a signal. How'd it go?"

CHAPTER NINETEEN

Ban Mai Nong Sai, Thailand

Niall was travelling in the second of the two RTP cars, well back from the three Arintaraj 26 SWAT teams ahead. Two teams, led by their Commander, had been designated to take the warehouse fortress, leaving team three to secure a residential address linked to the warehouse. They were now just minutes away.

Niall had attended the briefing. Team one would place charges on the roller doors, then enter to secure entry. The second team, two of which had performed a night creep around the address, would first shoot, then flail their way through the glass front doors. Once in, they would place charges around the door frame and a second set on the adjacent wall. The wall charge was designed to blow a hole big enough for the team to enter, should the metal door not give way. They had further charges if required.

They would storm the warehouse, secure everybody in it and make the premises safe before calling in the Cyber team to deal with the arrests and subsequent paperwork. Simultaneously, team three, led by the Deputy Commander, would take the nearby residential address. The front and rear doors would be smashed open using a ram. Stun grenades would be thrown in ahead of them before entry. They would then secure the premises and everybody in it.

Even though Niall was inside a car, and some distance away, he heard the explosions. They had been given two radios by Arintaraj 26 staff. One was tuned into the teams storming the warehouse, the other into the team at the residential address. The driver of his car, Boon-Mee, was listening intently to the chatter coming across the airwaves of both radios. After a while, he turned to Niall.

"They're in at both addresses. Just waiting for an update. Which one do you need to go to first?"

"The warehouse."

As talk over one of the radios began to cease, Boon-Mee picked up a third radio and tuned to the Cyber team's frequency. The front passenger turned to Niall, in the rear.

"The residential address is secure. The other team is going there. We will wait until the warehouse is clear."

Five minutes later they were called in. As soon as Niall got out of the car, he was met with the unmistakeable smell of cordite. He saw that the large roller door, although still down, had been blown in on one side. He followed his driver, Boon-Mee, who approached the front doors, which seemed to have been blasted outwards, with glass littered everywhere. Inside, in the foyer, he saw a wall with a large hole in it, and, lying on its side, a metal door that had been blown inwards. They were met by the Commander of Arintaraj 26 who spoke to Boon-Mee, who then interpreted for Niall.

"He'll lead us through. You cannot touch anything."

Niall was led through to a corridor and shown a room on the left. Inside, he saw a white male, the one that Coco had met, lying face down on the floor with his hands cuffed behind his back. There was a SWAT team member standing guard over him. In the next room there was another white male, this one naked, also face down, cuffed, again with a guard. He went to another room and looked in. It was clearly a torture chamber of some sort. He was then led to the final room on that side of the corridor; inside, it looked like a recording studio. There was a white male slumped in the corner with a handgun between his legs. There was a bullet wound in the centre of his forehead. He was clearly deceased.

The Commander spoke for about a minute before Boon-Mee translated.

"He says that this man had the gun in his hand when his team went into this room. He didn't follow commands and moved suddenly with the gun, so they shot him. We must follow him."

"Do we know who he is?"

"Not yet."

Niall stared at the man. He was sure the lifeless body in front of him was that of Michael.

He went to the room opposite where he found two children: one a white-skinned European, another of Asian descent. There were two SWAT team members with them who had removed their tactical hard hats and face masks to help build a rapport with the boys. Boon-Mee interpreted for the Commander again.

"They know that the white boy is the one missing from Cambodia. The other child is Cambodian and from Phnom Penh. Please follow."

Niall went into the next room where there were two males. Both were face down, semi-naked, also handcuffed. The guards over them had their guns pointed unwaveringly at their prisoners. There was a long exchange between the Commander and the two guards before he turned and said something to Boon-Mee.

"One is a Thai national. He's not saying anything. The other is Brian Kennedy. They both had handguns but responded to commands."

Niall was led back out to the car to make the short journey to the residential address nearby. They were met at the door by the Deputy Commander who took them in. Inside Niall saw two men. One of them had been shot. The SWAT team medic had clearly made valiant efforts to save his life, a battle he had lost. The other man was face down and handcuffed like the others. The Deputy Commander spoke to Boon-Mee in Thai, gesturing towards another room. Boon-Mee then translated.

"We think the dead one is a Malaysian called Umar; he went for a gun. They had no option but to shoot. The other is a Thai national called Chet. He's talking already. There's two mines and ammunition under his bed. This will take some sorting out, I can tell you; I'll be writing for the next month—but we got the children. The European back at the warehouse, do you think that's the person we missed in Bangkok, when you were last here?"

"Yes, Boon-Mee. I think that's him."

"For now, you will need to stay with me until we identify everybody and get to the bottom of all this. It could take a couple of days."

Three hours later Niall rang Tom.

"Tom, can you speak?"

"Hi, Niall, I'm back at the hotel. I'm with Deena, Sarah and Chenda."

"Who's at the safe house?"

"Narith and the locals. Why?"

"They need to be told there are two land mines set up either side of the moat bridge, between the bridge and the jungle. They're about twenty metres in, and in a direct line to each other. That's come from one of the arrests here."

"Hi Niall, it's Deena, they've found them. I asked Major Pich not to search the grounds until they'd been cleared because the area was heavily mined in the war. I pulled in a favour from HALO who had an expert in the area. He found them and made them safe. I'm now in the Major's good books. Thank you anyway."

"Thank God for that! First thing: Tom, are you OK?"

"Yes, I'm fine."

"So, what happened there?" the excitement in Niall's voice obvious to Tom.

"You first, Niall. Your result will affect this result."

"We got the European boy and a Cambodian, both missing from Phnom Penh!"

A huge cheer went up in Deena's hotel room, making Niall smile at the other end.

"Happy days, Tom!"

"Sure is, tell us more!"

"The Brit from the meet with Coco was there, but we know who he is. There was another Brit there. He's a former MP and something to do with the Catholic church. He's panicking and singing like a canary. They shot one dead. I think that will be Michael. They haven't identified him yet, but it's going to be him, Tom. We got him in the end, not the way we would have liked, but we got him. Then there was a Thai national, who won't say who he is, and Brian Kennedy, who we know can't be Brian Kennedy as he's dead.

There was a linked address, not far from the warehouse. There was a Malaysian called Umar, who went for his gun. He's dead. And another

Thai national called Chet. The Thai national is talking and trying to do a deal. They're putting the pieces together with his help.

From what we know so far, Kennedy, and the Thai national he was found with, ran the whole operation on this side in conjunction with Michael. It was Chet and the dead Malaysian, Umar, who got the children across with the help of Chakra and his gang. Huge sums of money were involved."

CHAPTER TWENTY

Home Office, London, England

"The Home Secretary is ready for you now, Chief Constable. Go straight in please."

The Chief walked in to find Home Secretary, Rachel Abrams, sitting at a small coffee table. On it was a tea pot, two cups on saucers, teaspoons, sugar and milk.

"James, thank you for coming. I've had some tea made for us. Do you take milk and sugar?"

"Just milk, please."

The Chief waited as Rachel poured him a cup. This would be one to tell Fenella about when he got home, the Chief thought, taking a sip. It was a fine cup of tea as well.

"Now that the media scrum has died down somewhat, I just wanted to personally congratulate you and your team for all that you've achieved. It can't have been easy to learn about your own staff, and I know for a fact that working with the Security Service can be a hard task. What you and Toby have managed is huge and cannot be underestimated. I'd like you to pass that on please."

"Of course, thank you."

"I've personally spoken to the Secretary of State for Canada. I passed on the sincere gratitude of this Government for the assistance that Deena Potts, their Ambassador, provided. Especially how she handled the intelligence of the mines."

"Yes, she handled that very well."

"She did. That leaves me with a few other people I'd like to talk to you about. I'd like to start with Jane King. What's happening with her?"

"That's been difficult. Finding out about her father has been extremely hard on her. She's carrying some shame and guilt. At the end of the day, her father hasn't done a great deal. He just did as he was told. But at the moment, she's not seeing it that way. Then there's Tom. She admires and trusts him; she loves working with him. I put him out there and left him out there! She knows that."

"As was requested of you, James."

"I know that, but nobody else can. So, you can see how it looks."

"Yes, I can see that—which is why I wanted to have this chat. When is she going back to work?"

"I'm not sure she will be!"

"I don't want that girl to throw away a brilliant career with the police. You must convince her not to. I have secured a security clearance from Toby, so you can fully brief her. Hopefully that will give you some leverage."

"That will help, thank you."

"Good. Now Tom. What's the situation with him?"

"He's an angry man at the moment. He feels he can't trust me or TVP, especially now that he knows the full story. You know what my thoughts were on telling him everything."

"Yes, I know. But I have a plan, and it's not open to discussion. Tom Ross will be seconded, along with Sarah Dorsey, to the Home Office under the direct command of this office. Effective immediately."

As the Chief was leaving the Home Office, the Minister for Security, Patrick Hall, and Arthur from the Secret Intelligence Service, MI6, entered the Home Secretary's office and sat down.

"How did Chief Constable Galloway take the news?" Patrick Hall asked, with concern in his voice.

"Initially, he was most put out and protested, as I knew he would. However, when I explained it would be a secondment, and that in politics nothing is forever, he came around to my proposal."

"And the Inspector of Constabularies role?" Patrick replied, with his eyebrows raised.

"That certainly sweetened the deal, Patrick. Arthur, once Tom arrives, I have an investigation that I would like him to undertake: a cold case review on behalf of a local sheriff's office in the US. It's a personal request from the US Secretary of State. I've agreed to it. I suggest you use that as your first point of recruitment."

"Yes, Home Secretary. Just so I'm clear on this: I have the authority to recruit Tom Ross as an operative to be used for a 'third direction' instruction, should Her Majesty's Government ever need to issue such a direction?"

"Yes, you do. And I am expecting we will."

At that very moment, Tom was knocking on the door of Jane's house. When she saw it was him, she burst into tears and threw her arms around him.

"What's a man got to do for a cuppa?" Tom said, caringly, gently taking hold of Jane's arms.

"I know! I'm sorry, it's just seeing you after all this. You could have died. My Dad's been arrested. Michael's dead. This whole thing's so screwed up!"

"About that tea?"

Jane laughed, wiping the tears from her face. Taking his arm, she led him inside and made them both a mug of tea. They then sat silently on the sofa next to each other.

"I hear your Dad didn't actually know the significance of what he was doing. He'd been duped."

"Yes. But he did it, because he'd had an affair with Maggie Burrows and was still infatuated with her! I'm so angry with him!"

They sat in silence again.

"I'm also as mad as hell we couldn't hold Michael to account. I wanted to see him sentenced and imprisoned. Has Niall confirmed it's him yet?"

"Not yet. It'll take some time to fully identify him. Even if he'd been taken alive, the Thais would have had the first go. He'd have got a big sentence, possibly even the death penalty. He may not have survived one of their jails."

"I just feel he finally escaped us again!"

Tom could see Jane was welling up, so remained quiet until it had passed.

"I hear you're taking some leave. Is that to help your mother?"

"Yes, it is. It's also to give me some thinking time. You know why I decided to stay on. Now I think I made a mistake; I should have gone then."

"You made the right choice then; the right choice now, is to stay—period."

"I just feel so much guilt. All that Masonic corruption. I'm his daughter. This will just stick with me all my career!"

"This won't define you, Jane. This isn't anything to do with you. In ten years, when you are doing JT's job, you can look back at this conversation and thank me with a good bottle of malt every year on this date. Do we have an accord?"

CHAPTER TWENTY ONE

Tom sat in the waiting room of his doctor's surgery. One of the requirements of going to work at the Home Office was a health check. His own GP was away, so he had got the last appointment with a locum, who, at the end of the day, was running late. It didn't bother him, he had nowhere else to be.

He was reading an article in one of the magazines about keeping chickens, when he heard his name called. He looked up, just in time to see the back of the doctor walk from view down the corridor. Tom got up, and as he turned into the corridor, he again saw the disappearing back of the doctor entering his consulting room. He caught up, went in and sat down.

The doctor was facing away as he typed on his keyboard, occasionally stopping to use the mouse before typing again.

"Sorry you couldn't get to see your normal doctor. I'm the locum," he said in a soft, faint Welsh accent.

The doctor slowly turned in his seat to face Tom. He had a warm broad smile, that put Tom at ease. His hair, which reached his collar, was greying, and, as their eyes locked for the briefest of moments, Tom felt a connection.

He had a round, open, caring face that wasn't for affect, just because Tom was the next patient. It was experience, it was who he was as a GP, and who he was as a man. Locum or not, Tom just knew he was in safe hands.

"I'm Doctor Mark Vernon-Roberts. Now, what seems to be the problem?"

IN MEMORIAM
Dr Mark Vernon-Roberts
1945–2019

When I first met Doctor Mark Vernon-Roberts, he was a retired GP from Wales, living between there and New Zealand. I was asked by his son: would I take his father out fly fishing? As a mad keen fly fisher myself, it was something I readily agreed to do.

That was the start of a short, but magical fishing journey for us both. Turns out, Mark was just having a few problems with spotting fish, getting his eye in. His casting and his fly tying technique were light years ahead of mine, and I consider myself no slouch.

Mark had another love—books. He was passionate about the correct use of English grammar, particularly the punctuation of quoted speech. When he heard I was trying to write, he offered to proofread the manuscripts. Which he did, devotedly, as chief editor over the next few years and two novels.

Editing is not an easy task. By the end of the second book, I decided to walk away from the series. I moved to a new house and lost touch with Mark, until, one day, I saw he had died. When I found out, I became overwhelmed by his death, lost fishing opportunities and that unwritten third book. So, I sat down to finish the job.

Mark, this was our last journey together. I hope at least some of the commas are in the right place.

Wherever you are, may there be plenty of soap suds and riffles mate.